THE PRESENT MOMENT

WOMEN WRITING AFRICA
A Project of The Feminist Press at The City University of New York
Funded by the Ford Foundation and the Rockefeller Foundation

Women Writing Africa is a project of cultural reconstruction that aims to restore African women's voices to the public sphere. Through the collection of written and oral narratives to be published in six regional anthologies, the project will document the history of self-conscious literary expression by African women throughout the continent. In bringing together women's voices, Women Writing Africa will illuminate for a broad public the neglected history and culture of African women, who have shaped and been shaped by their families, societies, and nations.

The Women Writing Africa Series, which supports the publication of individual books, is part of the Women Writing Africa project.

The Women Writing Africa Series

ACROSS BOUNDARIES
The Journey of a South African Woman
Leader
A Memoir by Mamphela Ramphele

AND THEY DIDN'T DIE
A Novel by Lauretta Ngcobo

CHANGES
A Love Story
A Novel by Ama Ata Aidoo

COMING TO BIRTH
A Novel by Marjorie Oludhe Macgoye

DAVID'S STORY
A Novel by Zoë Wicomb

HAREM YEARS
The Memoirs of an Egyptian Feminist,
1879–1924
by Huda Shaarawi
Translated and introduced
by Margot Badran

NO SWEETNESS HERE
And Other Stories
by Ama Ata Aidoo

TEACHING AFRICAN LITERATURES IN
A GLOBAL LITERARY ECONOMY
Women's Studies Quarterly 25, nos. 3
& 4 (fall/winter 1998)
Edited by Tuzyline Jita Allan

YOU CAN'T GET LOST IN CAPE
TOWN
A Novel by Zoë Wicomb

ZULU WOMAN
The Life Story of Christina Sibiya
by Rebecca Hourwich Reyher

THE PRESENT MOMENT

Marjorie Oludhe Macgoye

Afterword by Valerie Kibera

Historical Context by Jean Hay

THE WOMEN WRITING AFRICA SERIES

The Feminist Press
at The City University of New York

268778
MAY 08 2002

Published by The Feminist Press
at The City University of New York
The Graduate Center
365 Fifth Avenue
New York, NY 10016
feministpress.org

First Feminist Press edition, 2000
Originally published in 1987 by East African Educational
Publishers/Heinemann Kenya, Nairobi.

Library of Congress Cataloging-in-Publication Data
Macgoye, Marjorie Oludhe.
    The present moment / Marjorie Oludhe ; afterword by Valerie Kibera ; his-
    torical context by Jean Hay.
        p. cm. — (Women writing Africa series)
    ISBN 1-55861-254-8 (cloth : alk. paper) — ISBN 1-55861-248-3 (pbk. : alk.
    paper)
    1. Women—Kenya—Fiction. 2. Old age homes—Fiction. 3. Aged women—
    Fiction. 4. Kenya—Fiction.
    I. Title. II. Series.
    PR9381.9.M19P74 2000
    823'.914 21 ; aa05 06-30—dc00   00-057670

This publication is made possible, in part, by grants from the Ford
Foundation and the Rockefeller Foundation in support of The Feminist Press's
Women Writing Africa Series, and by the Nathan Cummings Foundation, with
the support and encouragement of Sonia Simon-Cummings. Publication of
this book is supported by public funds from the National Endowment for
the Arts and the New York State Council on the Arts, a State Agency. The Feminist
Press would also like to thank Joanne Markell and Genevieve Vaughan for
their generosity in supporting this book.

Printed on acid-free paper by Transcontinental Printing
Printed in Canada

08 07 06 05 04 03 02 01 00   5 4 3 2 1

CAST OF CHARACTERS

Women in the Refuge

BESSIE: Kikuyu. Does not remember her full name or age, or most of her lost family. Her last son, Leonard (Lucky), was born in detention.

MAMA CHUNGU (MOTHER PAIN): Seychelloise. Born Mimi Paul c. 1925. Brought to Mombasa by her father, a ship's steward. Works as a servant for "Mr. Robert."

MATRON: Kikuyu. A widow. In charge of the Refuge. Has four adult children.

NEKESA: Luyia. Born c. 1920 in Nairobi. Has lost touch with her family, except one brother. Friends and members of the Revival Fellowship, Keziah and Mama Victor, offer her help and support.

PRISCILLA NJUGNA: Kikuyu. Born c. 1923 in the "settled area," where her father works as a cook in a European house. Marries Evans Njugna, and both work for the Bateson family.

RAHEL APUDO: Luo. Born c. 1915, daughter of a soldier. Marries a soldier with whom she has a son and two daughters, Vitalis, Margaret, and Florence. Her husband and her co-wife also have several children.

SOPHIA MWAMBA: Swahili. Born c. 1912 in Mombasa Old Town and named Fatuma. With her husband, Ali, has three children, Hassan, Mariam, and Hawa. Hawa has married Solomon Wau and has several children, including Joseph Baraka Wau. After Ali's death, Fatuma marries a Taita Christian, Henry Mwamba, and been baptisted Sophia. Henry has a daughter, Emma, from his previous marriage.

WAIRIMU: Kikuyu. Born c. 1905, daughter of Gichuru with several sisters and a brother. As a young woman, is seduced by Waitito.

Nurses

GERTRUDE: Friend of Mary Kamau. Engaged to Sam Kamau.

JANE: Engaged to John, who is in the Kenya Air Force.

MARY KAMAU: Friendly with Jose Baraka Wau, and has a brother, Sam Kamau.

Other characters

"LADY FROM THE CATHEDRAL": Escorts Mrs. Reinhold, and has known Priscilla and Mama Chungu.

MRS. REINHOLD: An employee of a donor agency, observing projects in different parts of Africa.

THE SOLDIER: A vagrant, and subject to delusions.

REV. ANDREW WAITITO: Son of Nellie, brought up in an Ugandan orphanage.

Historical figures mentioned

ARCHBISHOP ALEXANDER: South African church leader who helped inspire the independent church movements.

JAMES BEAUTTAH: Kikuyu activist.

ARCHDEACON LEONARD BEECHER: Representative of African interests in the British Legislative Council and later Anglican archbishop of East Africa.

CHARLES BOWRING: Colonial secretary.

ARTHUR CREECH-JONES: Colonial secretary.

MR. DOORLY: Nairobi magistrate.

SHEIKH HYDER: Head of a prominent Mombasa family.

JOMO KENYATTA: Activist and later, first president of Kenya.

MARGARET WAMBUI KENYATTA: daughter of President Kenyatta and mayor of Nairobi

CHEGE KIBACHIA: trade unionist.

MBIYU KOINANGE: Founder of the Kenya Teacher Training College, minister of state under Kenyatta.

FRED KUBAI: Trade unionist.

ELIUD MATHU: Representative of African interests after Beecher.

MARY NYANJIRU: Protestor in the "Harry Thuku riots" of 1922.

MAKHAN SINGH: Trade unionist.

ABDULLA TAIRARA: Colleague of Thuku.

HARRY THUKU: Kikuyu political activist, 1895–1970.

REV. MR. WRIGHT: Anglican chaplain.

NOTE: In Kikuyu custom, the first son is named after the paternal grandfather, so there will be a recurring sequence of names.

CHAPTER
ONE

It was a beautiful morning. Wairimu could hear the birds singing behind the higher trees and the sun was already promising to warm the path before it got much higher. She would be hot in her goatskin from shoulder to knee, but since being circumcised she wore it always modestly, mindful of her grown-up status. The water-container bounced empty on her back, hardly enough weight to keep the leather thong steady round her forehead. Her bare arms and legs felt smooth and luxuriously conscious of the mild air: on the left arm was a metal bangle her brother had brought back from Nairobi when he went there to see the train and conduct some mysterious business with rupees and skins.

She rubbed possessively at the bangle. Even since she had started fetching water as a little girl the forest had thinned. The path was not so chilly and dank as it used to be. One was hardly afraid – as the mothers always had been in their girlhood – of hyenas or human raiders. On this path she had never heard the wailing of a baby abandoned or put out to perish beside its dying mother. There was too much light among the trees now, and too many of the white men's agents were on the watch. Beyond the ridges, it was said, the Roman Catholics would even pick up the babies if they were in time, and somehow nurture them without a mother's milk, not caring to find out whether they were survivors of twins or to examine the tooth order, let alone speculating what evil had brought death upon the mother of a perfectly formed child.

Wairimu quickened her pace. She was not really afraid of the forest, but she would need to catch up with the group of girls ahead to get help in hoisting the heavy skin once it was filled with water. It was strange that Nyambura had not caught up with her by now. This was the first time she had ever seemed reluctant to take her friend with her

1

to deliver a message to her second grandmother, and Wairimu would have waited for her nearer the homestead if she had not been confident she would follow soon. It was strange, but as people grew up you had to expect them to change.

Wairimu turned a bend in the path which brought the morning sun almost to dazzle her eyes, and there the young man was standing. Her head was not bent because her load was so light, and his eyes seemed to catch hers as she paused in the middle of a step, conscious of the weight on her forward foot pressing down the valley path, the yellow haze of morning light, the air caressing her braceleted arm, the birdsong overhead and the rustle of some small animal making for the river.

She turned, and the turning was slow and painful, stretched her left arm and found the bracelet gone, the wrist bony and the fingers hard with old burns and scars. Her eyes were still dazzled a bit and sore from the forward heat.

'Ee, Wairimu,' one of the other old ladies chided, 'you sit too near the charcoal fire. Your head gets heavy and you could hurt yourself when you fall asleep.'

'I was not going to sleep, Priscilla,' she replied primly. 'I was just resting my eyes from the glare and thinking of the next thing I had to do.'

'And I was just doing the next thing and stirring the thin porridge for both of us. Where is your mug, now, Wairimu?'

It was difficult to think that Priscilla had ever been young. She was all bones and corners. Her voice was sharp and her ears sharp, and though her eyes were a bit blurred she never seemed to forget which day it was, or whose turn it was, or what everyone was called, the baptismal name and the birth-given name and the mother-of name for those who had been lucky and the place names they were attached to. Priscilla, Wairimu thought, had never grown: there was no place where her skin was too big for her, where breasts or features spilt out over the bone structure, no hidden interior self. But Wairimu still enclosed within herself the springy footstep and the ancient ornaments, the gleaming rounded skin and the halo of sunlight encircling the young man with his shirt and shorts, his wide-brimmed hat and sandals, his knowledge of the world and other ways and women. That

2

had been the start of it all, of her going away, because after this revelation of what he shared with her she could not face either the shameful disclosure of the wedding day or the cloying sameness of all the days that would follow. The forest was no longer thick enough to hide divergence. She had to go away.

Rahel had gone from them in all but name. She had not spoken for two weeks now and could not hold a cup to her lips. She lay there, long and black and gaunt, her eyes sometimes following the others about. It was not her first withdrawal, but her longest. They mostly left Matron to feed her, for they were blamed if they made a mess, spilling things or letting her play with the food forgotten in her mouth. But Rahel too was wandering in the woods, gathering firewood with her friends, and as they found themselves far away from the homestead they sang louder and more wildly, practising among themselves the marriage songs and other forbidden chants, which they would not dare to utter within the elders' hearing and yet were expected to know and perform when the occasion arrived. One of the older girls had even seen the fearful twin dance performed and demonstrated, as far as she could remember, the women's part, until far from the usual path they came upon the dead tree and were struck suddenly quiet, alarmed by the silvery replica of living branches and the vivid green of moss. They turned away quickly, breaking no branch, but these days the image of the dead tree lay before Rahel's eyes and she clung to it for its symmetry, its detachment and its total recall.

Some of the old ladies said they dreamed a lot. Perhaps this was what they meant. For Luo people, Rahel used patiently to explain to the others, a dream was no such flickering thing as they described, although there might be fancies that turned into dreams. When someone brought a message to you he came, not just seemed to come. He came to claim what was a dead person's due – a chicken, a change of name, relationship with a child soon to be born – and even if you did not know him yourself, the elders would recognise who he was from your description and act on the message.

Suppose it were a living person, Priscilla had asked. And then does he appear at the age when he died, or younger? Does he speak in

3

known words? Do you see him in your bedroom or somewhere else? Do other people sleeping there see him too? Really, Priscilla should have been a European, asking so many questions. It was all on account of having gone to school so young and worked all those years in big, chilly houses, where the comfort of the cooking fire never penetrated to the upper air and chairs, shiny to the touch, kept you at a distance from other people.

Rahel could no longer answer these questions. She knew what she saw – and this time she saw the girls, young and noisy and mischievous. Her tongue had somehow got out of control since that night she had seen her father's eldest brother as she remembered him long ago, his thin shoulders bare, the little circles of gold gleaming in his ears (for he was a peaceable man and had bound himself to the self-restraint of the ear-rings as early as she remembered him). His fingers were pulling and working at the sisal rope. He had brought her no message, claimed no child – for her daughters had died long since and their daughters might, for all she knew, be married in distant places – only he had looked at her kindly, plaiting the rope, plaiting the rope, and from that time a chill had fallen upon her limbs and she moved with difficulty. Well, in Nairobi in June and July it could be chilly, but it was only when she saw the dead tree that she remembered the shadowed thickets that were always cold. It was many years since those places had been broken down for firewood and the land put under the hoe: nowadays, at home, you never wished for a heavier blanket unless in the midst of the rain. Of course now you were clothed. Yet in those days the stout calico petticoats the girls got from their own chickens, or as a present with the first instalment of dowry, seemed to their mothers finicky and quite unnecessary. A nice Luo girl was not expected to go in for these new-fangled fashions.

Unable to rouse her, friends pulled the charcoal brazier nearer to her bed and crept away.

The man clanked along the road and the old ladies called one another to come and see. After all, a fine figure of a man, crazy or not, is worth a second look at any age. This one was much more striking than those who appear on Sundays in the uniform of a three-piece suit, collar and

4

tie, as like to one another as the more splendidly dressed waiters and ushers who would move you on outside the big hotels where tourists sometimes offered shillings if you could get close enough, looking pathetic and detached.

He jangled as he walked. It was not in fact the row of medals – they were cut, actually, from the silver foil of cocoa tins and suspended by safety pins and laces from a length of cellulose packing tape – but pieces of metal suspended from the belt that made the noise and occasionally hit against a jerky knee, but most of the old ladies were not able to see that clearly. The man held his head erect and marched with exaggerated movements, his lips muttering directions to himself, 'one, two, one, two', when he was not speaking aloud. Coloured cords streamed from the shoulders of his khaki shirt and a piece of tinsel glinted bravely on top of the peaked cap adorned with red and green beads. The tatty trousers were tucked into well-shined ankle boots, and a small cane in his right hand emulated the movements of a newly commissioned officer, anxious lest he leave the baton behind.

A crowd of small children shouted greetings all around but kept their distance after the man had wheeled about with a meaningful tap of the baton on the iron bars. As he got into his stride again, Wairimu minced to the roadside and broke into a dance step, tightening the wrapper girlishly round her hips.

The man stopped and roared out a dozen obscenities in English. The children giggled. Younger women turned their backs and ostentatiously stooped to resume their washing. A young man stood still and saluted, then continued walking in the opposite direction. The words were too familiar to the older parts of eastern Nairobi to retain much of their original force. Some of them were untranslatable and therefore retained an aura of quaintness and sophistication. For some of the old ladies who were new to the town they had no literal meaning; for others they stirred memories which were better suppressed in their present, respected surroundings.

'Women have done me no good,' shouted the military man in Swahili. Mama Chungu remembered him from the days she used to hold a begging-bowl outside the mosque. But they were not allowed to beg once they had entered the Refuge, and each one made herself into a different person to fit the situation just as she had done on marriage,

5

motherhood, widowhood and time and time again, conscious at each stage of identity behind the expectant, narrow hips, the swelling breasts, the symbols of mourning and the simulation of distress. The man used to parade in town those days – he still did, for all she knew – wanting to flaunt his condition to the world and so using these foreign tongues and manners instead of the intimate birth language that would allow one to divine and assuage his grief. She did the same. They were all masked here for the sake of sharing, since they had been brought up to see sharing as the ultimate goal and there remained this sisterhood of constraint to share with. If he had been a real soldier in a real war, there would exist a kind of brotherhood, not needing to be sought out with dirty words and toy medals. It was like hearing on the radio a search for missing persons – fifteen years old, one metre 55, wearing a white school blouse and a grey skirt, black shoes, white socks – as though one could be found by sharp Swahili voices rather than by following the trail of home and blood.

The man made a derisory gesture and continued his march. Wairimu giggled. Some of her friends mocked her stiff movements. Priscilla pursed her lips at loose behaviour. Sophia was reminded of *beni* processions long ago, *Kingi* competing with *Scotchi* or *Kilungu*. But they did it so much better – those military uniforms, that imitation of bugle notes on traditional instruments, the marching rhythms tapped from the surface of the usually more subtle drums. Or was it only that at the coast things seemed sharper, better defined, more rational? Eeeee – these old ladies thought it was only your early days you cared about, saw them through golden sunlight, the days when feet never seemed heavy or belly slack and empty. But it was not that, not that at all. Even the day she left Mombasa with her daughter – the years not counted, but well past the time of childbearing – looking forward to living with the grandchildren, not dragging back or clouded with the knowledge of the tragedy to come, even then, she remembered, the minarets were set deliberately against the radiant colour of the sky, the palm fronds distinct, your fingers almost itching to plait them; every dress, every meal, planned, leisurely but just as you wanted them, till the purchaser, the husband, the client for hairdressing or medicine, would fall pat like a ripe mango just where you intended. The day was regulated by the call to prayer, the years by women's wiles and fashions, the lilting precision of the language, the delectable swing of argument and counter-argument, sharpening the wits and smoothing the gracious tongue. These women of shrill claim and counter-claim, of late-learned cleanliness, leaving old implements to rot beside their homesteads, patching their roofs with odd sheets of board and their dresses with clashing colours, they might stare at this battered old fellow. Even now with a clean *kanzu* and a decent haircut he might be made respectable.

But Matron, scandalised, sent the kitchen helper to call them in to tidy up before supper, because the nurses were coming next day.

Every term a group of Community Nurses in training came once or twice to visit the Refuge. The old ladies were pleased: they liked visitors and every event gave them something to talk about. Many of the girls were cheerful and laughed and joked to buck them up. A few even returned on private visits when they were in the neighbourhood or if, after finishing their first training, they went on to do midwifery at Pumwani just round the corner. These, though, were the strong-stomached. Many of the old ones seized on the opportunity to relate in clinical detail their own and their daughters' confinements, and most of the nurses felt that enough was enough. But the old ladies also benefited by having the place spruced up for visitors and more fervently inspected to see if their clothes and bedding needed renewal. One time the girls had brought them packets of dried milk.

'She is very weak,' frowned one of the nurses examining Rahel. 'Don't you think she would be better in hospital?'

'No,' said Wairimu firmly. 'She likes the company of people she knows. She is better here with us. What more can you do for her in hospital than we do here? She's not going to start riding a bicycle, now, is she?'

'But isn't it depressing for the rest of you?'

'She got worse last time they took her to hospital,' put in Sophia. 'And it's not depressing to have her here. What would be depressing is to think that we would be kicked out if we got like her.'

The others nodded assent. Just then Matron appeared in the doorway.

'Ladies, I hope you aren't hindering the girls in their work.'

'Discussing things with them *is* our work,' the nurse insisted bravely. She found the very name of Matron alarming. 'I thought this one could be moved to hospital, but they are reluctant to let her go.'

'I believe they are right.'

You never knew with Matron. To your face she would never admit that you understood anything, but eventually she would allow some respect for your experience.

'The community has a strength of its own. Some of them have not much else left to live for. Rahel's leg was healed, as far as it can be, in hospital, but you do not have a cure for her years and her losses.'

The nurse swallowed.

'All right, I won't report this to Sister Tutor, then. But if she complains, I hope you'll stand up for me.'

'Don't worry. The hospital is so overcrowded I'm sure they will be grateful to any of us who can look after our own patients. When shall we see you again?'

'You won't, officially speaking. We're going back to classes next week and the new lot of girls will be starting as soon as they've had their short leave.'

Mary was one of those looking forward to joining the public health section: she was still on ward duties, with tests and leave to come before they changed over. She hummed as she walked briskly down the long corridor to collect the day's issue of medicines from the dispensary. This was the first time she was doing it alone. She still delighted in her crisp uniform, though the belt was uncomfortably tight and it took long minutes of wrestling to pin the cap straight on her long, springy hair. The watch on her left wrist was also a pleasure to her. It was one of the most expensive items on the list of pre-training requirements and her eldest brother had bought it for her to reduce the strain on her parents. She remembered him every time she studied the second hand to register the rate of pulse or the gradual suffusion of temperature.

The corridor was by now familiar, the doubts of the first training days long overcome. She could not, of course, remember being wheeled along it as a newborn or again after she had broken an arm in standard five. In fact the place had grown grubby over the years. Some of the light shades were broken and the repeated pressure of bodies at visiting time had left lines of grease along the wall, but she was hardly aware of this. Though some people criticised, your hospital, like your school, was not exchangeable. Its very ordinariness made a claim on your loyalty.

It was just where the passage branched off to the dispensary that she met the student doctor. He did not appear to be gliding round with his hands full of important papers like the seniors. He was just standing by the intersection looking about him, empty-handed, his white coat gleaming as though very new over his expensive-looking shirt and slacks, a striking light brown face, loose, curly hair, an exploratory look in her direction. She almost stopped, then lowered her eyes and tried to even her pace. After all, she had seen medical students before. Everybody warned you about them. It would be foolish to let them get you flustered. But something about this one was different. When she walked back with her loaded tray he was still there, in conversation with one of the specialists who attended her ward. She was not at all surprised when he appeared there later in the day.

Suddenly one morning Rahel woke up and asked what time it was.

'Half past seven,' Priscilla told her, careful to express no surprise. Bessie and Mama Chungu helped to prop Rahel up against the pillows. She insisted that she would get up, but soon found that she could not stand and submitted to their ministrations.

'Well, where have you been?' Wairimu demanded, after they had fussed over her, fed her, prepared clean clothes and found some pretext on which Matron could call in before breakfast to observe the change.

'I've been trying to sleep: haven't we all?' retorted Rahel. 'What with bugles blowing and crates crashing about. I almost thought my leg was gone again.'

'Well, you take care of what you've got left after all the time it took them to patch you up. See, here's your leg, a bit stiff but you can walk on it when you're stronger. Not that you'd better go climbing trees, now.'

'I never did, you know. And I never even touched the special tree.

But it was a noisy night, wasn't it? I seemed to be ages getting to sleep.'

'You've been ages waking up,' said Matron gently. 'You've been quite ill, you know, so you'd better take things quietly. Let's put you in the wheelchair while we make the bed up again. It's only in your head you were hearing bugles.'

'And people have been asking for you,' added Sophia. 'The Community Nurses – perhaps even the soldier.'

'Well of course,' Rahel began, making up for time lost to speech and heedless whether they had heard it all before, 'soldiering is in the blood, as my man used to say, and I can't just ignore it.' Sounds of the past kept on reverberating, that was what she meant to say. But her tongue still felt clumsy, prodding in an exploratory way at the Swahili words, whistling over the sibilants, whispering the final vowels, *jes'i, tarumbet', ssstand-at-teasss*. 'I could picture myself joining up if I were young now and had my two good legs, like those young women we saw in the TV news, remember? My father was a regular soldier and he was away in Tanganyika when I was born during the Great War. My next brother was not born till three years later when the KAR came home, so he was one of those called Keya. We did not live in quarters and all that as people did later on. The soldiers had a really rough life in barracks, sometimes, or out in camp: my mother would weep over it but of course we children just thought the stories were exciting. But the men were very loyal to one another so it's not surprising that I married a soldier too. Many of my father's comrades used to come and visit us at home, and I dare say some were specially picked to look at me and my younger sister. I was second wife to my man down in Uyoma – we were not baptised then, and my father thought that was good enough for me. It was a little while before they built Jubilee Market in Kisumu, so that would have been about 1935: some African soldiers went to London for the procession and I remember my father had a photograph of them. So I was all right in Uyoma. My co-wife was ten years or so older than me, but not jealous. . . .'

'Careful, sister, careful,' interjected Wairimu. 'So she was my age. Are you saying that by 1935. . . ?'

'I am not saying anything bad, Wairimu my sister. I am only saying that Luo women have a certain dignity as they get older, if you take

10

my meaning – and it's no use swinging your skinny old hips in here. There's no one to admire you, even if some people have forgotten the meaning of taboos. Not to say what would happen if Matron found you skipping about like you were not a day over forty. Well . . . so I was all right in Uyoma. I got used to preparing fish for the market and getting water straight from the lake, but the harvests seemed poor to me. I got Vitalis first and then two girls before my husband went away to the war, to Somaliland first and then to Burma. We managed, somehow, through the famine of Otonglo and all that, with no money coming in. We had fish and water at least, so the children stayed alive.

'After the war our husband came home. Everyone was happy. Vitalis was ten years old and wanting to go to school. My daughters were at the toothy stage. My co-wife had a little girl she said was five – I think she juggled with the dates a bit myself. She encouraged me to go on a long visit to my mother about the time she said the baby was due. But I didn't feel it was my place to say anything, and when our husband came home from the war he didn't ask any questions either. He was changed, very quiet. He was glad to see the children, especially the boys, asked them questions about fish and plants and different kinds of wood, got them into competition, throwing stones and sticks, making traps. But with us he was reserved. If we asked,
  ' "How do those I-talians talk?"
he would make us laugh,
  ' "Al-la-la-ali-lu-la-it-to-ta," up and down the scale like Sophia when she gets some of her real Swahili friends together. Or
  ' "How do you know when you meet a general?"
  ' "At – ten – shun. God – say – king – mai God – hel – lo – ol – boi – at the double – cheers!"
(But sergeants' voices we already knew. We thought he might be a sergeant by now but he didn't even show us his sleeves.)
  'But if we asked,
  ' "What is the ship like? Did you go in an aeroplane? What do they grow in Somaliland? Were the people in India friendly?" he would just sit silent and tell us,
  ' "You wouldn't understand. It is better for you not to know. These are not women's matters."
  'And on that leave he would sit hour after hour, just looking out

11

from the front of the house or walking down to see the fishing boats and back without answering people's questions. The little girls asked him once,

' "Didn't you bring us a present back from the war?" (For he had money. He put some in the Post Office at Kisumu and with some he bought meat and bottled beer and sweets for the children, but nothing from those distant places.) And he said to them,

' "I have come back to you. No one can ask for more than that." Later that day he called Vitalis and showed him the big scar on his left thigh, and said to him,

' "This is the best present you can get in a war. Do you know that? It is worth two weeks in bed and four weeks of not being directly shot at. It is therefore a very valuable experience." Vitalis did not understand, but he never forgot. The rest of us never dared ask what caused the wound or whether it hurt: he shut me up angrily when I tried.

'Then when one of the women from the neighbourhood, a grubby old thing, always making trouble, came to greet us, she started saying to him,

' "Don't you think that Auma is very small for her age? I have been surprised ever since I have been seeing that child. My grandchild whom my son left in the womb when he went to the war and did not come back seems to be much healthier."

'She kept on about it and I was trembling for what he might say to Min Auma, but he only fixed his eyes on the old woman.

' "Have you ever seen a woman with a big belly and her head shot off?" he asked.

'She shook her head.

' "Can you imagine a hot, marshy place – you may think it is hot here, but really it is hardly warm – and a man who has been dead three days with his feet in the marsh?"

' "No, my brother-in-law, these are evil things."

' "You, who love to slither and slide, have you ever marked a trail by counting the dead men near the path, and picked up their weapons to use against their brothers as you go forward?"

' "In our custom you let the enemy's spear lie where it falls, since it can operate only for your enemy's benefit."

12

' "So I was taught, but Luo custom is for little Luo wars, fought by the rules for a bit of land or a few cattle. But in a real war, that aims to destroy rather than to get, every weapon is a weapon pleasing to war, and every death is a death pleasing to war, and every fighter is a sacrifice to war. Do you understand me?"

' "These words are beyond my understanding, my brother-in-law."

' "Then keep your small concerns for small minds and do not bring your tittle-tattle here to me," cried my husband, and she scuttled away and never made trouble for us again to my knowledge. But trouble comes and these days we do not think to ask who makes it.

'We did not have any more children, my co-wife and I. He did not neglect us, but perhaps some strength had gone out of him in the wartime. And even when my father sent word to him of my youngest sister, thinking that such a marriage would strengthen my position in the house and also bring the girl some protection, for she was rather lazy and wayward, not likely to organise a home well, he was not interested at all, but said he would prefer to invest his wealth in the children he already had. Since some of these were mine, of course, my father could not object. Although he was still strong, my father did not go overseas during the second war, but helped to train the young recruits until his time came to retire. There was one time, in 1947, he was sent specially to Gilgil. He said afterwards it was a matter of discipline, something that could not be avoided. That was all he would say, but we could see he was deeply hurt and he did not live long after retiring. He had been in different camps, but my mother never travelled further than Kisumu till the day she died.

'But it was different in our days. Although my husband professed not to listen to stories about my co-wife, it was only I who went with him to Gilgil so that Vitalis could go to school. I also learned to read there and to look after a military house. It was an easy life if you had a good man. Don't you see I even speak Swahili as well as you people?'

Wairimu did not really think so, but as she had learned it at an earlier age and had a more sensible mother-tongue to start with she did not press the point. Luo people generally did not tell the difference between one and many till they got to the end of a word, and could therefore be very careless about the vital first syllables in Swahili.

Rahel, admittedly, was better than most. Whatever you learned in the army you were likely to learn well.

'But it didn't work out like that, did it?' asked Wairimu. There was no need for tactful silences between them. The boundary of talk was where the lack of words or experience drew the line. 'I mean about investing in the family. Or else you wouldn't be here, would you?'

Rahel sighed.

'Whether that old lady really left us alone or tried to work witchcraft on us I couldn't say. Or whether the evil that my husband had seen during the war preyed upon him and upon us after he died. He just collapsed and died, you know, in 1952. Same time as the old king. He would have liked that. Great ones for kings and generals the army people used to be. Of course, we hadn't started thinking about *Uhuru* then.'

'I had,' insisted Wairimu.

'Well, I suppose you had, and our top people had; but I hadn't. That's all.'

Rahel held her peace. Since 1947 she had dealt with these Kikuyu people, their history of loss and assimilation, their long, hidden malice, their quick calculations and the terrible bent backs of their burdened women. She wanted to shout at them to hold their heads up. Was that only because she was a soldier's wife or because she had grown up to a graceful carriage and a steadily balanced water-pot? Was it because her ancestral land had been protected by the mosquito and the tsetse fly or because plain speaking, back in her father's time, had matched the British in their own stiff-necked way?

She subsided back into sleep, dreaming of grainy millet porridge with bitter greens (for in recent years she had quite gone off fish heads), of the cool earthy corner of the house where the filled water-pots were stored according to their use, of drums in different rhythms and starched uniforms with gleaming buttons. When the Community Nurses came they were astonished at the improvement, but let her rest.

CHAPTER TWO

Mary was taking Wairimu's pulse and the old lady was looking at her attentively. She knew that she must be quiet till the count was finished.

'You're Mary, aren't you?' said Wairimu. 'You looked after me before.'

'That's right. It's clever of you to remember.'

'I remember because I used to be like you once, though you may not believe it. Only more flighty, perhaps.'

The girl smiled, and the old lady was gratified to see her that much better.

'There's something the matter, though, isn't there? You don't look well to me. Are you – overdue – is that it?'

'No I'm not.'

'Sorry, you think me rude. It is only that when you get old you can tell: perhaps that only means you have nothing to do except minding other people's business. I think I would be a nurse if I were young now. But in my day there were only two choices, picking coffee or looking after men.'

'And which did you do?'

'Both.'

'And I bet you didn't miss out on a good time either.'

'You can say that again. And you?'

The weariness came back into Mary's face.

'I guess if I'd been young then I'd have done both too. I'm still a student and – don't tell anyone, now – last month I *did* think I was pregnant. Thank God I'm not. But what I do know is that I wouldn't have had any help if I had been. He didn't even answer my letter. Well, I suppose it's better to find out too soon than too late, but it depresses you, doesn't it?'

15

'The old, old story,' said Wairimu softly. 'You don't imagine there would have been such punishments for getting into trouble in our old laws, do you, if it hadn't happened pretty often? Is he a student too?'

'A student doctor. Nurses are just there to be trodden under their feet, I guess. My big brother warned me already. He helped to educate me and he would be just furious if he knew. He's engaged to my friend Gertrude, the tall one over there, and I'm certain he'll treat her right.'

'Yes, I had an elder brother too,' smiled Wairimu. 'He died long ago, of course. He was the first one to tell me about Nairobi and I'm sure afterwards he wished he hadn't. But cheer up. They say what can't be cured must be endured, and old age is one of those things you can't cure.'

Wairimu thought the young man would take her to Nairobi. Years afterwards she saw how foolish that had been, but when a fairy-tale figure appears in your life, do you not expect the surroundings also to burst into a fairy-tale? It was many years later that she saw children creating a fantastic world of drama in their playground and acting up to it. Then she realised how it had been with her in those few passionate days. Or like the film of Adam and Eve which she had seen in some outdoor church arena, with the serpent wriggling up all over again and someone in a seat behind her shouting out loud, 'You fool, don't eat it – don't EAT it!' and subsiding with a hiss of despair as the sempiternal wrong was enacted once more.

She knew him, of course. He was Waitito the son of Njuguna. Nobody came as close to home as that without your knowing his name. He had probably come to visit his friend and age-mate, Nyambura's brother. But again it was days before she began seriously to wonder why Nyambura had not accompanied her to the river that morning, and she never put the question afterwards; what would be the good? As though there were not more serpents than one wriggling through the dirt, and how would Eve know – Eve who was older, after all, than Mumbi, if she remembered it right, though what she had learned afterwards never seemed so clear in her head as what had actually happened in those far-off days – how could she know that the serpent was not one of the good gifts she was surrounded with? It was something that had worried her once upon a time when she was having church lessons, time hanging heavy those days on her hands and limbs, how did those first people find out that they must fear a caterpillar but crunch up a locust, that a goat was good to eat but not a dog, that nettles could be tamed by water and fire but bright berries might kill. Perhaps the first Eve found these things only when she was put outside the garden, but Mumbi had the whole mountain.

The young man kept the golden haze about him even when he drew her out of the path into the chilly shade of the trees, and if he could put a spell on her so far outside custom (for even when custom was customarily broken there was a time and place for it, a known penalty and a known outcome), must he not also draw her into that world where custom did not rule?

She asked a lot of questions, those three days, about Nairobi, but he said it was not easy to get a place to build there and on the fourth day he vanished and there was no one she dared ask. Later she heard that he had come to arrange his marriage and he bought the girl, Miriam, a white cloth dress and had a service for her in the mission church, but before that happened Wairimu was away in the coffee.

She used to wander away from the other girls and sit thinking. Her mother was worried and asked if she was ill. What, otherwise, was there to think about? If she feared her daughter was pregnant, there was soon clear evidence that she was not. They even asked if she was displeased with the marriage they were arranging. It was not that either. He was healthy and good-looking enough and as yet unmarried. It was not even that she would not pass the test of virginity, though that too was frightening. It was more that she had touched a magic world and been left behind.

To go to the coffee was also a new thing. It was one way of choosing for yourself. Otherwise for girls there was almost no choice. Boys might choose school or be marshalled into school, and as a consequence they might be chosen for one kind of work or another – in the time of the Great War, recently ended, many boys and men had been forced to go either to work or to fight – but for girls there were very few school places and as yet little choice: when you came home again there was still the marriage to be arranged. It was rumoured that the Sisters might try to keep the girls with them, but in fact the novitiate was not started till later when converts showed they really wanted it: the girl had no alternative to marriage until the coffee came.

You had to walk for about three hours – one of the other girls had pointed out the way. So, since it was not safe to go before light, you had better make an excuse for fetching water early in the morning – perhaps spilling a load the evening before and blaming it on a baby or a calf – so that it would be an hour before you were missed. Then you had to present yourself at the gate of the European farm and ask if they wanted workers. Usually they did. If they didn't, she supposed you would have to trail home again and face a beating. But once you were taken on, given a place to sleep in the long, low buildings, a blanket and some staple food and taught which berries to pick and where to put them, they would not let you out even if your parents came to cry and shout for you. At the end of the month you got some money, and so you were like a man and could do a lot of choosing for yourself.

One or two girls may have gone there because they were pregnant. But more often it was because they felt overworked at home or harassed by an unkind stepmother. They might go planning for a certain object, like Lois, who went with Wairimu and had been baptised as a baby far down the mountain where her father was working at the time. She was engaged to a Christian and was determined to buy herself a white dress and a pair of shoes to be married in. Even those who did not specially mean to save, she told Wairimu, would buy themselves a yellow cloth to replace the leathers they walked in, and new ornaments. So they slipped away one misty morning, leaving the water-skins by the path, and before midday they were written on for the coffee.

Nobody thought of going for good. If you came home with your money and your experience it would be as a chooser and a doer, able to send your younger sisters to the river and have food brought from the kitchen. But in fact not many went home. When Wairimu left Lois there she had still not got her white dress and they heard that the fiancé was not pleased with her running away. There was more to being a Christian wife, he said, than dresses and shoes.

Wairimu was a strong girl, though not tall, and used to working hard. She was not shy – ever since that morning on the river path she had known that she could not go back to childish behaviour again – so she got along with people, sang about her work, joined in the evening dances, held her own against the men's demands. The golden haze had never come back. None of them could put a spell on her and she always said no.

She had got her yellow cloth and an extra wrapper for cold days and a few more bangles, but she also kept some of her rupees. For the coffee had not brought her what she wanted, except just for avoiding the wedding day. She would have to go to Nairobi.

One day the young master was walking round inspecting the berries. The old master did not often do that: he left it to his foremen. The young man sometimes came for a couple of months. They said he was still at school in England, though he looked grown-up and dressed like a man.

'How are you getting on?' he asked in good Kikuyu, looking into her basket.

'I want to go to Nairobi,' she answered, taking the chance.

'It's a long way to Nairobi,' he laughed.

'But I want to go there. There is something I can do for you if you take me.'

She looked hopefully into his face and danced a few steps.

His colour changed as she did not know white people's colour could change. He became red like the pinky-red in the ear-coils. Then he slapped her hard.

'Keep your place,' he shouted, and hurried away.

Well, she had made a mistake. Fortunately no one had seen it. But the next time she saw a rainbow pointing outwards and downwards she knew she must go.

You could walk it easily in three days – to Mbiri one day, Mbiri to Thika the second, Thika to Nairobi the third. But people did not walk alone. Besides, you were not supposed to leave your work without being signed off. You could be brought back, and that would be worse than a slap. She began to lay her plans.

The coffee was taken by bullock cart from various parts of the estate to the factory. There the first processing was done, but it had to be worked over again in Nairobi, so it was packed into enormous bags, twelve to a ton, and sent out by lorry to the railhead, near Fort Hall. She could not even lift one of the bags, a bitter humiliation, since she considered herself grown-up and as strong as her granny. Her mother, always fussing over babies, was not quite in the same class. The men

19

would lift the bags, two working together, on to the lorry which would take them to Nyeri town, where a coffee transporter would combine the loads from the different estates and deliver them all to the railway. The little estate roads were not in good enough condition for the big lorry to collect direct. The foremen grumbled at the expense of all this changing over, and the better profit that could be made if you were near the railway.

Wairimu made herself agreeable to the Kikuyu driver of a local lorry. She had once before got a lift of a few miles from him when she had taken a day off for shopping in Nyeri: that was her first experience of wheeled transport. He agreed, on certain conditions, to speaking for her to the long-distance transporters and telling her which day they would be travelling. She must go near the beginning of her ticket so as not to lose too much pay: if she asked to be signed off she would be questioned about her plans and perhaps laughed at again.

She slipped out of the lines early one morning, wearing her yellow cloth and ornaments, a small *kiondo* slung on her back. She was almost as excited as she had been when leaving home that first time. The air was cool and crisp, the earth road still damp and chilly beneath her bare feet. She had decided not to go home first. They would only try to detain her. They knew where she was, for her brother had been to see her once on his way to look for casual work in Nyeri town, so the whisper must have spread. At that time her father was still trying to avoid having to return the first goats paid to him towards her dowry. But he would not so demean himself as to come and wrangle with her away from his own homestead.

She waited by the roadside, out of sight, for the lorry to drive up to the estate, load and start its return journey. She climbed up among the huge sacks and enjoyed the jerky movement and the wind whistling by. In Nyeri town the driver introduced her to the turn-boy of the regular service, with whom he shared a room. She agreed to cook for them both that night, but the turn-boy had to negotiate with his Indian driver, so she had to part with one of her precious rupees as well. She had been paid three rupees for each thirty-day ticket. They rested on Sundays and could take other days off for sickness or visiting provided each ticket was completed within forty-two days. She had completed ten tickets in about a year and had managed to save about ten rupees – only now they were talking about changing the money.

It was a big climb into the high lorry and she did not see much of the countryside because she was half-hidden among the bags, but she had the sensation of going down and down, and when she stood up at an occasional halt everything looked familiar. The roads looked wide and smooth to her, though not to the driver. These were the same, she realised, on which the women had been forced to work until Harry Thuku had got a telegram from London saying they must stop. She did not quite know what a telegram was, but all the women praised Thuku and they were already singing songs about him as the Chief of Girls.

At Fort Hall there were a few stone buildings, a *boma*, donkey carts, a motor car or two. These must be what had made it Fort Hall instead of Mbiri. The driver told the turn-boy to put her off before they came to the railway, in case he were asked awkward questions, but the turn-boy had a better idea. He stopped another lorry just outside the town and consulted with his opposite number. Then he dragged Wairimu out of her hiding-place and over to the other vehicle.

'You'll have to put up a good story,' he whispered to her, 'but it will be better for you than waiting for the train.'

She had to confront the Indian driver herself, but found he spoke excellent Kikuyu: his father had a shop in the small town and he had grown up there, only going to Nairobi for a few years of primary schooling. She told him that she had a sick brother working for the railway in Nairobi and her aged father was not able to travel that far so had sent her to look after him. The Indian looked sceptical but he told her to hop up so long as she agreed to take care of herself in Thika where she was going to change loads and spend the night. She joyfully agreed and made the most of the ride, seeing the country grow flatter and more fertile as they passed. At Thika the turn-boy took her to a tiny shack beside the market and brought her a bowl of maize and beans to eat.

Next morning there were more wonders. Not only was the train to be seen near the road but you hardly passed five minutes – time to fill the water-skin, as she might have said then – without encountering traffic, people riding bicycles (some of whom were pointed out to her

21

as European women), donkey carts piled with fruit, firewood or assorted bundles, motor cars (most of them the same Model T Ford as the master had at Nyeri, but she hardly knew that any were different), a few machines which were used, according to her companion, to till the fields, and occasionally huge carts pulled by teams of oxen which were heading for uncivilised areas where the roads were not properly made up. This one was swampy in places, and at Ruiru they passed strange machines where the river roared by, which could, he tried to make her believe, light huge lamps fifteen miles away. True, there were poles beside the road, too tall for any fence, and so they drove on, past tall houses and on to hard grey roads, and at last this was Nairobi, the other side of the river. They put her down at the corner of Government Road and Duke Street, on their way to the mills, gesturing towards the station in token reference to her story. There was an awe about everything then which had faded for her since. The sun was high: she sensed once more the golden haze. She had been right to follow her rainbow.

People swarmed about. Roads were wider than she had ever seen. It was like a dream, but a dream without anyone to direct you where to go or what to do. And, like a dream, without edges to it – bare and patchy as it seemed in memory, everywhere you looked (even across the race course, even to the roads you had traversed the other side of the swampy river bed, even to the wide plains south of the railway workshops) it was still Nairobi.

All the same, she was getting tired. There was some money hidden away inside the *kiondo* but she did not know how to buy anything to eat from these strange buildings filled with men, or how to ask her way to a market. She did not understand most of what was being said around her, and began to see why people had said it would be hard to find anyone you knew in Nairobi (but in any case she did not know anyone). She had seen Indian shopkeepers in Nyeri, and an engineer or two coming to do repairs in the factory, but here there seemed to be Indians everywhere.

One of them pulled up a car near her and out of it stepped not another Indian, as she had at first thought, but a young Kikuyu man dressed in a suit such as the master would wear only on Sundays or for attending *baraza* in town, with a wide-brimmed hat and shiny

22

European shoes. He shook hands with the driver of the car and started to walk away.

'Thuku,' a whisper went round the crowd, 'Harry Thuku.'

Thuku! She had not seen him before but she knew he had been to Nyeri and they had all sung songs in praise of him because he had protested against the women's road work and was going to free the people from forced labour and European taxes. This was seeing life indeed, and she felt an urgent need to participate, to make herself also known. She was about seventeen years old and she too was part of a new world. So she began to sing one of the praise songs, swaying in time with the music. Some people laughed, others clapped their hands out of beat, for which she did not see the reason. Thuku himself stopped and turned round.

'So you know me?' he asked with a smile.

'Everyone knows you, sir, even if we did not see you when you came to Nyeri.'

'But I do not know you. Who are you?'

'My name is Wairimu wa Gichuru, sir.'

'And what are you doing in Nairobi, Wairimu, if you come from Nyeri? Are your parents here, or do you have a husband?'

'I came alone, sir, to see the city and find work.'

Some of the men laughed. A woman in European dress was about to take her arm.

'Leave her,' Thuku ordered. Then he spoke in another language to a man in the crowd.

'Wairimu, you are brave, but you do not know how hard a thing you have undertaken. Your people ought to have explained to you. This friend of mine will take you to some Kiambu people who will teach you what you need to know. Perhaps they will give you some work for a while. Will you trust us to arrange that?'

'Yes indeed, sir. Thank you, sir.'

He smiled again.

'It is good to be brave and wise. People have said that I am brave. But sometimes it is wise to be a little afraid.'

The group dispersed as he walked away and the man he had pointed out signalled to Wairimu to follow. She went with him to a narrow, dirtier street and in it to a small corrugated iron building where men

23

were eating and drinking tea. The foremen and clerks at the estate sometimes had tea and bread but she had never tasted any herself. The man indicated a bench she should sit on and a young boy brought her *uji* to drink and pieces of bread, at his command. The friend of Thuku – she later learned that he was called Tairara – went to talk to the man and wife, Samson and Nduta, who ran the tea room. Then he went away and left them to talk to her in Kikuyu.

First they asked whether she had run away from home, whether she had ever been married, if she had a baby or was expecting one. Well, they said, it was not according to their custom that she should be alone, but the world was changing and Nyeri was perhaps less strict than Kiambu. She could help them serve and wash the utensils: they would give her food and a corner to sleep in and, if she stayed, some money at the end of the month. They supposed she must know what Nairobi was like and how men were bound to pester her. That was her own affair but they did not want any trouble in the tea shop. Outside, they had no way to protect her, women being as few as they were and all the old rules set aside. Straight away she had better learn numbers in Swahili and the names of the main foodstuffs. This did not take long and she revelled in her own ability to learn.

She was amazed by her luck. Although supposed to be working most daylight hours, she was soon able to find pretexts for going out to buy provisions or help someone with a load to the station. She was fascinated by the streets, where ox-carts still mingled with the motor cars and at night big lights (just as the turn-boy had told her at Ruiru) shone from poles along the wayside.

In shop windows there were white people standing and sitting to display the clothes – it took her some time to realise they were not alive – and some of the buildings were higher than the tallest tree. Inside, people said, you walked up stair after stair, like the four that led up to master's bungalow at the coffee. Water came out of pipes – not many of them: you had to queue for a turn to fill your bucket. Some people preferred to go down to the river, but Nduta refused to use river water for tea or cooking. When you slopped through the marsh and reeds to get to the bank (for there was nowhere else you could decently have a bath, and even so there would be men prowling about) you could see why. For this was not like the river that came down from the

24

mountain and people had not respected it. Sewage and hospital waste poured into it, rubbish and dead cats floated in it, rats invaded the garbage heaps left beside it, the only natural life connected with it was the loud croaking of the frogs at night. It was only after heavy rain, which could fall even out of season in Nairobi, that its pace would increase and the water might seem clean as it gurgled along, but then it would overflow its banks and still more refuse would be carried into the stream when the water subsided again.

She learned in a rough and ready way to recognise the different kinds of people. There were arrogant Somali, with their elaborate headscarves and bony features: some of them condescended to oversee labour on the estates, demanding enamel dishes, tea and special times to pray, but now she saw their women for the first time and learned a new concept of elegance. There were big, black Luos, Uganda people with white robes and commanding eyes, Kamba porters and woodworkers with their pointed teeth – good mechanics, they were reckoned up country – Goans, like brown Europeans, deft, jerky, decorative, and Hindu and Muslim Indians in every kind of dress and every walk of life. Arabs and coast people came often to the tea room, speaking in a way the inland people seemed to understand but did not imitate: Nduta said they avoided bars because of their religion. The men were very clean; there were only a few women, but Wairimu was studying them carefully. Then there were the Europeans, hundreds of them, it seemed, in the middle of town, because many of them had work there instead of being hidden away in kitchens and workshops like the other races. By complexion, tilt of the head, clothing, tools carried and, most especially, by the state of their boots, you gradually got to identify European official, farmer, soldier, railwayman, police. The women all seemed to be young – though people said the ones with the shortest hair and skirts were the youngest – but even here you could soon learn the difference between a visiting farmer and a town wife. Many of them were not married at all, she was told, but served in shops (European shops, of course) or wrote things in offices, earned their own money, bought dresses or cooking pans or groceries for themselves (you could see the parcels being carried out by shop attendants to a waiting vehicle), some even drove their own cars. Indeed there was a lot to think about.

Wairimu delighted in the different food smells, horse smells, tobacco smells and cosmetic smells that wafted across the pavement from each group. She was interested and amazed by the skin colours and textures, more various than she had dreamed of, and the voices that ranged from gruff and guttural to shrill and staccato like those the old people said you used to hear at night when the forests were thick and full of life.

She was summoned from her reverie by the kitchen attendant. Clothes would be brought tomorrow, they were told. Everyone was expected to be *very* clean and to be wearing something *decent* underneath so that they could be fitted without making anybody ashamed. Please remind everyone to be ready early in the morning. Well, there was some pleasure still in getting a new dress, just as there used to be in selecting the six goatskins, turning and matching them this way and that to make the best of the colours and the patterns. Of course she would remind the ladies and inspect them too. Seventy-eight years had never yet taught her to mind her own business.

The local donors' committee had come up with thirty dresses and two of the ladies had come down to distribute them. It was an occasion they always enjoyed, an opportunity to give pleasure through their generosity and to show how free they were with the old women, patting them on the shoulder and helping to pull the garments over their flabby chests. It was an agony for Matron, who knew that the gifts got together must vary greatly in their appeal and durability, and also that at least half of them would be too small. One of the ladies was an Asian diplomat's wife, the other a Kenyan lawyer, glad to find excuses to get out of the house during her maternity leave. She had hopefully brought along a sewing kit for alterations, but Matron was envisaging long weeks of complaint as she presided, smiling, over the coffee and biscuits. She wrote out a list of the residents under the headings large, medium and small and advised the visitors to divide the dresses in the same way to reduce the area of dispute, and to call in ten ladies at a time. Then she firmly withdrew. Let the charge of favouritism land on other heads for the time being.

26

Of course the residents enjoyed themselves at first, holding up and fitting, admiring themselves in a mirror brought for the purpose from Matron's quarters, having photographs taken. But as the actual allocations were made discontent began to show. In the large category Rahel was no problem: if it was long enough, not much else mattered. Priscilla was so used to fitting into things that the shirt-waist that was too narrow for any of the other tall women suited her very well: it happened, in fact, to be trimly cut and sedate in colour. Sophia got hold of the most glamorous dress of all.

'You'll be able to put a *buibui* over it when it wears into holes,' Mama Chungu commented acidly.

Bessie was easy-going in the medium class. She was used to regarding a dress as a raw item that would go through various metamorphoses before it dropped into grey and musty rags. Nekesa was satisfied with the print dress she got, though they had to borrow a wide belt from another outfit to cover the gap at the waist fastening. The 'small' group were the most constrained, most having substantial muscles, in spite of their apparent skinniness, compared with the teachers and secretaries from whom the clothes had come, but Wairimu managed to land a sturdy dress with red and purple flowers by leaving the zip undone under her *shuka*.

'You see,' she said next day, pouting, 'Sophia got the best of the dresses. She always comes in for favours.'

'It fitted her,' Priscilla answered patiently. 'I liked it, but it would have hung like a sack on me. And you are shorter – it would not fit you.'

'I am not saying I wanted it. But they favour her. Just because she is a convert. Why didn't they send her back to Mombasa?'

'Why didn't they send you and me back to Nyeri? Because there is no one to look after us there. But for her it is worse, because she is now a Christian and some of the family would take revenge on her. I hear that her son will not even have her name mentioned in his house.'

'Sophia, Sophia,' repeated Wairimu. '*We* hear it often enough for goodness sake. Fat and flabby and flaunting herself like a young girl. Look at her hands – never did a hard day's work in her life. And all those bangles – *jingili, jingili, jingili!*'

Wairimu tossed her head in a way that might once have been called flaunting and remembered just in time that it was forbidden to spit on the cement floor.

'Work for them is different,' said Priscilla gently. She did not feel at all gentle, remembering how long it was since she had held a hoe herself. Remembering that she was as tall as Sophia and had once had heavy limbs and loins that would have rounded out with bearing children, breasts that were eager to be filled and fill again.

She had seen Mombasa several times, the first long ago in the war days when Jim was a baby and she had gone down with Mrs Bateson during the school holidays to help. Mr Bateson was busy on the farm and could not go. She had seen, even then, that the women worked. Those outside the town dug their vegetables and kept their chickens and goats, but inside were people who lived on money like Europeans. They traded, made sweets or *mandazi* for sale, sewed, plaited mats or baskets, bargained at great length, looked after their homes with satisfaction. True, in that hot sun and staying close to home, you might have thought them lazy in movement. But they were not lazy in the things that concerned them.

Sophia was pleased with the new dress. It had cunning pleats and big sleeves and a pattern of sequins. Some diplomatic lady of mature age and figure had once had it made for cocktails, for leisurely hours on ships or terraces. She felt queenly in it, as she remembered in her young womanhood poring for hours over materials in the bazaar and making them up with such long delight to emphasise every good point in her figure. So that one shuddered with pleasure, even under the modest *buibui*, waiting for the other women to pull and touch and handle the fine work. This one would be hard to wash, she knew, especially in cold water, to dry in a dusty compound, but one could not always be prudent, and in a place like this death stalked around the corner: one need not for ever be thinking of making things last.

As a child she had been taught to be careful, but not too careful. In her pleasure at the new dress she dared to think back to those days – endlessly warm days; even when the rain pelted down and made streams of the alleys of the old town, pools all over the too-flat roads of the new town, you were paddling in warm water, still comfortable. You were always crowded, but not in want, and the air was fragrant with spices, oiled bodies, coffee, fish, salt, tar. Perhaps this was why

28

the Refuge always felt so empty, the vacant atmosphere of disinfectant and boiled potatoes, the clean earthy smell that clung to these Kikuyu women and the sour, outlandish, yesterday's gruel of those others from the west. It was not that she did not like them, but they seemed to lack any notion of pattern, ordered their words in grunts and cackles.

She remembered as a little girl the excitement of people always coming and going. The rails still ran through the streets all the way down to Kilindini port, with trolleys pushed by men in uniform, carrying Europeans and other important people or crates and parcels for the big ships. In spite of the conflict between Arab and Swahili, everyone took notice when the town crier went round, with his buffalo horn and little stick, to make the announcements, or when the elders turned out richly dressed for the seasonal religious ceremonies. She remembered the lamplight procession and the fireworks after they heard that the Great War was over and that King George had won it, and the other time, when she was about ten years old, that Swahili and Somali had all at once been lumped together with the 'natives' from inland and had to carry passes. At least Mombasa prided itself on still having more civilised men than other places, exempt from some of the 'native' ordinances because they could read and write, interpret from Arabic to Swahili or English, and were engaged in government service or skilled in the law.

She did not go to *madrasa* with her brothers but learned at home to read a little in the old script and count for trading purposes. So when, long afterwards, they wanted her to read the Bible (she who had a memory like Scheherezade and could have driven them crazy with story-telling from the five books and other ancient memories) it was not too hard to learn the new letters with their intrusive a-e-i-o-u, all starting unpropitiously from the left side.

By the time she matured she was expert in weaving the mats which her mother took to market. Around this time her uncle, the one who carried his coffee-pot round the town, clinking the cups together in advertisement as nowadays the ice-cream man rings his bell on hot days, married a young wife who was expert in sewing and from her Fatuma – she was not yet Sophia – learned the art of needlework.

Her first marriage occurred at the time when the port grew dull for lack of business, sisal and coffee fetching so little that it was not worth buying sacks and putting them on the train. This did not prevent the customary ceremonies and the formal dowry payment. Fatuma made no objection to the match and, after the public proclamation that her virginity had been demonstrated, the couple were not reluctant to be enclosed for the seven days traditional *fungate* honeymoon. Ali had managed to keep his job as a clerk at the docks and had furnished a neat apartment for her, two upstairs rooms, where his friends would come to drink coffee and read the newspapers, one of them even to play the accordion. This surprised her, for it was generally considered to be a Christian instrument, used to accompany the seductive and debilitating beat of the waltz or quickstep. She was more accustomed to vigorous group dances, to the high wail of the long trumpet or massed drums, heard behind canvas screens when a ceremony was going on in the old town. But keeping a job was no joke in those days, and Ali was always having to pay out to assist some less fortunate colleague or sometimes, she suspected, to protect his seat in the rickety office where there were fewer and fewer invoices to write. (But in retrospect the old crafts and diets of the island survived in perpetual sunshine, as they had survived many another trial of history.)

Ali was lean and muscular, dressed ordinarily in white shirt and shorts, with the white embroidered cap pressed firmly on his curly hair. On Fridays he would expect his long white robe to be spotless and would take Hassan, similarly dressed, to the mosque while she stayed behind with the little girls. Before each Idd he would give her money for the fabrics, embroidery thread, whatever else she needed to turn them out smartly to his credit.

Indeed, the memory of her first marriage was punctuated not so much by births and miscarriages as by fragments of her art – a sailor suit she had made for Hassan to wear when some Governor or other was arriving at the port, a shimmering loose gown for carrying a baby that had slipped away when she was barely showing, a white-sprigged bed cover she had quilted for the wedding of a Goan teacher's daughter.

In Sophia's memory the strike seemed to be the beginning of the end. It was a good thing – Ali said so, and therefore she must believe it. Although they continued to live in the old town way, in which

Muslims considered themselves a cut above the inland people, Christians or pagans, kaffirs all, except for a few who had seen the light and were beginning to follow civilised ways, Ali was one of those who resented the Arab feeling of superiority. This feeling had grown since the Arabs, despite all their talk in the Coast Arab Association, had kept the votes for a Legco member to themselves. So Swahilis had begun to talk about unity with inland Africans, and once one started to think about them as brothers it was impossible not to see that they were suffering. Their wages were extremely low for a place where you could not even partially apply the theory that food was coming free from the home place; a house, however overcrowded, was hard to get and sure to cost more than the small allowance paid to those who did not get a room in government quarters; worse than that, the casual labourers might not get more than a few days' work a month. Disorders and riots had occurred before. Now, Ali said, it was time to show what organisation and solidarity could do.

It alerted government and employers to labour problems. It was not able to do much else. Only the Conservancy Department had given proper notice of their intention to strike. The Municipality therefore recognised a dispute and came up promptly with a very small offer. The night soil workers accepted it but the sweepers did not, so that although there was not a sanitary emergency, the rubbish piled up. Casual workers at the port were the first to come out but the 'permanent boys' had too much to lose: however when the strike spread to the African Marine Company police stopped all work in the port for fear that strikers would carry out their threat to invade the dock area. Pickets did their best to bring building to a halt and also to call out domestic servants, but some domestic employers and hotels were accommodating their staff or driving them home.

Permanent labourers on the railway did not actually strike – they presented their demands and were promised investigation. This greatly weakened workers' co-operation, but even so about six thousand people were off work at the same time. The Texas Oil Company paid off their daily workers and brought staff from Nairobi. The Mombasa Electric Light and Power Company signed off strikers and engaged new staff locally. Dairy workers settled their dispute within a day. So unity was sabotaged and people drifted back to work.

31

Only the very poorest got much out of the interim award, and the planned further investigations were postponed in the excitement of war breaking out.

To Fatuma it just seemed messy, outside forces spilling over in the untidy order of island life. Rubbish piled up in the streets and round the fish market, goods lay undelivered, some of them rotting, gangs of unemployed wandered about, no greater hazard to life and property than usual but irritating, the extra police making a great show of breaking them up while, as a result, new groups formed up like a wave behind them. It gave her a funny feeling, but she tried to believe Ali that it would make for improvement in the long run.

Then, almost before one was back in routine, war. Knowing as usual, Ali said the awards, the restraint on police action, had been to keep the people loyal in case they were needed to fight. There was no very promising alternative to be loyal to, from what one heard of the Italians in Ethiopia, but even so in 1940 the government managed to lock up some political activists on a charge of being in touch with the enemy, and to ban three political groups.

It was not what older people thought of as a war, with soldiers nipping across the boundary to shoot one another beside the railway while you stood back and waved flags. This war meant work – the port full of ships, carrying troops, carrying food, carrying mail, which sometimes failed to arrive and was always wanted in a hurry. Everyone was busy. Everyone was tired. There were long queues for goods in the authorised shops, high prices in the others. Routes, and so manifests, might have to be changed at the last minute, documents delayed to reduce the risk of careless talk. One morning a load slipped and crashed down from overhead. Ali was crumpled, reduced, died on the way to hospital. He was buried, as is customary, at sundown. Overnight, order was reversed, and all Fatuma's faiths disintegrated.

Eleven years they were together, good years, until the disaster that in her mind marched always with the troubles of the Second World War, when you had to pretend to be an Arab to qualify for a rice ration and your menfolk were too busy in the port to come home to their beds. But all that was behind her now. . . .

The cement floor was chill and damp to the touch. Draughts reigned under a cloudy sky. One had to speak to these faded old ladies in simplistic terms, dull and devoid of ornament. Admittedly, she did not know their treasured languages, but they prided themselves on knowing hers, and drained it of cadence and colour as they spoke.

Sophia smoothed the new dress lovingly. Once she would have scorned to wear anything that had been on another woman's body. But this was neutral. It held no perfume of other days, no fragment of shell or fish scales, no healthy smell of babies bathed at sundown, of hard soap or new cloth redolent of dress, of coconut oil and peppers, cloves or rough sticks of cinnamon that were good to chew. No kohl, no hennaed patterns on the skin, no moist, milky breasts, no mystery here behind neat curtained windows where clerks and technicians and their lumpy wives lived in bland discomfort as the whites had taught them. Selecting the gayest of her wrappers as an invocation to warmth, she cocooned herself under the blanket in the hope of dreaming herself away.

'No, good, Soph-i-a,' said Matron sharply. 'You will complain to me again that you can't sleep at night because of somebody coughing or somebody snoring, and you use up all your sleep in the daytime.'

But Sophia hugged herself more tightly and kept her eyes closed.

CHAPTER
THREE

She was so determined to sleep that she even missed the soldier marching by again. Perhaps he had moved house (whatever passed for house) or had chosen the Refuge particularly as his audience.

'Lef' ri' lef' ri',' today he was really drilling in style, causing the traffic to slow down as he followed one side of the road, stopping and starting to his own orders.

'Might as well have a band,' commented Nekesa. 'I remember before I went to Uganda there were often military bands in Nairobi, European ones, I mean, in those days. Livelier than we get now, with always the same DA-DA da-da-da DA-DA. Everyone used to turn out to watch.'

'Better they had been thinking about their freedom,' growled Mama Chungu.

'You can think and still watch.'

'Nobody wanted to be watched in the forest,' put in Wairimu. 'Quiet you had to be, deadly quiet, or else you were a dead man.'

'Can't we leave it alone?' asked Priscilla. 'The Emergency finished twenty years and more ago. We are free now. Let us not keep chewing over it.'

'Some of us had losses,' insisted Mama Chungu. 'You may not like to be made to remember it, but it's true. We cannot get away from it.'

Indeed we cannot get away from it, thought Priscilla. But we can try to keep it in the past instead of living haunted with the images of blood and iron.

She looked curiously at Mama Chungu, who had spoken so little of herself since she had been picked up from the pavement and brought to the Refuge that some of them thought she had no memory at all. No one knew where she had come from. But memories, of course, need not speak in loud voices. They may gibber at a tantalising distance like a bat in the rafters, or swoop upon you like a moth, soundless but soiling you with a residue of filmy substance. They are the more terrifying if they wake you up, unaware of where you are, or weave about from real places to the fantasy of story-books or the falsity of postmarked letters. Perhaps, after all, Mama Chungu was resuming shape, particularising herself, and the birth-pain of which she used to babble was not that of the mother but of the newborn child.

'Rubbish,' Rahel used to say when Priscilla tried to steer away from Emergency talk. 'I've had to do with fighting all my life. What's the use of pretending our menfolk can do without it? But I admit it was a tough time for you in the fifties. My Vitalis was a young private then, and it turned him up some of the things he saw. Young men don't talk all that freely to their mothers, but he told me some things that seemed to haunt him, feeling he was taking it out of his own people. (Not that anyone spoke of freedom fighters then. Not where we lived, anyway. We were taught to feel superior to them and with their jobs and houses falling our way it wasn't too hard.) But I used to tell him it's not up to a soldier to choose his side. Other people have to do that, and sometimes they get the chop for it. A military man takes his orders the same as a bus driver. No good saying "I'd fancy a run to Nakuru today instead of Mombasa." Once you do that, every rut in the road will be your fault. Stick to your orders, I said to him. It lets you out of taking responsibility.'

'And look where that got us,' Wairimu would retort. 'Sharing a house with twenty-eight other old busybodies who praise peace and talk war, without a man in sight except the Reverend coming to tell us to mind our women's business.'

Wairimu was by far the oldest, so she felt she had a right to slander old age if anyone did. She looked on Rahel, ten years younger, as her lieutenant, but one already failing in health. Sophia actually came between them in age but she was set apart, not by her colour, not by lack of experience (for they all respected her conversion and her tribulations), but by something less definable. It was not only her lack of the countrywomen's skills, for Priscilla might also have seemed town-born if you did not know better, and Nekesa could hardly tell a potato from a groundnut till it was dug up and put on the market. There was some other timeless quality about Sophia that kept her out of the age-ranking order, friendly enough to all but not near neighbour to any.

'Isn't this a bit extreme?' the donors' representative had said when the Vicar brought her to see the Matron and go through the record books. She was a sandy sort of person, all pale and dappled, standing for some kind of corporate European personality.

'I mean you have to be able to observe a lot of heartbreak to get the funds administered properly. It is a bit like the love of God: you take it in full of feeling and then have to learn to live with it inside the bounds of society. But we have been trained to think that it is only white people who can be completely ignored by their relations. These old bodies seem to have survived disaster after disaster.'

'Of course the cases are extreme,' said the Vicar gently. 'Ours is not a very wealthy country. We don't give out our resources to help the middling poor unless they have had other kinds of distress. Most of us have been middling poor at one time or another in our lives.'

'Yes, yes, I see. Everywhere there are disasters. But one is dwarfed by disasters without any savings or security to relieve them. Care is one thing. The rebuilding of utterly shattered lives is another. Of course people were doing this with displaced persons in Europe at the end of the war, or after partition in India, but where society has not broken down. . . .'

'Do our old ladies look shattered to you?'

'No indeed, that is the wonder. Except the one who keeps nattering about her baby. Of course the one in bed has had a stroke by the look of her – I didn't see that entered in the record. But still she has a kind of serenity about her, even after all those troubles.'

'In England, you see,' the Matron took it upon herself to expound to the Vicar, 'people will take their old folks to a home, even if they have to pay quite heavily for it. They are more easily defeated by the care than by the expense. We are not like that, though there are a few who abandon their relations. And usually those who are willing to pay can employ someone to do the work at home.' She had now turned her attention to Mrs Reinhold. 'Wages are not so high, and in the countryside a helper might not even demand a wage, just expenses paid now and again. So those we get here are really problem cases.'

'Now, now, Matron,' the Vicar interrupted. 'They are people with problems. They are not themselves problems. That is what Mrs Reinhold is saying.'

'Of course I did not mean to imply. . . .'

'And we know that the Lord is able to deal with every problem,' went on the Vicar firmly, 'and He sends people like you, Mrs Reinhold, to assist.'

'Yes, I agree,' said the social worker cautiously. 'I happen to agree, though I'd be a bit careful about saying so when a number of very good and devoted people think they have sent me themselves. And on their behalf I should like to say how much we appreciate the care you are giving here. But surely not every one of these residents is an out-and-out Christian? And yet they have a resilience, a self-confidence that is hard to find among institutional cases – if you will allow the word for once, Vicar – and not to be taken for granted among people who have been buffeted so much in ordinary life. I mean, even a shared disaster – an earthquake wiping out a town, for instance – gives people an urge to support one another and put a brave face on it. Much of my work is concerned with that kind of situation. It is all these individual tragedies that reduce me to a jelly.'

'You seem to be holding up very well for a jelly, Mrs Reinhold,' answered the Vicar gallantly. 'But I think perhaps you have a different time-scale for disasters than ours. Don't forget we had the first man – a sort of raw material for Adam – in Kenya. William the Conqueror and Genghis Khan and Hitler, all these people are mere episodes for us. We have lived, traditionally, a very eventful life as regards plagues, famines, migrations, raiding parties. I don't think any of these ladies grew up in the expectation – I don't say not in the hope – of a calm course of life in which your husband was always nice to you, your children mostly stayed alive, you were surprised if there was nothing palatable to eat and were sure that your daughters-in-law would look after you in old age. We had the picture of that kind of life, but it wasn't one to take for granted. If it had been, perhaps people would have resisted the changes the colonialists brought more strongly. I think perhaps it was not that they were too surprised to protest but that they were not surprised enough to believe that the new order was going to last. And the Emergency was not a single catastrophe but a repetition on a large scale of the kind of situation people had already encountered on their own. So it is not unimaginable to these women to be situated as they are. Perhaps it would be unimaginable to people who are young now in this country – we must hope so.'

'They are tough all the same.'

'To be eighty years old in Africa is to be tough. Particularly for a woman, because she has learned from childhood to look after others rather than to be looked after.'

'In Europe and America,' chipped in the Matron, 'women live longer than men because they are exposed to less hardship. But in our pastoral areas, men live longer, because the women's work is so much harder.'

'Even Rahel,' the Vicar went on, '– Rahel is the one who may have had a stroke – has a story you could hardly bear to hear. The record book only gives the bare bones of it. And yet she is not from the Emergency area and indeed Luo women have a relatively high status in their community. Would you like her to tell you about it?'

Once roused, tidied, introduced, Rahel was more than willing to go over it all again, and a schoolgirl was summoned from a neighbouring house to interpret from Luo into English. Friends gathered round to support even though they might not understand. Mrs Reinhold sat obligingly with a notebook, conscious that an example was being set up for her.

'Vitalis was getting on for eighteen when his father died, and mad keen to follow in his footsteps. So he joined up. It was probably the best thing he could do. I took it for granted, really. It was the only kind of work I knew much about, and he was not all that good at school to look for an office job. Margaret – they had all been baptised by then – was nearly sixteen, and soon afterwards she married a man from Seme and they moved to Tanganyika. Florence studied up to standard four and she stayed with me. After the town kind of life we lived in quarters I didn't much like the idea of being inherited by some old man in Uyoma. My co-wife had a grown-up son by then, so she was able to stay with him in our own *dala*. So we arranged that she would prepare the fish that end and I would collect them off the bus in Kisumu and sell them in the market. When Florence was a little older she got a job as a ward-maid in the hospital and was able to help me pay the rent of the little room we had. I wasn't really a very keen churchgoer then – in any case you lose a lot if you're not in the market on Sundays – but my church friends were pleased that I had refused to be passed on to another man, and so they tried to teach me more and I got some comfort out of it.

'But then our troubles started. I don't mean to say that our husband's death was not a trouble, but that was in the course of nature. He had put a lot of his Post Office money into a boat for his eldest son, Omondi, and that's where a lot of our fish came from. But Omondi, the first child of my co-wife, was perhaps not meant to be a fisherman. He was a bit clumsy. He was not properly a saved man but he did not go in for the full boat-rituals either.'

There was a pause here, because the schoolgirl came from an inland area and had no idea of the mysteries of the lakeshore and the fishing cults. With a long explanation and a few Swahili words thrown in, she managed to convey the idea.

'He said they were expensive and a waste of time. But a man who does not believe in anything will surely come to grief, and unfortunately the end came on a day when he had taken his younger brother out with him. None of the men came back and there was no trace of the boat. For a long time my co-wife was completely broken down – sons gone, boat gone, and the families of the other men blaming her for what had happened. It was a terrible time. Her elder daughter had been sent to boarding school up to standard eight and was training as a teacher, a great thing in those days, but she got pregnant and ran away from the college and we never heard what became of her or received any dowry. The little one was now about thirteen and doing well at school, but of course she had to leave because there was no money for fees, and she was needed to help her mother with the fish business.

'We managed to keep on, but not very easily. We worked – *jowa*, that time, in the 1950s, we worked. We were happy in a way because of the *Uhuru* we were hearing about. But these young people think that to have a job is just enjoyment – money at the end of the month and the rest of the time sitting around drinking tea – that is far from it, mama.'

The schoolgirl giggled. Her fees depended on the commission her mother made getting orders for shoes and knitwear from bored girls in office after office she dropped into for a chat during a carefully planned working day. Mrs Reinhold frowned: one of her daily problems was the clamour for jobs from people who had never learned what it meant to have a job.

'Florence had her little bit of money but of course she wanted shoes out of it, a handbag, skin cream – you ask Wairimu, she has worked for wages ever since she was young, she knows what girls are: but work, running here, running there, carrying the dirty pans, going to rooms where people were half-dead, cut open and stinking, or even completely dead, that is not easy, and without the praise a nurse gets for it either. Whether you had a bad head or what, always running, and mother always asking for rent out of your money: myself I was providing the food, the market payments, the charcoal, the fares to Uyoma. I think if we had been working alone we might have made a fair profit, but having always to allow a share to Min Omondi, who was in a very low state anyway because of the expense of that big funeral, it was a hard grind. Often we had only the leftover fish to eat, the ones that would not last till morning, and the smell seemed to be around us day and night.

'So I was not surprised that Florence wanted to get away from it. She started to spend nights at her girlfriend's place in railway quarters. I could not object so long as she was helping me. Girlfriends, of course, have brothers, cousins, uncles: don't suppose I hadn't thought of it. Soon she was wanting to be married by a Kisumu man.

'Well, of course I asked, "What about the dowry? Where are your uncles to speak for you? Where is your mother from? Do you have regular work?"

'He was a gardener and groundsman at one of the schools.

' "It's a bit late, mother-in-law, isn't it, to be asking these questions?"

'That's what he said to my face. No respect at all.

' "I reckon you've got less than four months to get them answered, Min Florence. I'm ready to give her a roof and a name for the baby," he said to me. "And if my brother can help me to scrape together five hundred shillings, that might pay your rent for a year, I suppose. As to talk about registering the marriage, leave that till we see how we get on. If you think with all that education she's fit for a doctor or a

40

lawyer, then you'd better look after the bastard yourself, hadn't you?"

'And what could I do? It wasn't like now, when a girl goes back to work a month after she's had her baby whether she's married or not. I couldn't have kept the two of them, and in any case she was set on having this husband. But I felt my heart sinking, for he was not clean in the way that a man who has come home from honest work and respects his neighbours makes himself clean, and not careful, even in the way that a man living under begging eyes on low wages can be careful. It was a weary year for me. If it hadn't been that Vitalis sent me a few shillings out of his pay now and then, I don't know how I'd have got through it.

'By this time it was the late fifties: conferences going on, elections, parties forming and reforming, Women's Progress movement, more and more children going to school – it was exciting if you think back over it. And me getting near the end of my womanhood, almost crying at the waste of it, but getting some strength from those church women I worked with. I knew in any case that none of those layabouts who tried to get on visiting terms with me were fit to stand in the same drill yard as the husband I'd lost. Besides, I was a grandmother already, though Margaret did not write to me, and not wanting to give Florence any excuse for misbehaving either (as though she needed one). Perhaps I was a fool, as some of you think, to refuse to be married again in Uyoma, but I swear to God I never gave my husband cause to be ashamed of me when he was alive or after he was dead, and now I'm glad of it.

'So it went on, fish, fish, fish till *Uhuru*, and the rest of you remember that too, how we all expected that the sky would light up and everyone would pay twice as much as before for whatever he bought from you. Did they now? Somehow in these twenty years we've got more dresses than we ever expected then, and shoes. Children of people we know are going to the university. You go on a country bus without picking up any bugs – that's something, I suppose – there are better jobs for women and all those good houses filled with our own black people. Yes, things have got better, but slowly. Then we were looking for miracles.

'All right, *Uhuru*! Flags, fountains, shouts and songs. And then you remember what – mutiny! Perhaps it did not sound so terrible to you

41

compared with all the other new words we've got used to – hostage, hijack, mugging. But to those of us who had grown up in the military it was like a thunderbolt, the extreme evil, the breaking up of all the rules you live within. Change of flag, picture, tune had not before meant for me the splitting of the framework.

'People in the market had radios. They came to tell me. Yesterday it was a far-off event in Uganda and Tanganyika. Today it was among us. Vitalis was at Lanet. The road was closed. Vehicles were not going through to Nairobi. Trains were overloaded. One of the saved sisters came and handled the money for me. She could see that I was half-blind with tears. It was like a sort of death.

'In fact to other people it was not what I meant by a mutiny. There were no symbols of disgrace and death, and in a couple of days it was all over. Perhaps a new country, I thought, can teach people new rules. For the first time I began to doubt whether I could cope with changes to come. For the army, I was thankful it was no worse. But Vitalis – Vitalis was gone. A deserter.

'I haven't seen him for nineteen years. He is my only son and I don't know whether he is alive or dead. But it isn't just that, you know. Some people's children go to America and stay there. Or even to Nairobi and stay there. They get a letter now and again or perhaps a photograph. Even if your son doesn't have money and presents to send you, you still have a son. Even if he doesn't keep in touch, you have some idea how he is making out. Even if he was buried in Burma, you have the measure of his life. Take my daughter Margaret. She was in another country and we got very little news, but the family carried on. Then in 1975 the border was closed. A little while after that we heard that she had died of cholera. There was no way to go to the funeral. I have grandchildren there that I have never seen. There is nothing they could do for me even now that there is talk of opening the border. I am settled after four years here in the Refuge and there is nowhere I would be better looked after. But Margaret has had her life. One is not ashamed.

'Vitalis has broken his father's greatest taboo. He must have had reason, I suppose. As you grow older, you find loyalty is more complicated than you used to think. Why should a woman be ashamed before all other men except those picked for her from

Uyoma, if there is even that much choice? Why should you hear talk from your daughter's man that even your own brother would be ashamed to use before you? Why should you not ask the DC, now that he is your fellow African, the same price you asked of the DC when he was a white man? I may perhaps still have an only son. But because of these taboos we taught him he dare not come near us and we do not know where he stays or even what name he is using. As though the taboo means more than being a son. Is it not strange?'

'And Florence?' asked Mrs Reinhold gently, aloud, but silently asking herself whether it was not better, after all, to be childless and not disappointed. 'Is not Florence able to help you?'

'Florence?' Rahel seemed surprised to be asked. 'Perhaps she went further away than either of the others. She stayed with that man and got a second baby. Then he took them to Nairobi, and she waited a long time but at last started a third. This was after Vitalis deserted. By now her man was drinking badly, and he beat her and beat her until she died: neighbours took her to hospital, but it was too late to save her or the baby. When that happened, the husband was so frightened that he ran away. She was already buried in a Nairobi cemetery before I heard about it from a Kisumu girl who was training in that hospital. Because the father had run away, the children were taken to an orphanage. The police could not trace relations. I suppose the Kisumu people thought if they came forward to claim the children the man would be identified and arrested. My friends advised me not to say anything, or I might be asked to pay for the children's keep, and what could I do? They look after them well and send them to school, I hear. At least in the Children's Home in Kisumu they used to do that. Of course they will be grown-up by now, Jimmie and Janet, but I would not know them if I saw them, and why should they bother about me, since I was not able to make a home for them?'

She turned to her friends and spoke in Swahili. The girl still translated, with only a little hesitation, into English. She was not considered very bright at school. The teachers wished she could give a more detached attention to problems in chemistry and home hygiene.

'I keep remembering the dead tree, Wairimu, the dead tree.'

'The years are long,' said Wairimu. 'But do you not have any people at all?'

'We don't always know. It doesn't seem possible, does it? When we were young, we could not have helped knowing, because everybody was attached to a place – though I hear your people moved about more than ours. My co-wife and her youngest daughter died in the cholera – that was after I had my accident and came to Nairobi. I believe the daughter had some children – she had left her husband – so perhaps they live on that little bit of land. But even if I did not have this bad leg, I could hardly get a living on it without the fish, and who would help me with the fish now?

'The accident happened when things fell on me off the top of a bus when I was reaching up for the fish baskets – Matron must have told you about that. First I was in Kisumu Hospital for six months and the landlord took the few bits and pieces I had in the room for the rent I owed him. I suppose he thought I was going to die there. Then they sent me to Nairobi and I was in the ward for a year. They said someone must come from Kisumu to fetch me when I could walk a bit – there's a laugh, isn't it? Then when they found there was no one they brought me here.

'My middle brothers and sisters died long ago. The youngest – the one my husband refused to take – well, laugh with me: her husband was a DC before he retired, and he has a big farm nowadays. But of course he does not have to help his wife's relations. His responsibility is to the nation.'

The old ladies cackled together at this, after Mrs Reinhold had signified her thanks and left, looking burdened, choked.

'I don't blame him at all,' said Rahel, wiping her eyes. 'I know how he treated his first wife, you see, and all the worse after he took up with my little sister, and I've told them both what I think. But she's a match for him, I'll tell you that.'

'And so here you are in a home with one bad leg.'

'Here I am in a home with one good leg and a number of grandchildren whom I hope I may be proud of. They have no reason to be ashamed of me. And so I still don't see why the fighting looks so terrible to you Kikuyu ladies.'

CHAPTER
FOUR

'It was not terrible just to us, but to everyone who sees the gunshot end of it,' said Priscilla primly, the screams echoing in her ears as she bent her head to pick a thread of cotton from the front of her dress, where the blood from the child's throat had flowed. Pangas, she thought to herself, knives, not guns, and it was not guns, either, which had caused her brother's shame of which, to this day, no one in the family had ever spoken openly.

Wairimu also was thinking less of guns than of banana arches and rings of hide, the silent garotte and the evening roadblock. But she said simply, 'I was there at the Harry Thuku riots. We heard that there was a big meeting and that everyone was going, so of course I had to join in too. I learned early enough about terrible things.'

She paused. That was more than sixty years ago, beyond the memory of many of the women in the home, beyond the experience of most, who had grown up with the certainty of being initiated, manipulated, screened, divided into categories and the hope of being ultimately provided for. How many had ever initiated, developed, understood that they were the providers? And yet when she had been near the heart of things – which was, she supposed, the sense of that calling, the flash of sunlight on the dreary path – she had run away. Just like the Lord's disciples, in fact, but one was allowed to read into it that their womenfolk had a little more sense of occasion. As for these fellow-residents of hers, perhaps they were not all as dull as she was tempted to think them. When they muddled the years and answered out of the question, perhaps they were only hiding the memory of their own retreats or, like Bessie, closing their minds to the unthinkable.

'Thuku had been arrested with some other people and we thought, somehow, that we could get him out. The police lines were not far

45

from where Central Police Station is now, and the place where it all happened is now called Harry Thuku Road, just there beside the university. The Norfolk Hotel was already there and the Native Civil Hospital was nearby. Opposite the Norfolk, where the National Theatre is now, there used to be a sort of market for horses and other livestock brought down from the north.

'People were already disturbed. On Tuesday, the day before the arrest, there had been what they call *hartal* at the bazaar. That means that most of the shops were shut – it was something to do with Mr Gandhi in India, and there was a big meeting of Indians in Jeevanjee Gardens. It seems they wanted fairer dealing in India as we did here, and someone explained to me that that was why they were friendly to Thuku, but none of them came to our meeting, though a few were walking about nearby.

'In fact everything was out of order, though I was too new to Nairobi to feel it coming. Well, by the 1950s I had acquired more sense of trouble on the way. Men were talking about a strike in the mines in South Africa. In Kavirondo (that is what we used to call Nyanza and Western – you know it's true, Rahel, so don't shake your head at me), people were also restless because of the rise in tax and because they were not getting compensation for their men who died in the Great War. There was famine at the Coast and – we heard later – freak rainstorms at Naivasha. You might say it was like the signs of a storm – the sky seeming to harden, the sudden chill, birds chattering, a kind of hush in the air, people running for cover, before you actually hear the thunder or feel the first big, slow raindrop. In fact, what was happening was Nairobi drawing together, becoming, on the African side, a community. The crisis was just like the shedding of blood at circumcision, a mark of the maturity which, if you gave it a chance, would be coming about anyway. Most of us were Kikuyu, it is true, in that meeting, but everybody knew what was going on, even the Somali and the Luo kept their children home from school and their wives from market that day. And, as in the storm, the thunder did not last long – we ran away soon enough. But the rain went on. The ground was ready and the community began to grow.

'We went there on Wednesday evening. I was supposed to be at the tea room, but most of the men were going to the police lines so I went

46

too. Mr Doorly, the magistrate, spoke in Swahili, telling the people to go home. A lot of them did go, and so did I when it was getting dark. I had stopped being afraid of meeting a rough man at night, but those shiny bayonets the police were holding were another matter. I did not like the idea of one of those sliding up on me after the street lights went out, or the prospect of someone herding us into the police cells.

'But those who remained stood where our leaders told them, looking angry but not making a fuss. I suppose it must have got cold in the middle of the night, because then some started moving about and praying aloud. Then the police got restive too, and started blowing bugles to call out those who had turned in, and both sides complained about the noise disturbing the sick people in hospital. The African police must have been fed up by the end of it too – on duty day and night, with people shouting at them from the front and giving them orders from the back.

'Before light in the morning men with bicycles were all over Nairobi calling on house servants and others to come and join the crowd, and when I got to the place at eight o'clock there were already three thousand people, it was said, and others still pouring in. All the same it was very calm. Most of them were men, of course (there have always been more men than women in Nairobi) but in one corner, where the Europeans used to play with bats and balls, there was a big group of women, and I wriggled my way through to join them. Some Europeans were talking to the crowd in English and Swahili – I knew the difference by then, though I could not understand either – and our leaders translated some of the speeches into Kikuyu. Six of us came forward – these were the men chosen to go and see Bowring, who was next to the Governor. There was no dispute about who should go. Other men were walking about telling us to burn our registration *kipandes* and refuse to pay tax, but I didn't have a *kipande* or pay tax either. This was when we started feeling more restless and some people got hold of sticks. Afterwards some stones were thrown, but I didn't see many stones about, except perhaps some pieces of tile broken off from some building work.

'After a long time the delegates came back and told us in Kikuyu that Thuku could not be released until he had talked with the Governor, but we had better go home as they had had a chance to put their points. They said it with very straight faces and some of us were not sure whether they meant it or not. That is one trouble with our people – it is not easy to read our faces. Some men who had been sitting on the ground stood up as though to leave, and then some of the women called the men cowards and urged them to fight it out. That was when we found ourselves moving forward towards the iron fence. You couldn't stand against the crowd, you were just pushed forward, which meant that most of the women were in front, and the European officers who had been walking up and down between the armed police and the crowd were knocked forward too. There was a young Kikuyu man about my age carrying a white flag. He had been there in the evening and in the morning he was still carrying it. The shooting started after he had been knocked down in a scuffle with a white officer, but it was difficult in the confusion to tell exactly what was happening. Mr Doorly had read out some orders in Swahili and at the same time soldiers arrived behind us in the open grassy place near the Scottish church. All of a sudden there was one shot, then some more. I don't know how I knew what it was, but of course we had been watching those armed police for hours and I never had any doubt about it. Mary, the bravest of all, was there with blood streaming from her. Mr Wright, the European padre, was standing nearby. He didn't throw himself down like others, and some of us girls got as near to him as we could, somehow thinking that shots could not go near a white man. Poor man, it was as close as he ever came to sinful women, probably, but he did not look frightened, only distressed that we should be bewildered, divided and in pain. It could not have been more than a minute or two, though it seemed an age, before people were turning to run away, and that gave space for us who were crowded at the front also to run, and again be carried along with the rest. I was expecting more shots from behind, but although we had seen the policemen being issued with more bullets (I've learned a lot about bullets since then) they were so jammed together that they couldn't possibly have reloaded until we were already on the retreat, even if they had wanted to. There were some whistles and bugles blowing, everything in confusion.

'I tell you, I was scared. For all I thought I knew the world, I was still a kid, not yet eighteen. It was quite clear to me that I had seen

48

people die. And remember, this was not supposed to happen, however old you were. You put people nearly dead out in the forest rather than meet the shame of seeing them die. At that time I would rather have faced the police bayonets a dozen times than worked in the Native Civil Hospital. It was obscene to be face to face with sickness, touching, smelling, hearing the death-throes. But I understood that this was real fighting. I had seen our great hero and come close to where he was shut up in prison, and not even a great crowd of us could get him out. I learned something about power that day. They took him away for years and years and his name was hardly mentioned. . . .

'I had seen that golden haze over the city turn black and smoky, and the women who looked so smart and strong to me that first morning I had seen slinking into back alleys in dirty wrappers, smelling of drink and weakened by disease. The men whom I admired for their knowledge of other languages, their clothes, their command of town life, mostly showed no respect for either girl or woman, and little enough even for elders. The dream had turned into a nightmare.'

But Rahel could not understand nightmare. Sophia could not understand the excitement of first seeing paved streets and storeyed buildings. The younger ones, even those to whom Wairimu could have spoken her heart out in Kikuyu, could not remember the crying in the forest or even the rupee (they could not connect it with the word *mbia*) and had no memory of seeing their first bicycle or their first Indian or being afraid of a big, black Luo who was said to eat people. Wairimu found the pictures blocked in her mind, unable to get out.

She had run through the streets back to the tea shanty, only afterwards noticing that the cuts and alleyways had become as familiar to her feet as the twists and turns of forest paths. She had not even paused to think where she could rush ahead, where she must give way to an important pedestrian: the knowledge was buried in her. She poured out her story to Nduta – Samson, of course, had been at the meeting, though she had not seen him in the crowd. Nduta was boiling huge sufurias of maize and beans. Whatever else, people would be hungry today and some would be afraid to go home. And if you were searched, it was better to be about your normal business.

Wairimu was sobbing.

'I did not know it would be like this. It would be better if I had never come. I do not want to get like these sour, smelly women. I like working for you here, but in the town I see no escape from changing. I want to go. . . .'

'Home?'

'No, not home. I am afraid to go home. I am no longer a girl in their eyes. They would taunt me, and – and –'

She did not want to say that she thought she was barren. By now she had enough experience to suspect it. Enough, anyway, to know that even with a child she could not settle back to life within the ridge. That would neither expel her fear nor satisfy even the narrowest part of her dream. She had chosen and so she was destined to go on choosing.

'Not home. Perhaps back to the coffee.'

'Yes, do that. Go today – go now. The town is not yet ready for you. Unless you have a man – a husband, best, or a father to speak for you, but at least a steady man – you get the worst of the bargain here. You can get money, but as yet there is no way for you to get good from the money as you would from beans or sweet potatoes or wood if you had plenty. One day it may well be different. And we do not know what kind of trouble the day will bring, but trouble it is bound to be. So let me advise you. Pack up your dresses and your new beads. You could sell them here, but perhaps away from town you will get a better price. Put on your old cloth tied over your shoulder, pick up your bundle and go. But you should not walk alone, and if you show money for the train they will ask you a lot of questions. Is there any older person who can accompany you?'

'I think this, mother; please help me. When I came I had no thought of going back or of anything but seeing marvels. But I know it is not only from Nyeri that the coffee comes. The drivers have told me that sacks are brought together in great numbers for sale. So, since I do not want to go home yet – perhaps I may go when I am older and they have stopped trying to make a marriage for me and when I have presents for them – is there not somewhere nearer where I could get the same work?'

'Of course, if you are willing. There are plenty of coffee farms nearby, and because of the dispute about the wages some of their

50

workers will have gone away. Get your things ready now, and I will tell you how to get to the Kabete road, but if I can find anyone going that way it will be safer. You don't need to wait for Samson to come: you tell me he was not where the bullets were passing: he has money and knows how to keep himself safe. I do not know quite what we should give you, but take these three florins for now – hide them, but remember you will have to change them for the new shillings when they come. We are sure to see one another again and you can bargain with Samson then.'

Wairimu had not actually been expecting money: she had got some from the men who called her to their rooms and had learned from other girls what to ask for and what to pay for things, since in town you had a choice of traders, not like the farm store where you had to pay what was asked. That was a lesson it was well to learn early, reflected Wairimu as she took up her story again.

'In the little room at the back I changed into my old yellow cloth and just enough beads to look natural. In the *kanga* I had bought I wrapped my two "European" dresses and other ornaments, a tin mug that was my own, a bar of soap, a headscarf of which I was very proud, a calico waistcloth and my little bit of money. I also had a small knife, some brown sugar twisted in a piece of newspaper, and a leaflet of the East African Association that I had bought for five cents although I didn't know how to read it. I folded this carefully inside my clothes, put the lot in the *kiondo* basket I had come from Nyeri with and slung it round my forehead. I was ready.

'But Nduta told me to wait a little. She was talking to a smart man I had seen before, and giving him tea in one of her best cups. This was a family connection of hers, she told me, who usually called when he was in town. He worked in the house of a *Mzungu* along the way to Kabete, and was sent in for post and shopping once a week or so. He would take me part of the way and explain to me what Europeans wanted of their staff. His name was John Wanyama and I should address him as Mr John.

'Mr John soon let me know that he was an important person, skilled in the handling of European stoves and water-sources. However I need not offer to carry his burdens, because this was his master's jacket back from the tailor's and he could not trust it in the hands of such a person as myself. In the streets he expected me to keep submissively behind him, but once we were by the old railway track – where Uhuru Highway is now – he allowed some conversation. He wanted to avoid the scene of the meeting, though that might have been a short cut, and even down to Sixth Avenue soldiers were inspecting the town in pairs, hustling out any Kikuyu they found in alleys and doorways and directing them towards Pangani Village. Since there were armed *askaris* cruising the streets in cars, it was easy enough to see that the people followed directions, and seeing the way they were handled I was glad enough that the soldiers had had no part in the morning's clashes. But John's packet of letters and his employer's chit kept him safe, and I suppose the *askaris* took me for a wife of his, ignorant of what standards a paragon like John would impose upon a wife.

'We walked up past Chiromo where, he said, his master had camped in a tent by the river when he first arrived in the country long before, and past the *mpaka* or boundary of Nairobi town. The place still looked to me full of people, but more homely, through woody lanes, and Mr John kept telling me that the way to advance in work was to join a European household. I could take him as an example – his neat shirt and shorts and tyre-rubber sandals, his pair of keys, his baptised status, his children going to school, his self-contained house – I thought all houses were self-contained until he explained – and two servants under him. Domestic service, he explained to me, was really important work for men, but some ladies were beginning to take black nursemaids for their children or to do a bit of laundry, and this would give me better status and security than agricultural work – that was what women did at home and anyone who wanted advancement must look for something better. His own master did not have small children, but some of his friends employed Swahili, Seychelloise or mixed-race women, and it was really a great concession for them to consider local girls or widows.

'I promised that I would think about it when I had got some experience and had learned to speak Swahili, as this was necessary for getting along in town. Was I crazy or what? Two hours ago I had been sobbing in the urgency of leaving Nairobi. But this was a balmy place where you could hardly imagine the sound of gunshots, and all the

52

Africans in sight were skipping nimbly about some sophisticated business of their masters. John said I was very sensible. I did not tell him that I thought myself too grown-up to be looking after someone else's babies or washing her dirty clothes, but I took note of the place he lived in case I should have any more questions to ask and followed his directions about half an hour further on to the first of the coffee farms.

'We had left River Road, I suppose, after three in the afternoon, a couple of hours after Mary's shouts had flowered into blood. So the sun was well down by the time I reached the first farm and in Nyeri, I knew, the plantation office would already be closed. I wondered what I could do if left alone in a place that did not seem to have any familiar homesteads. Perhaps here too a line had been drawn between the coffee and the places where people lived. I should not have liked to be forced to appeal to Mr John with his fancy airs, but perhaps it was safe to walk among European houses even after dark. Fortunately I did not need to try.

'The clerk at the first farm said he could not register any more people that day but they were short of workers and I could come back in the morning. I told him that I was far from my place. I had gone to see my brother in Nairobi – that was what I thought I had better tell him – but he had gone away and his friends had told me that I could not fail to get work on the farm since I had experience in coffee. Well, he agreed, that was so. Some workers had got above themselves with the troubles of these days and therefore they were short-handed. He could perhaps find somewhere for me to stay the night if I had some money left from my last job to compensate the lady who would put me up. I said, of course, that I had no money left but a little sugar and soap that might make me welcome, and so he called one of the older women passing and she agreed to take me with her for the night. Next morning I put my fingerprint on the form.

'I was, in a sort of way, happy. I knew the work, and how to get advantage from the work, better than when I had first started in the coffee at Nyeri. I was safe from the danger of yesterday. I was safe also, for a while, from questions at home. I had seen Nairobi. I was not yet satisfied – even to this day I cannot say I have seen all of Nairobi – but there was the city within walking distance, with people I knew and streets I knew, waiting to be explored. On a Sunday I could go and come back and not be much more tired than if I had made three trips to the river for water. I had not yet got shoes, but I had enough money for shoes now and was going to earn some more. Surely I should be content.

'As I picked, I thought and thought, and I realised that this was the gift Waitito had given me in return for what he took from me. He had opened a door through which one could see picture after picture, more lively and colourful than the black, dead pictures which get on to each side of a page on a newspaper, and try oneself out on each, accepting or rejecting. Before there had been pictures – Wairimu, girl – Wairimu, bride – Wairimu, mother – Wairimu, elder's wife – Wairimu, grandmother – but nothing to choose between them, only to be chosen. And if one was not chosen to have a child then the pictures became very few indeed. Not many people were like Mary Nyanjiru, who had a song sung about her even after she died outside the police lines – *Kanyegenuri*, you remember. We used to sing it all the time, and I still sing it now when I need to get my courage up.

'So I picked and thought, picked and thought, earned enough to eat and a bit to save, made friends enough for day to day but saved a bit of myself too, undisclosed, ambitious, special. What must I aim at? First, to know Swahili, not in order to be a servant like *Mr* John, even a rich servant, but to enter a wider world than the Kikuyu world, to understand Nairobi, even if it were only on a Sunday, to go home with power – that meant with presents and knowledge, like a boy. So that even if they wanted to pair me. . . .'

'Do you know the time?' asked Sophia. 'I do not want to miss the TV.'

'Really, Wairimu,' said Priscilla, taking advantage of the interruption, 'there is nothing wicked about being a servant. Most people are servants of somebody and all of us are servants of God, and Jesus Himself. . . .'

'Yes, yes, I know. I did not mean it like that. You started by being a servant and ended up a friend to your madam. But someone like John would never be a friend to anybody. He can only be Mr.'

'Mama Chungu was a housemaid,' cried Sophia, hoping for further

54

revelations. 'You told me that much once. Were your employers like friends?'

'Bosses are bosses,' replied Mama Chungu with a shrug. 'It would not help to remember them. You have your own life to live.' She would not be drawn any further.

All the same, Wairimu continued the recital of memories to herself. Some things one could not share. At least, not with virtuous, desiccated old women. The very best one might, for a little while, share with a man. Some people did. . . .

'So that even if they wanted to pair me it would not be only within the daily tramp for water, digging and shelling, peeling and digging again, bent under firewood. I did not despise these things, and don't – fire, food and water, even here in the Refuge, our life centres on these three – but already, at eighteen, I had seen that it is not necessary to being a woman to be bent against the painful forehead-strap, with a little hump down on your spine and danger in bearing children because of it. I have seen hairy white women, big-eyed Indian women, big-nosed Arab women, big-boned charcoal-black women all standing straight and not lacking for food and fire and water. My body, too, can be respected.

'Respected but also used. The circumcisor's knife has not cut away the urgent need for that. So I must find out what there is for me before I become withered and shrunk like some of these women at the coffee, whose husbands went away to the war and did not come back, whose land was given by their "chief" to the strangers and cannot be got back, whose strength is used up in weeping and protest, roadwork and terracing, and cannot come back.

'That is what I thought – are you awake, Rahel? I am trying to share, I am trying – and that is what I still think. Though I have never had a child, it is not struggle and weeping that have dried up this body of mine. I have a good age and have had good times, sister. If I had then pictured old age, shivering, feeding the fire under the porridge-pot, I should not have seen it as lively and comradely as this we have.

'So I listened and practised, listened and practised, talking with the ayahs and the house servants and the clerks of other tribes until I had mastered this language I speak to you now – not as Sophia speaks it, I grant you, but well enough to describe what I have seen.

55

'Nine years I stayed in that place. The men surged round me with offers because I was the youngest, bright and not all that much used, flaunting my town dresses and telling my stories of Thuku and Nairobi. I told them that for marriage they must consult my father, who was far away, but I shared house for a long time with James, one of the drivers, because he was handsome and cheerful and took the trouble to teach me to read a little. As yet no church people were coming to the farms to teach us reading. I said to him, "Because I am like a man I can choose how I live. Let us try for a while."

'But after more than two years there was still no baby, and he was moving to another job, so I told him just to go. No one would approve a marriage after that, and I had no need to share my house with another woman who would crow over me. We parted friends and one of my questions had been answered.

'It was then that I decided to go home. I had been waiting for the railway to take me all the way, but in fact I still had to get off at Sagana. I think it was late in 1926. I had filled up my work tickets and told the clerk I had not been home for a long time. He told the white boss and the white boss said I was a good worker and had not taken much time off sick, so I could be taken on again if I wished. All the same he offered me a letter in case I decided to look for work nearer home. I told him I wanted to come back, but it is always a good thing to have a letter. When I went to collect it I was also given an old cardigan belonging to the boss's wife because they thought I had forgotten how cold it was up the mountain. I thanked him, but of course I rolled it up in my *kiondo* and hoped the letter included a "receipt" in case anyone thought I had stolen it. Sweaters were rare then, but right up to Independence, you remember, people liked to have a "receipt" for anything that looked valuable enough to steal, in case they should be charged with being in possession of it.

'They let me ride into town on the back of a lorry and I went to the station to book. For third class, of course, there were no reserved places: you had to scramble in as you do now. Even with my big ideas it never occurred to me that I could go any other way than third, and I found it exciting. I had never been on a train before. One thing that puzzled me was that the Thika line had always been called a tramway, and trams, someone had told me, ran flat along the streets among the

56

motor cars. But I afterwards found out that it was quite an ordinary railway. The word had only been used to evade some British Government regulation about building new railways. I have learned a lot since then about how the world works!

'But at the time I thought I had reached the peak of knowledge, sitting in a corner seat with my big bundles among a lot of men and a few families going about their business. I don't think there were any passenger buses going to Nyeri then, though there was still a freight service going ahead of the railway at its various stages. One or two young Kikuyu had started a kind of taxi service, but ordinary people could not pay that much. It was a help to the missionaries. Even after the Second World War, very few Africans could afford to use the buses which the Indian traders – they did not yet have cars – used to bring their stock in trade from Nairobi. But there was never any doubt that the railway was meant for all of us – you only had to look at the 1,2,3 marked on the carriages.

'The third class was not very comfortable, even compared with crowded plantation quarters, but I liked being on the move and when they told me we were getting near Sagana I went to the toilet and put on one of my dresses and my scarf and canvas shoes so as to go home in style. I was disappointed that the train did not go right to Nyeri, which had been laid out in communal sections since I left, but when I saw it again, with its high pavements and dusty streets, it looked dull after Nairobi. Meanwhile I did not really know where I was, except when I caught a glimpse of Mount Kenya behind the clouds to let me know I was home. I got directions and found I should have a walk of nearly twenty miles, so I thought I had better put my shoes away again rather than spoil them but before I had organised my bundles two white nuns came along in a truck with a driver and said they could give me a lift part of the way. They spoke perfect Kikuyu and were very surprised to hear that I did not know my way home. They asked me if I had been educated somewhere else – I suppose because of the way I was dressed. I explained that I had never been to school but had worked near Nairobi and learned Swahili. It seemed they had spread their work out near my village in the five years I had been away, and knew some of my friends.

'They did not know my parents, and I suddenly realised that in all

57

those six years I had imagined things just the same at home (if I ever thought of home), not thinking that the baby would be a big girl now and my brother perhaps married. I had not thought, either, that the land might have been seized or exchanged. Since it was so hilly, I had taken it for granted that it would always be "in the reserve", and indeed it was so. Belatedly I began to worry, during the hour or so it took me to walk from where they dropped me, not recognising anybody till I got close to home, and then trying to avoid long explanations of where I had been.

'The homestead looked just the same from the outside. I was not comparing it with others. For all those years I had not set foot in a family home. I found myself running, crying, "Mother, mother!" A big girl came out of the smoky house holding a toddler by the hand. She stood still and stared at me.

' "Is it Kanini?"

' "Yes, I am Kanini. Who are you?"

' "I am Wairimu. Do you not recognise me? And is this Njoki?" They looked puzzled and seemed afraid to embrace me, fingering the hem of my dress, the little one hanging her head.

' "No, of course not," said Kanini crossly. "Njoki is a big girl now. There was a boy that followed her, but he died. This is our brother's child. Wairimu, you frighten me. I thought you were lost for ever."

' "Well, you see I'm not lost. Where is mother now? Go and call her quickly. And father?"

' "Mother is in the sweet potato field. Why don't you go to her there? I am not supposed to leave the fire. Father has gone to the Better Farming meeting. He will come at night. Njoki has gone to school. Our brother is working in Nyeri and his wife has gone to hospital with the small baby."

' "The baby is sick?"

' "Oh no. These days you go to hospital before being sick. Do you not know this? Where have you been? Are you married? Do you have children? You must be quite old now. Father says I need no longer wait for you to be married first."

' "You are a child," I said, upset all the same by being so lightly tossed aside. "It is not for you to question me. Do you think you are old enough to be married?"

58

' "I am as old as you were when you went away," replied Kanini pertly, "and I do not think I shall get to your age without becoming a mother."

' "Perhaps not," I barked. Kanini did not understand my sharpness. "Don't touch my bundle, now. I'll go to find mother myself."

'Mother wept for joy, of course, but there was still a little reserve between us. Father interrogated me about each place I had been, the work, the housing conditions, the transport, the kind of people, but he did not, that first day, refer to marriage or future plans. I found that the girls were now sleeping in a separate house in the parents' homestead, not in the communal dormitory any more. The sister-in-law was a slant-eyed, bare-shouldered girl. I wondered how such a one, smooth-skinned and soft-spoken as she was, could interest a man who had been to Nairobi and seen the world. But she knew about her husband's work, even what he was paid, had stayed with him in Nyeri town and could tell you the price of sugar and of the petrol tins you nowadays used for carrying water. Also the two children seemed closer in age than custom allowed – perhaps that had something to do with it. I did not expect to be so uneasy at watching the little boy sucking from the still firm and shapely breast. My sleep was troubled, and I seemed to hear my parents' voices rising and falling in the next building long after the usual hour of rest.

'Njoki was up early the next morning, getting her chores done before she put on a European-style cotton dress which was her school uniform. I had bought a scarf for my mother, tobacco for my father, yellow cloth which I was going to cut with a razor blade to fit the two sisters, but now it was far too small, a wooden comb for my brother and tea and sugar for them all. My mother already knew how to prepare the tea, and she boiled it up with milk. There were matches in the house, and condensed milk tins to use as cups. Father was wearing khaki shorts and a sleeveless shirt. This made him look younger than before, but he spoke with more authority than I remembered. He talked to me of roots and seeds as though I were a boy, and of terracing steep slopes against the rain. My mother had to do her share of this work, though they were too far up the mountain for her to have been called out for the women's roadwork before I went away. That second evening they wanted to hear about my meeting with Harry Thuku, about what happened outside the police lines and the consequences. Now, somehow, I was detained when the younger girls had gone off to their sleeping quarters and my sister-in-law to settle the children down in her own house.

'I thought I was the one who made choices, but it seemed mothers and fathers still had power of manipulation. The firelight was dim, just as I remembered it. The elaborate trellis under the thatch was blackened by smoke and kept mosquitoes off. I was back in the world before the dream, for though there had been other dark nights and low fires since, they had not enclosed me like this. If Njoki continued at school, I thought, out of random knowledge, she will need a light to study by. In the brother's house there was a tiny lamp, though not for everyday use. That is how things would be, how light, indirectly, increased.

' "Have you come back for us to find you a husband on the ridge?" my father asked, embarrassed, staring into the fire. This was not the way these matters had ever been discussed.

' "That was not in my mind, father."

' "The time, you see, is past," he went on gravely. "It would be difficult. And I hear that out there people make their own marriages."

' "There have always been some who married outside the ridge," I replied quietly. "Did not Thaira give his daughter to a Maasai? And Nyambura is the daughter of a Kamba woman."

' "That is so, but that is not what I meant. Is no one offering me dowry? Do they take you so cheap? I do not think you have had a child. Or can you live alone, like a man?"

' "I can if I must, father. I had to go away to find this out. I was young – I am sorry if it hurt you more than I thought. I should have been away from you in any case as soon as you had got me married."

' "Was it something wrong with the boy?" my mother asked, in pain. "I remember speaking about it before when you were so miserable. I hoped you might be happy somewhere else rather than sitting at home as though your head were lost in the mountain mists."

' "It was not the boy's fault, mother. It was just that I had another – dream, let us say, not to do with dowry or with babies. There was a man long after that who would have offered you dowry, father, but I

60

did not – that is to say, if there had been a child he might have been satisfied. You understand? And so it would be with others."

' "So you are going back?"

'Was this what I had meant by being free, like a boy? If so, I was glad to be a woman instead. On the whole I have always been glad.

' "I am going back to the work, father, but not to that man. He has moved elsewhere. I refused to go with him. I like it better there at Kabete."

' "You are sure, my daughter?" my mother asked. "I know that you might be humiliated by other wives, flaunting their children, but sometimes it is better to be humiliated than to be alone. And there are wise women who can sometimes open the way for you."

' "I am sure, mother."

' "He got you so cheap, then."

' "Not very cheap, father. He taught me to read. That is not a little thing. He taught me how to live in a cement house and keep it clean. That is also something people pay money for their daughters to learn. And how to wash and iron heavy clothes for men. I could earn a lot of money if I went to work in a European house, knowing these things. But I prefer to be more free. I will go back to the coffee. And since the dowry of learning has been paid to me rather than to you, from time to time I will send you money out of what I have learned through my brother in Nyeri. It is not all you would have wished, but it is better than nothing."

' "I do not understand all this," said my father heavily. "But it is better that you go back. Your brother was able to go and return and build a life here, but for a young woman there is still not that kind of freedom."

' "I will send a present for Nduta who helped you in Nairobi," said my mother, acquiescing. "There is no way to keep a grown-up daughter like you at home, Wairimu. But I am glad you came to see us. Please stay a bit longer to greet old friends."

'I stayed for a fortnight, visiting my agemates, most of them mothers of families now. I called on aunties and grannies with twists of tobacco and sugar, went to hospital with my sister-in-law, a shady place where they weighed the babies, out of earshot of death and groaning, and once walked into Nyeri town to see my brother and go to the shops. I went over Njoki's standard two lessons with her and had a look round the school. But I could see that I was neither child nor woman in other people's eyes and was soon restless to be off. Having finished my money, I walked the three days to Nairobi, changing companions from time to time – women going to market at Mbiri, or Fort Hall as people called it, men going down to Thika to work on the sisal plantations, workers from Thika going to Nairobi to see the sights and look for a better job, so long as their passes were signed off. In Nairobi I visited Nduta and picked up a friend here and there, but pretty soon I went back to Kabete and signed on for another ticket.'

CHAPTER
FIVE

Some days later the soldier came right into the Refuge. The gate was not manned in the daytime and not locked unless one of the residents was going through a depressive phase or particularly likely to wander away. This did not often happen. Although those who knew Bessie's old habits were at first afraid of her taking them up and forgetting where she now lived, she had become twice as timid since being deprived of her shanty, and never went out unless tailing meekly after one or more of the others. They wondered whether she had quite forgotten where she was and thought herself transported into some totally strange place, except that she could always identify the Maternity Hospital with talk of babies. Clearly, however, her own lost baby had been born with the minimum of help in a detention camp, and it was unlikely that Bessie had ever set foot in a hospital in her life.

The soldier marched straight up to the house. The kitchen help walked out to intercept him and ask him what he wanted. He said that he had heard there was a home for retired officers and wished to put his name down. Persuaded that no men's home was available, he still stood surveying the scene and several of the old ladies came out frankly to have a look. It was the slack time of the afternoon when they were making tea or *uji*, and those who had shared an ambitious lunch were still sleeping it off. A mandasi or a cup of soup was really enough for them, but once in a while it cheered them to put their heads together and, with an onion from one, a handful of beans from another, flour from a third and the wisdom of generations, make a morning pass over the charcoal burner and review their little bits of household possessions. Supper and morning porridge were provided, more efficiently, as Matron was always pointing out, but with a distasteful briskness in the institution's dining room.

'Hallo,' said Mama Chungu cheerfully.

'Oh, this is your new place, is it?'

You remember him, he may reasonably remember you. But it is better not to be remembered. Mama Chungu had experience in making herself unobtrusive. The habit stays with you, and seldom provokes generosity from passers-by, but it is better than attracting attention and still finding someone ungenerous.

'*Ça ne fait rien*,' she thought – *sanfaireean*, even the English sailors used to know. *Haidhuru*, she corrected herself hastily, and went to set a pot of maize and beans to boil, furious that she had so nearly betrayed herself.

'You looking for a good billet?' asked Wairimu. 'This one is ladies only, you see. Besides, you're young enough to look after yourself. Haven't you got a wife to cook for you?'

'Women have been no good to me.'

'Perhaps you haven't been good enough to them,' said Nekesa. 'Are you visiting anyone in particular?'

'Just inspecting, madam. Have to put a guard on, you know. But there was another one – one with a bad leg. I used to see her with you at the gate.'

'She's lying down,' answered Nekesa quickly, before one of the others should interfere with her pet theory. 'She hasn't been very well. We aren't supposed to disturb her. Apudo, you mean?'

'How would I know your names, woman. Garrison check, that's all.'

'They took her to the hospital,' cried Sophia. 'They let the medical students practise on her so now she's worse than when she went in.'

'Not worse,' Nekesa insisted, 'only not much better yet. Rahel will mend. She's a tough one, from an army family.'

The soldier seemed to have stopped listening. He made an elaborate mimicry of presenting arms, then turned on his heel and marched off down the path, counting to himself. Nekesa had already begun a campaign to get Rahel out in a wheelchair on sunny days so that she could be roused a bit and put on display if the man should come again. But the next week he arrived one evening after Suleiman had come on duty, and failed to get admission. He did not argue but eyed the watchman nervously and strode away. A third time he started to come in one morning when Rahel was dozing in her wheelchair but Sophia headed him off.

'Don't go near her,' she shouted. 'She's only interested in real serving soldiers. We've seen enough of the other sort.' Nekesa was out and not able to intervene. Priscilla was a little more circumspect.

'There is no need to shout, Mrs Mwamba,' she insisted, turning towards the man. 'This is a private institution, you know, but if there is anyone in particular you want to visit, perhaps I can direct you.'

The man saluted her, turned about and marched off. Rahel did not wake up and Wairimu, looking out for a bit of fun, was afraid to detain him under Priscilla's disapproving gaze.

'My madam,' Priscilla murmured, 'would never have anyone turned away from the house roughly. She used to say that in one place or another we were all strangers and pilgrims.' And tried to remember what it was like not to be a stranger, a sojourner.

'Mrs Mwamba'. So that was her name. The second marriage – no one would expect it to have the excitement of the first. But it was as though a madness had seized her. For centuries her people had lived at a few miles' distance from pagans and savages, traded with them, sometimes converted them, even married with their women and yet preserved their distance. One had seen, closer and closer to the town as people moved in to work or strike their bargains, the frenzied dances in which they abandoned themselves to the spirits – *jini*, *pepo*, *mwazindika*.

And now it was as though a spirit had taken hold of her. She was nearly thirty when Ali died, an experienced woman, mother of three, surrounded by respectable kinsfolk and in-laws. She banked the compensation money in her little red book and let them think she had used it all on the mourning ceremonies. One day, she thought, Hassan would need it to learn his way into the new world. Once the prescribed hundred and thirty days of mourning were over, her people would have made proper provision for her. The Prophet (Peace be upon him) had himself married a thriving widow; when one is skilled one does not need also to be passionate. There is fertility, housewifely competence, an adequate income. Why need one go mad as well?

Fatuma – the handsome young Fatuma who still dwelt within Sophia – went on refusing to have a marriage arranged for her, saying

65

that she was still weeping for the loss of Ali. Probably it was so: she could not recreate the memory. Hassan was going to school – not to *madrasa* but what one now considered 'proper' school, wearing neat shirt and shorts. Mariam was attending private classes in the home of an Ismaili Muslim lady. Hawa was two years old, mumbling and singing all day among the bright pieces of cloth on the floor. Because of the war, ships could not be spared to bring in fashionable clothes as they used to do. Stocks of cloth in the shops were running down. So every lady wanted sewing done, and if you had hoarded some pretty pieces, meant for your growing daughters, you could get a high price for them, as well as for making up the dull, market cloth in decorative styles.

Fatuma's sisters and cousins hovered about to protect her modesty, and Ali's workmates came, two by two, to offer their condolences and, later on, to see how she was getting on and bring sweets or cashew nuts for the children out of their now healthy wage packets, for wars make money. Among them came the accordion player and, with him, the Christian friend who had taught him to play. And this time her eyes dropped and her hand trembled, holding the coffee cups. The new world was coming, they said. India would soon be free of the British. Our own soldiers had taken Ethiopia from the Italians and handed it back to the little black Emperor, while British generals and ambassadors stood smiling by. Kenya needed dockers now and next time they made a strike, after the war, their demands would be accepted. She smiled and tried to think about Kenya. She had been a short way up and down the coast but never a dozen miles inland. But some of the women she talked with in the market had come from as far as Kisumu, two nights' journey on the train, to visit their husbands working in the docks. All this was Kenya and all those people were Kenya too. Ali used to say so.

She seemed to see Henry all the time. She met him in the bazaar, looking for dresses for his little daughter. His wife had died with her second baby and the girl stayed with her granny, at the home place. She found him playing the accordion at an open day in Hassan's school. His Swahili was very good. He would come to the Old Town for shopping and chance upon her calling out to the water-seller, or buying thread or fetching Mariam from her class. One day he asked if he could go and see her father.

She was even more flustered than other times he called. Why should he want to see her father? To talk about dowry, he said, since he had no brother or uncle here to send for him. Because of losing his first wife he might not be able to offer very much, but he wanted to do the right thing. Only, of course, he added, looking at her very hard, his wife would have to become a Christian.

She could not now remember whether she had stormed or wept, for in all her hopeful imaginings no such demand had ever crossed her mind. Did he want her to go away, then, to some distant, dusty place, far from the sea and the coconuts and the call to prayer?

No, he conceded. Mombasa was a good place to stay and work. His little girl could be brought here and go to school with Mariam and Hawa. For of course he would insist on their going to school. If he went home, the children of her other husband might bring a difficulty, but his parents would not object to their staying in Mombasa, might even make a visit. Only, he was a baptised Christian and – he swallowed hard: she took the point, not circumcised – and so he was not offering to take her as a concubine but a legal wife in church who would bear his name and be proud of it. He had a steady job and a decent house to offer her. Hard and angular she knew it would be, after the old home, but fashionable by the standards of the time; as more and more workers came into the city, houses were even more at a premium than in 1939. She hung her head and said that she would come to look at the house.

Of course there was no question of going to see her father. To him infidel dowry would be an insult, and she had already been rebuked for receiving visitors too freely. Then one evening Hassan did not come home from school. He had been rude and moody for some months now. She understood the difficulty of a boy without a father. After searching frantically in the neighbourhood of the school, she found her father had collected the boy and sent him to live with her brother in Kilifi. However much she stormed, she was told, the Kadhi would uphold the transfer of a believing boy to a believing household. Her mind had been made up for her. That night she told Henry she was moving in with him.

To her astonishment, he refused. He said he did not want to sin, which she did not understand, or to do anything to put himself in danger of the courts, which she understood. He transferred her and the children to the home of a married neighbour of his to learn the customs, attend church classes and have the banns called. Her bridges were burned now. Anything could happen.

With a docility foreign to her nature, Fatuma learned what lessons were set for her and severed the links with her old life. Hassan was nearly a man now and she knew her brother would not let him go. Mariam was eleven and would surely soon be betrothed. She had left her classes now and helped with the plain seams, but she was restless and unreliable. There were whispers in the old town that she wandered too much while her mother was in the bazaar. A move would be good for her, but the idea of school would not go down easily. She was rude to Damaris whose house they lived in for a while, but Damaris was gentle and did not protest. Henry bought food for them all, and the father of the house did not bring in much. Mariam sat quiet while Henry told her stories about Issa – for she already knew something of Musa and Ibrahim and Nuhu – but Hawa laughed and played at being Zacchaeus up the tree or at lowering the sick man through the roof, and sang the new songs with gusto.

Sophia remembered getting her new name and promising truly to make a new life. The wedding was strange to her, in an ugly white dress, with people singing songs that still seemed to her untuneful and gathering outside to shake her hand. She had only a hazy recollection of the ceremony, but she had moved into Henry's house and they were happy together.

CHAPTER
SIX

'Ladies,' announced Matron, in a voice that compelled attention wherever the old people might be hiding away, dozing, pottering in the garden, knitting or counting the minutes till TV time, 'I have brought you a new visitor. The usual padre is away on leave and he has sent the Rev. Andrew from Uganda to pray with you today. I am sure you will give him a nice welcome. Now, you will excuse me, Reverend, because the book-work to keep this sort of place running is heavier than you can possibly imagine; I can get on with it at a time like this, you see, when I can be sure they are all healthily occupied.'

The records were, indeed, orderly and up-to-date, and it was not often that an old lady would intrude upon the work of keeping them so, unless in case of accident or a sudden bout of illness. In fact, since breakfast and supper were served to the residents on time, their private food allowances for other meals issued like clockwork, surgery held every morning and clothes and bedding inspected once a month, they had little cause to disturb Matron. Since they could move in the daytime as far as their strength permitted, there were other neighbours who could hear their whispered confidences, a message delivered through the church from some old friend, a private visitor or a strikingly successful act of barter. Matron contrived in the course of the week what she thought of as a private chat with each of the thirty old ladies and what they regarded as a trick interview to find out whether they were approaching the institution's limit of physical or mental degradation. This was not fair on their part since, unless they became spectacularly noisy or incontinent, Matron would stretch the rules as far as possible to keep her flock in healthy and familiar surroundings – witness Rahel lying so often inert on her bed and Bessie sobbing at night for the full-grown baby she said was snatched from her.

It was rumoured that Matron had been taken to England for a course and, the missionaries sometimes suggested with a grin, instructed in the management of Women's Institutes. (Only Priscilla, among the residents, had an inkling of what amused them.) Certainly she had cultivated a sort of kindness which it was difficult anywhere to lay hands on. The racier of the old ladies speculated – but quietly – on how the long-dead husband had ever managed to get on her two sets of twins, all of whom made discreet Sunday visits in spotless little cars with well-turned-out spouses and children. Not even Wairimu knew their names.

'*She* thinks we'd be entertaining our boyfriends if we didn't always have somebody's eye on us,' giggled Wairimu, shoving the pastor in the direction of the best chair. It was a licence of speech that was allowed her as the eldest, though she felt she might have claimed it anyway as having the best features. She had to admit that Sophia was well-preserved, but some of these uncouth old women ran to fat if not to wrinkles. Not Priscilla, of course, but no one would have imagined Priscilla sticking her neck out in any circumstances.

'Well, naturally,' the young padre replied with a easy smile, 'a set of beautiful girls like you can't be too careful.'

The old ladies cackled appreciatively.

Getting them quiet, he spoke very simply about the fiery trial in Uganda during ancient and modern days, the strain put upon Kikuyu Christians in Emergency years, and Satan still like a roaring lion seeking whom he may devour. He gave thanks for their place of domestic safety as second best to an individual home, but reminded them that there was no spiritual safety zone, that even the strains of living in community led to the lonely forest edge where you could be asked what side you were on. Just because of their loneliness – for the company of age-mates could not, he knew, take away the longing for children and grandchildren – they had wisdom and experience to share with younger neighbours, and he urged them to make that offering of love, because many young people were also deprived of the full affection of their families. And Christian love was always ministering to the present moment, not to past sorrows or future fears.

They nodded assent. This was a message that came close to them

70

and they prayed and were blessed and sent the steadiest-footed among them to collect tea from the kitchen. It was laid on every Wednesday, in case they should come to blows in deciding who was to entertain the preacher.

'Your Swahili is very good,' said Mama Chungu. 'We should not know that you were a Ugandan. Have you lived here long?'

'No, I am just studying here for a year. But you see I actually had a Kenyan father. I did not know him, but my mother said I was to be called Waitito after a grandfather.'

There were ooohs and aaahs from several of the old ladies, while others busied themselves with pouring out and passing the cups of tea. Wairimu tried to question the pastor in Kikuyu, but he shook his head uncomprehendingly.

'So your father,' asked Priscilla, hardly raising her eyes from the Kikuyu Bible where she had been trying to find a place, 'where was he from? Kiambu, Murang'a, Nyeri?'

'I do not know,' replied the padre, 'and I am sorry not to know. My mother told me that he had been a priest and had run away, but I think perhaps he was just studying to be a priest and had left the college. She thought he was going to marry her, but he left her a little while before I was born. But whether it was true or just an excuse not to get married, whether they caught and disciplined him, perhaps returned him to Kenya, or whether he went back and confessed to having lived with my mother, I never knew. She died when I was seven and I went into a Protestant orphanage and was educated there, and so was led into the ministry. And I do not think I shall run away.'

Priscilla was looking at him intently. She was known to be a most militant Protestant, so the others supposed her to be wondering how the illegitimate son of a priest could be in a position to preach.

'You were in Kampala, then?' asked Nekesa. 'I was in Kampala myself from 1953 to 1960, and I speak Luganda because my stepfather was from Uganda. I used to trade in that market at the foot of Namirembe Hill. Perhaps you were a little boy there with your mother?'

'Indeed, you could have known my mother. Her name was Nellie. She told me I was born in the country, but I cannot remember anything before our little room in Kampala. I suppose in those days a

71

family in the countryside would feel very much ashamed of a child like me. I never knew my grandparents. I sat beside my mother when she haggled over goods in the street, and often stayed alone at night. When she collapsed by the roadside one day – I think now she must have been having another baby, but it was never explained to me – they took us to Mulago Hospital and I hung around there till she died. And then I was taken to the orphanage and never, never spoke of these things until I was saved by the Lord Jesus.'

'Yes,' said Nekesa quietly, 'in the Lord one can speak. I may even have known her. But there is a rivalry among young women, as you know, and also a sort of – privacy, I suppose, abstaining from asking questions. It is the only sort of privacy one can hope for. I might have landed up like her if I'd had kids. That really puts a limit on what a girl can get, living as we had to, and so people drive themselves to a breakdown. But I never had a child. I'd had to look after myself from an early age, since my mother could never stick to a man. I was brought up in Nairobi, so I knew how to speak Kikuyu, and it was difficult for us women on our own to prove who we were, even though I was in my thirties by the Mau Mau time and thought I knew the ropes. I suppose my own father must have retired from the railway by then. In any case he would not have known me, for I was only about ten, and my brother younger, when he chased my mother away with us. Later my mother went off to Busia somewhere, and my stepfather had no time for me anyway. So Kampala seemed a good place to go during the curfew years. It *was* a good place, too, with money around like dirt, fancy shops that made us blink, not much colour bar. I think it's not like that now.'

'Indeed not,' said Pastor Andrew. 'Now it is the bright lights of Nairobi that dazzle us all. But why did you come back?'

'I was not saved then,' continued Nekesa, 'and I was still on the game. Sorry to refer to it, Reverend, but if a man saves you out of a well it is good to know how far you had fallen when you thank him, isn't it? But by 1960 I was pushing forty, not able to compete with the young ones, and I'd learned how to trade in combs, mirrors, handkerchiefs, that kind of thing. Business was more advanced in Uganda than here, you see. We knew things were going to get better in Kenya, with *Uhuru* just round the corner, so I thought it best to come

72

in early. Maybe a few little troubles I had with the Kampala police helped me to make up my mind. Of course we did not know how difficult things were going to get for Kenyans in Uganda later on. But in my case the Lord was waiting for me here in Nairobi. Not that I was ready to listen, though I was trading straight and fair at Machakos bus stop, but when I went to hospital the first time He saved me, and from then on I kept myself clean and decent until I was too sick to work. They brought me here three years ago when all my stock and savings were used up. *Tukutendereza*, let us praise the Lord. That much Luganda we all know.'

The ladies resumed their chatter and the pastor excused himself promising to come again, and took leave of them one by one. Priscilla followed him quietly out of doors, and with an instinctive courtesy the others turned to putting the chairs back and arranging the tea things.

'So your father may still be alive?' she asked abruptly.

'It may be so. I have no means of knowing.'

'I hope you pray for him. You have the look of someone I used to know. Even a great sinner can be helped to repent.'

'It is so, my mother. May God be with you now.'

Priscilla turned away to hide her tears. If my old employer had taken me to England as I once asked, she thought rebelliously, perhaps I should have visited the Women's Institutes too and built a hedge round myself to keep the feelings out of sight. Complaining that the dust in the compound had quite spoilt her sandals, she spent a long time closed in the shower compartment scrubbing them noisily.

Yet even Mrs Bateson, calm and sensible as she ordinarily was, Priscilla remembered, would look restless and heavy-eyed on some mornings when she took up the early tea, particularly when there were violent incidents in the news, but also on some undefined days which she thought might have been birthdays or anniversaries. And when Priscilla asked respectfully,

'Did you not sleep well, madam?' she would reply,

'Thoughts, Priscilla, thoughts. It is better to keep busy so that they do not get the better of you. I think I shall cut the hedge today.'

A little while before she died, one of the bad nights when Priscilla was sitting up with her, she had spoken clearly, aroused momentarily from her heavings and mutterings.

73

'Be brave, my dear, when I am gone. It has been hard for you but at least you did not have to see your man die. He has had some sort of life, and it may be a good one.'

As she watched the last struggles, Priscilla could not shake off the memory of that night. It was a former clerk from the farm who led in the gang – he had resigned two years before, saying he had been offered a job in Nairobi, and there had been rumours that he was in the forest. Everything seemed to be clothed in rumours. They did not visit the homesteads any more, though it was still the time of homesteads: the security forces had not yet burned them down and moved the people to the new villages. Priscilla was glad that she had been spared that at least, safe in Nairobi and her mother sheltered in the church compound, while other workers in farms and schools were peering by night at the encircling fires and guessing, is that my home destroyed, my brother-in-law's, my best friend's? The hammering had come at the door and the clang of *pangas* until at last the wire frame had given way. They had stabbed at the Master first – he had ordered Mrs Bateson to the other room on the pretext of locking up what heavy tools they had. Then Priscilla's father had come running from the kitchen in his cook's apron, a carving knife in one hand and a heavy iron range poker hot in the other, short-sighted, grey-haired, utterly pitiful – they had jumped upon him in a moment and, knowing she could do nothing for him, Priscilla had run into Anthea's bedroom – Anthea whom she had cared for since babyhood like the child she had never had. There was no key, but she had shoved furniture against the door, pushed the child into the wardrobe and herself stood trembling in front of it, but of course to no avail. The men had knocked down the flimsy barrier, pushed her aside and dragged the screaming child from the cupboard. One blow, mercifully, had been enough, a slash across the throat, gurgling blood and then the police whistles had begun to sound and the men had run off into the night, leaving maid and mistress alive and sobbing in one another's arms. Her own mother was unhurt in the servants' quarters: only two of the farm workers from the distant lines were missing.

She grieved for her father, but he would have suffered in any case; after thirty years of service in that home where his children had been nurtured and some kind of respect achieved, what new

74

patterns of life were there for him? And yet all the patterns (they believed) were going to be new. He, like others, had spoken with resentment of land taken away by the whites and unjust taxes. And yet he was one of the lucky ones according to the terms of the time. The brandishing of the carving knife showed not only loyalty to an employer who could be termed a friend but also knowledge of his own doom and perhaps a faint hope of saving his womenfolk. But Anthea, with her perfect Kikuyu and her openness to new things, what purpose could be served by her death? Mercifully her older brother and sister were away in boarding school. And mercifully – perhaps for the only time in her life it struck Priscilla as a mercy – her own man was far away and could have no part in this shambles.

The police came and found her cradling Anthea's body in her arms while Mrs Bateson bent over the Master's. Themselves now stained with blood and scratched with broken wood and mesh, they answered question after question. Mrs Bateson had had to plead that she needed Priscilla, trusted her, knew that she had risked her life for the child, or she, too, might have been marched away among the suspects. And so they had moved to Nairobi, found a flat, started to live again, put a manager on the farm until in better times it could be sold, made a home for Jim and Susan before the term ended. And when preachers and politicians promised that all the patterns were going to be new, Priscilla alone remained as she had been before, a domestic servant, educated as far as girls could be educated in her time, working for a European with whom she always spoke good Swahili, not the kind with which employers sometimes insulted the kitchen. For although Mrs Bateson had urged her ahead and into the English-speaking classes, it was a kind of custom to speak Swahili with the servants, and perhaps a kind of courtesy, too, for neither of them to take refuge in the language of her own tribe. If it had not been for her man, she might have gone away to train as a teacher, but that man had changed everything. So Priscilla continued to take in morning tea, cooked breakfast (for no one ever spoke of engaging another cook), wearing a uniform, living in quarters, attending a different church from Mrs Bateson, eating different food, buying in different shops. Because when you have gone through so much together, how can you face any more changes?

75

Except that gradually times had changed and moulded them. Jim and Susan grew up and left the country. By *Uhuru* they had stopped coming for regular vacations. When Mrs Bateson broke her arm in a motor accident she asked Priscilla, as a favour, if she would sleep in Susan's room in case of difficulties in the night, and they both felt more secure. They got into the habit of sitting down to morning coffee together and both took to wearing bright smocks to save their good dresses when they were doing chores in the kitchen or garden. Mrs Bateson even suggested teaching Priscilla to drive, but that was more than she could face. They simplified their way of life to suit the strength they had left.

She lay wakeful, turning it over in her mind, while Bessie in the next bed sobbed for her baby – a five foot ten baby with a rifle and corporal's stripes. Susan had come when Mrs Bateson died, offered her whatever she wanted of the furniture and found her a similar job with another widowed lady. It sounded the same, but of course it was not. The house was larger and harder to clean. There were more guests to cook for and Priscilla was finding it harder to lift and carry things. She was under the doctor herself, and after a couple of years was told that her heart would not stand such heavy work. She wrote to Susan, since she did not communicate very well with the new employer, and Susan, after enquiring round, had got her a place in the Refuge. She was under sixty at the time, and knew she must look favoured to the others, but Matron looked upon her as an ally and, as she suspected, donations came to the home from Susan and her friends. Priscilla asked someone to store the few pieces of furniture she had chosen before the flat was sold, and kept her own savings against emergencies. No one knew better that anything may happen.

Jim visited Kenya once on a business trip and came to see her, bringing a hundred shillings from himself and a dress from Susan. She asked him if he would like to take any of the stored furniture away, but he had looked scared at any mention of the old home, showed her photographs of his own children and avoided any mention of early days on the farm. In her prayer book she had a picture of him on a pony, looking as though nothing would ever frighten him. They are good people, she thought, to remember. Some employers don't remember. But she did not dare to think any further back than that. She did not dare to think.

But one is never quite safe from reminders. On one of her visits Mrs Reinhold was to be collected by a lady from All Saints' Cathedral, since streets and districts grew blurred to her as she moved from one African country to another, confusing the greetings, the currencies, the landmarks, but never the tabulated criteria of aid. The lady herself held the geography of the city clear in her mind: when she occasionally needed to visit the eastern districts it was a matter of honour to do it efficiently. She felt this the more in that her imagination had never been able to grasp the kind of life lived in these overcrowded little boxes of houses or sprawling tenements of many doors and court-yards. Her husband's elder brother, jack of all trades and master of none, had lived in Eastleigh once before she knew him, before the glutinous mud and the influx of cheaper lifestyles had driven the last few, unachieving whites away and changed the race course. But she could not picture it, and the rest of the family preferred not to try.

Like many of the white Kenya-born she was tall and bony: she had tried, theoretically speaking, to bow her head and shrink her needs – her simple widow's single bed and dressing-table, her armchair, desk and footstool, her few serviceable dresses and pots and pans – to fit the bare, square rooms without convenience of windowseat or mantel-piece, and knew that she had failed. The failure made her not less generous but less capable of compassion: objectively, the acknow-ledged ignorance enriched her. So many of her neighbours knew, in their own conceit, everything worth knowing.

She put her head through the door to where the women were gathered round Rahel and greeted them. Then she took a longer look.

'Why, it is Priscilla, isn't it?'

'Indeed, madam,' Priscilla answered in precise, simple Swahili. 'How are you and what brings you here?'

'I am well, Priscilla, and delighted to see you. I shall never forget how you cared for Mrs Bateson those last months. Are you working here?'

'Oh no. I had one job after my madam died, but it was not the same, and the doctor said I must rest, so they brought me here.'

'I am sure you had earned a rest after all those years. I am retired myself and live very quietly since my husband passed on. Perhaps you did not know?'

'I heard, madam, in my last place, and I was sorry. I know you had nursed him for a long time.'

'Indeed. I wonder now what is left worth doing. But I am lucky. I did not have to face violence as Mrs Bateson did and, I believe, you also.'

She glanced at the wedding ring and Priscilla bowed her head.

Wairimu pricked up her ears. Sophia, mercifully, was sucking up to Mrs Reinhold and Matron, so she did not hear.

'But isn't this someone else I know? Where have I seen you before? Forgive me: we are all getting old and I forget things.' She was looking at Mama Chungu, who giggled and turned away.

'This is Mama Chungu,' said Priscilla in English. 'She does not talk about herself. I think she got her name because if you ask her about the children she says, "It hurt me, it hurt me". She can talk all right about other things.'

The ladies gathered round. Their endless curiosity had always been defeated by Mama Chungu's attachment to the here and now.

'So, Mama Chungu,' went on the white lady, 'I ought to know you. Where can I have seen you?'

Mrs Reinhold had come out of Matron's house with Sophia and joined the group. She did not understand Swahili.

'Perhaps by the mosque?' someone suggested. 'She used to beg outside the mosque.'

'No, I do not think it was there. Where before the mosque, Mama Chungu?'

Of course there would be record cards, but Matron did not discuss record cards in front of residents.

'Flowers in the market?' offered Mama Chungu quietly.

'I don't think so. I have a garden, so I never buy flowers. Where before that?'

Priscilla gave a start. A memory stirred in her of chasing someone out of the gate, the white marguerites she had taken without permission scattered on the ground. And later seeing the same woman hustled along by policemen, one of them holding incongruously the big bunch of flowers she had picked, a few at a time, from gardens along the way, until one angry householder had turned her in. Priscilla had never given it another thought. But the Cathedral lady had lived beyond the city limits until her husband's illness circumscribed them. It could not be a simple matter of picking flowers.

'Before that dobi Ngara.' Mama Chungu was reciting as though in a trance. Everyone in Nairobi shopped at Ngara at one time or another. They did not recollect her, but everyone changes. Mama Chungu had become sturdy again once they had brought her in from her pitch outside the mosque and fed her properly. She had begun begging too late in life to do well out of it, and her body had never adjusted itself to the angles of the pavement or the cocoon of polythene bags and wrapping paper. One could imagine her, at fifty, say, scrubbing at khaki uniforms in a backstreet laundry.

'No, it was not in Ngara.'

'Housemaid at Kamiti,' Mama Chungu replied to the unspoken question. Bessie raised her head but turned the movement skilfully into a need to scratch her armpit. Who was she to give away secrets? But she remembered, in her usual fuzzy way, being taken outside for grasscutting during that endless cleansing process for detainees that she could never understand, Leonard tied to her back – or was he still in the womb? – and seeing a chubby, light-skinned woman hanging clothes on a line. Someone her own age, fortyish she thought, whose babies would be behind her, someone safe, busy, defined. 'All these Europeans like to employ foreigners,' one of the other women had hissed. A foreigner, with soap-sore hands, in an ayah's dress? It was beyond her.

'My husband's brother worked at Kamiti for a time, but we never went there. Did you live anywhere else?'

'Mombasa.'

'Mombasa? But you are not one of us,' protested Sophia. 'You do not look like it. You do not talk like it. You might have had a grandmother. . . .'

'No,' agreed Mama Chungu softly, trapped now, acquiescent. 'Not from Swahili. From Seychelles.'

'You come from Seychelles? You speak French?' asked Priscilla, suddenly understanding. There would be wrangles about citizenship, calls for papers.

'Not much French. I come when very small, my mother say. I grow Mombasa, speak a bit English, work there for white people. I get old. I forget,' concluded Mama Chungu in English. They all stared at her. 'Two babies hurt me. I not get any more. I go Kamiti.'

The lady from the Cathedral sat down suddenly. She blamed herself for fumbling after a memory, forcing a confidence, set off on the trail by the thought of Eastleigh first and then Kamiti. That brother-in-law, rolling stone, drinker, had for a while, just before the war, got a job in a Mombasa trading house. She and her husband, newly married, had been glad to stay with him for a cheap seaside holiday in those lean years. And one day she had seen, outside the servants' quarters, a young, light-skinned girl who had never, since their arrival, come into the house. She would have been pretty if not strained by sorrow, and in her arms was a sickly fair-haired baby with Robert's bony forehead and chin. 'My husband's nephew,' she had thought, stupefied, and begged Robert to take the child to hospital or fetch a doctor. But by the time he was persuaded, at nightfall, it was too late. The girl came home, big-eyed and trembling. She thought she would never forget that anguished face, and it appeared she never had.

'Don't take it to heart,' Robert had said to them. 'It won't take her long to get another.' The brothers had quarrelled and they left the next day.

Robert had served in the war, then drifted into the extra security forces taken on during the Emergency. He had married and been posted to Kamiti, and for the wife's sake they never referred to the past. It had never occurred to them that the girl would still be with the household. Eventually, after his wife had left him, Robert made his way south and out of contact.

'It must have been Mombasa,' she managed to say in a steady voice. 'If I remember right, you were a pretty girl: you still have the features. You won't remember me, but it was I who asked someone to take you to hospital. We felt very sorry for you.'

'I was always good at washing, madam,' replied Mama Chungu in a servant's Swahili. 'I cannot complain of lacking work. It is only because the babies died that I could not do better for myself.'

'Yes, I understand, Mama Chungu. I do not know where your –

80

your old employer is, or even whether he is still alive. He did not keep in touch with my late husband. But if there is anything. . . .'

'Matron looks after us very well.'

'Yes, yes. I know Matron looks after you. . . . Mrs Reinhold, we must hurry to get you back to lunch before your next appointment.'

The ladies all waved the car off.

'Does she have children herself?' Mama Chungu asked Priscilla.

'Two daughters, I think. But probably they are overseas. She used to be a friend of my madam.'

Priscilla knew better than to ask questions.

'Let her have joy of them. It is not her fault,' Mama Chungu summarised without explaining. 'I am going to water the beans. It is better to work than to keep on nattering. Bessie, why don't you come and help me? It is time you started taking a share of the work. If you just sit about you will get so fat you will burst out of your new dress, and that would be a pity.'

Mumbling something, Bessie obediently began to fill a tin with water. They understood her to mean that she would be prepared to look after the chickens if there were any.

Bessie was the newest comer and also the nearest comer. She had lived, as long as anyone around could remember, in one of the wooden shacks on the edge of Eastleigh. She was only heard to speak Swahili and the few words of Kikuyu common to the town, and she could not tell you where she came from before or how she got her name. Even when old neighbours came to see her in the Refuge – till most of them drifted away, in the frequent movement that marks off our cities from the place called home, or grew embarrassed when she failed to recognise them – she would only weep for her dead baby and turn away from them.

There had been a sort of order in Bessie's life, though not one fitting her very well for the routine of the Refuge. Her little home was full of things – benches and old pillows, tin cans, a couple of china plates, odd calendars and pieces of matting. She spent a lot of the day, her decent dress encrusted with dirt, a nylon scarf elaborately tied round her head, picking up fragments of charcoal round the dumps and carrying them home in a bucket. The dealers ignored her unless she came too close: she would peer into dustbins in search of other oddments to build up her fire. A few chickens scratched around her place and a few leafy plants grew there, though one did not see her tending them. And from time to time the boy came – always in civilian clothes, but by his bearing and the vehicles which sometimes dropped him off one saw that he was in the forces. No one remembered old Bessie having a child, but there he was. He would go to the door and she would smile and start at once to chatter. And then one would see the old clutter of the house put out for airing, and sweeping and washing going on, and Bessie would put on a brand new dress or wrapper while the old one hung out to dry. He must have brought food, for she was plump and healthy, though you did not see her cooking: perhaps someone was persuaded to keep a little store for her or make a phone call when she needed attention. It seemed a danger contained.

And then came August, with the early morning stutter of guns through darkness. Then the daylight of vehicles swerving and skidding, some picked up and driven by clueless youngsters, some carrying armed men here and there, slouching and uncertain. Long lines of people passed, laden with goods looted from the town or from neighbours. Others were grumbling and empty-handed because they had been stopped near California flats and robbed in their turn, some losing what they had worked for as well as what they had stolen.

And then by evening, as the tide began to turn, young men running and hiding, leaving the roads strewn with boots, weapons, uniforms, sobbing, begging, threatening for civilian trousers, an identity card, a place to hide. Some of them drunk on unaccustomed spirits, all inflamed with fear and the poison of defeat, without having known what they fought for. And so the boy came, homing on the little shack, not seeing it the most dangerous of all places for him. And they came in the evening, those who had no need to put off their uniform, those who had not been defeated, and fought to avoid defeat, demanding to search, search, and as Bessie smiled and babbled the young man, in his vest and pants, stooped at the doorway and came out, hands high but too late, a shot ripped away his mouth and they left him there where Bessie wept and mumbled, and moved to flush out the next block.

There were many forlorn mothers in those days, some searching for their sons or not daring to search for fear of giving them away, standing in queues at the mortuary till warned of curfew time approaching, hunting for receipts for their household goods as homes were searched and boxes ripped open to find stolen goods, striving not to offend. More folk than usual took for a time to parading in the streets, mouthing pitiful words, raving of the past, attempting to forget their recent hurt. But Bessie sat sobbing and sobbing, her fire unfed, her little store of flour and sugar snatched away.

One day a policeman led her to the Refuge. It needed investigation, Matron said. There was a proper admission procedure. But by morning Bessie's skinny hens had been eaten, her fence pulled down to build a fire to roast them. Curfew was over. Everything was back to normal. Anything less than normal had better be kept out of sight. Sponsors were found and Bessie stayed.

She submitted to being cleaned up, did not even (like most) reach out for her old dirty garments when she was given new. She ate what was set before her, learned the use of the bathroom, accompanied the others silently to church. A tendency to genuflect led people to think she might have been a Catholic once. She would gather up the smallest scraps of charcoal and present them to Priscilla, whom she seemed to look on as a leader. Priscilla nodded gravely each time and found a cardboard box to keep them in, until enough were accumulated for a ceremonial brewing of tea. And after a silent day, as soon as the light was put out Bessie would begin to weep.

'My baby, my baby! I thought you would grow up to be a soldier and look after me. But they took you away, my baby – oooh, my baby.'

One day, when a new lot of Community Nurses came, Bessie, who had submitted silently to the girl's examination, appearing not to understand her questions, suddenly spoke clearly in Swahili. The kitchen assistant, who had been helping bring in their equipment, was very surprised but careful not to interrupt.

'Do you know about babies?'

'Why, yes, a bit. We have not done our midwifery yet but we learn to work in the children's clinic.'

'They took away my baby,' persisted Bessie. 'Who can I ask to get

83

my baby back? You see,' she whispered, 'most of these poor old women could not have babies. They are jealous. They don't want me to get him back.'

Jane was puzzled, but she was a good enough nurse to recognise when somebody needed help.

'That must have been long ago?' she asked gently. 'Where did you have your baby?'

'I had him here, in Pumwani, at the Maternity, and I took him home from here. It was afterwards he got lost.'

'Was he very little then?'

'No, not little. He was a big boy. He helped me. He was in the Air Force, you understand.'

Jane's face began to crumple, but Bessie was too absorbed to notice her distress.

'But then he was not a baby, if he was in the Air Force. And it is no use asking at the Maternity if he was grown-up. Have you tried the Headquarters?'

'How can I ask when it was they who took him away? They sent a truck and they picked him up like a baby, his arms and legs all bare, and they took him away. Where did they take him?'

'Was he . . . was he able to walk, my mother?'

'They picked him up like a baby and they took him away. Even they left the blood. In the Maternity they would wipe up the blood. . . . But why do you cry, my dear – Gertrude, is it? – did you lose a baby too?'

'No, my mother, I am still a girl, I did not have a baby. I wish to God I had had a baby. And I am Jane – Gertrude is the tall one over there. I did not have a baby but I lost a – a friend. Do not ask them too much, my mother, it is over now. Remember the good things. What was his name?'

'His name is Leonard, but his friends used to call him Lucky. Lucky Leonard. He was not your friend?'

The old woman was trembling. Jane wondered if she would be in trouble for upsetting her. But this was more important than taking temperatures and inspecting the bed.

'No, he was not my friend. My friend was John and he was – taken

84

away – too. But I am sure I met Lucky Leonard. We used to go for dances, you know. It all seems so far away.'

She covered her face in her arms.

'Yes, well, we have all had our dances,' said the old lady quietly. 'I think your teacher is looking for you. Just try to find out for me if you can.'

'Jane – Jane, haven't you finished yet? We want to compare notes.'

'Just coming, tutor, I'm sorry. The old lady had some questions, you see. . . .'

Gertrude was interviewing Priscilla and giving her a quick health check. She was a long-limbed, round-cheeked girl, just like Priscilla, who, at the same age, had loved games at school and taken a great pride in her own strength. She had hugged to herself the prospect of marriage when the dowry was first settled – she was already twenty-two, having returned to school, at Mrs Bateson's urging, when standards five and six became available locally to girls. She had come to regard the processes of school and of a European house routine as natural – she had never lived in a village – and had never been circumcised. There was a church wedding in a modest white cotton dress and afterwards in the farm clerk's house she and Evans had come together with a passion such as none of the grannies had ever hinted to her was possible. She had continued to work in the house – Jim was quite a baby then and Susan a couple of years older – but her thoughts were always straying back to the night. Her whole horizon was lighted up by her feeling for Evans. It amazed her afterwards that in those two years she had never conceived a child. Yet at the time she was so happy that she never yearned for a baby as other girls seemed to do if a year passed before they became pregnant. She made cloths and covers for the house. Both of them earned money. They were able to dress and eat well. . . .

She pulled herself together. Why open it all up again just because she had met a healthy girl who would soon be married, and she was hardly used to meeting young people any more? Gertrude was asking about the action of her bowels and making notes in a little book.

'You seem very healthy,' she said. 'I am sure it is because you know the rules of health.'

'Rules of health? I suppose so,' answered Priscilla. 'I had a good

85

schooling as things went in my day, and I always worked in nice, clean houses. But when I was nearly sixty the doctor said I had to stop because of my heart, and I had nowhere to go, so, you see, they brought me here.'

'You have no family?'

'No, I never had any children.'

'You are a widow, then?'

'No, or rather perhaps not.'

'It must be yes or no,' said the girl, smiling.

Priscilla felt very weak. She must not become a gossip. But the girl had a strange attraction for her.

'I do not talk about it with these old ladies,' she said stiffly in English, dredging up the words from the far past. 'But my husband went away, you see. He went away to get more education.'

'And did not come back?'

'And never came back. He wrote to me twice.'

'From America?'

'No, not America. In those days we did not know much about America. He said there were chances in Uganda. But perhaps after that he went overseas. It is possible.'

'That was long ago?'

'Of course, long ago. I was a big strong girl like you then. It was about the time Mr Kenyatta came back from England after the war. We were all thinking about education. My husband had gone up to standard eight. He was a clerk on a farm. But he wanted more.'

'Nearly forty years. . . . And you waited?'

'Yes, I waited, I worked. I had a good employer,' she was back in Swahili now. 'I was kept comfortable.'

'I don't think I could do that. I am getting married soon to the brother of my friend – that one over there. But I don't think I could bear it if he left me like that.'

'I was married in church,' Priscilla said primly. 'It was a matter of duty. One does not ever discuss these things – please don't. . . . But then,' she added under her breath, half hoping the girl would not hear, 'I loved him.'

'Yes,' replied Gertrude solemnly. 'I understand. And I see that you do. The tutor is calling me now. Thank you for telling me. I'll come and see you again and show you a picture of my Sam,' she called over her shoulder, pledging the most precious thing she had, the cheap ring flashing on her left hand as she strode off to join the group comparing notes.

'And I see that you do.' I must be getting old and crazy, thought Priscilla. Bringing it all out like that. Or did I just want to stop her going on to the next questions – father killed; brother maimed; mother died; sister widowed. . . .

Was it really because there had been no baby? That was what most people thought afterwards. But at the time it hardly even struck her, they had been so sure of each other. It had come out of the blue.

'I am not satisfied. I need to learn more. You also should one day get more education. There is a power in us that is not being used properly. In Uganda they say the standard is higher. I have to go. I know that I can get employment if I need to. Then I will send for you or come back for a holiday. You will be all right here.'

He gave his one month's notice and left. The Batesons tried to persuade him to plan ahead, to travel with his wife, but he was so consumed with restlessness that she had to let him go.

The house had to go to the new clerk – the same who would resign after five years and then creep back with a *panga* in his hand – but they found a little room for her in the servants' quarters, and she moved there with their bits of furniture and embroidered pillowcases. Anthea Bateson was born a few months later, so she had a baby – for a few years – to keep her busy after all.

The first letter from Evans came from Jinja a month after he had left, saying he thought he had fixed a place in high school. He was working in the school office meanwhile and had enough money in reserve for the first year's fees. Then after about three months came a letter without an address saying that the seminary offered everything to fulfil his ambition and he had now had his eyes opened to the claims of the true church. Of course a priest was not supposed to keep a wife but perhaps she also had mistaken her vocation. It would be better to keep apart for a while to test out the situation – perhaps at the end of a year they could discuss the matter. That was the last word she ever had. Evans's father, Waitito, and his mother, Miriam, had heard nothing. No rumour of his return ever reached the district.

87

She moaned and rocked herself on the bed they had shared, prayed at first passionately for his return, then, more mildly, that his apostasy be forgiven, at length doggedly for strength to bear it. By the time the other blows fell and they moved to Nairobi she was over thirty and Kikuyuland full of widows and detention-widows. She buttoned herself into her uniform dresses, polite smiles, sensible shoes. The only thing that surprised her any more was to be told she had heart trouble. Did she really have a heart?

Wairimu watched Priscilla talking with the girl and wondered what it was all about. Mrs Njuguna, Priscilla was called, and spoke little about herself. She must have been a baby when Wairimu first went to Nairobi but a mature woman when the bad times came, the times she refused to talk about. Well, no Kikuyu had come unscathed through those years and very few were eager to talk about them. Look at me, Wairimu reproached herself, full of stories of Thuku and roadwork and terracing, but how much else is bottled up inside? All of us keep something back – even Sophia, for all her talk. Thirty of us, mostly withholding something we know about ourselves, some, like poor Bessie, withholding something we don't know. The stories we learned when we were children were all about big people – braver, stronger, fiercer, cleverer, even wickeder, than anyone we knew. The ordinary people got passed off as hares or hyenas or birds. But if we knew the secrets of those little people, or the littleness of the big people – what they were afraid of, what they were mean over, what they wasted – then there would be the true story of our people. But it is easier to think in headlines. 'Prince Charles goes to school' was one the clerk had translated for her at the coffee: and then the small print on an inside page told how many 'terrorists' had been hanged.

After all, Wairimu decided, if she were young now she would not be a nurse. She would be a journalist. Why had she not thought of it before? She spread out a shaky hand, scarred with burns and prickles, and laughed. She had always found it an effort to scratch out a message on paper. Nowadays she could hardly hold the pencil to scrawl her name on the allowance form. And now she could only read the big print. Priscilla could read aloud well, using her glasses, and sometimes they got a visitor or a schoolgirl in to read the Swahili paper. As though, Nekesa pouted, it would ever have anything to do

88

with them: the New Testament was all she wanted to hear. She had come to it late and couldn't have enough of it. But even from these ragged readings, with old ladies jogging one another to see the pictures, or the younger ones, who knew their birthdays, wanting to hear their stars, Wairimu could see how it ought to be done.

'Harry Thuku saved me from a life of shame. Amazing revelations of old Nairobi.' (Well, partly saved me, anyway.)

'The Thika tramway, a first-hand recollection.'

'Freedom fighters or labour activists?'

There was a regular TV programme, *Wazee Hukumbuka*, Old People's Memories. Why had they never called her? But a documentary film – if she had a granddaughter, it would be done.

She had stayed at Kabete till 1931, when things were very bad in the coffee. About then Sophia would have been having her first baby, Priscilla would be in elementary school, Nekesa was getting used to living at the quarry with the rough stepfather, Rahel would have been a big girl, learning the songs and starting to go with the bridal parties to bring home the evidences of virtue. Once you knew it, you could see them young, catch them out as girls by the turn of a head, the choice of a word. Even she must betray her history to the others by jerky movements and squared shoulders. The basket of coffee is not so heavy as the firewood or water. The plantation is not so steep as the home ridge and valley.

The plantation at Kabete was barely working. Prices for produce were low and overseas countries had mysteriously become so poor that, even so, they could not pay them. The Master's family were living mostly on what they could grow in their kitchen garden. The car hardly left the garage. The Seychelloise sewing lady did not come any more. Then came the locusts. Wairimu had not yet learned about the plagues of Egypt, but when she did the locusts were the ones she understood first from her own experience. There would be others later.

She had heard about locusts consuming grain, seen small swarms pass. Somehow she had never been able to connect them with the coffee, the tough, shiny leaves, the round, hard berries. The first thing was the getting dark – not just shadowy, as before rain, but thick, black dark, so that if you had a lamp you would want to light it. Then came

89

the feeling of wings and bodies all round you. Some people are afraid of bats squeaking in the rafters of a house, or of rats. In town houses, when a shanty site has been cleared, the rats flee from it, squeezing into every crack and aperture that seems habitable with the smell of food and human ordure, jumping from a high window into your hair, crawling up the bathroom exit pipe in search of warm slime and company. Even this can hardly be compared with the air that fluctuates with locusts.

The men knew what to do. They had already met the menace several times. First there had to be noise – people beating on tin cans, blowing whistles, shouting, all in the eerie darkness, instinctively feeling that the threat could be frightened away. Then you took sticks, sacks, lengths of rope – but no *pangas*, since in the mêlée you might easily find yourself swatting a friend or neighbour – and went on banging against the creatures as they weighted down the bushes and bent the lower branches of trees. But it was more to show willing than in the hope of being effective. For each one that fell to the ground and cracked like a cockroach under your feet, five more tangled with you in the air, and who could say how many flew on, surfeited, to the next battle area? Some of the workers wanted to set fires to suffocate the locusts with smoke, but the Master did not agree since he was afraid the fires might destroy more than the locusts. Wairimu was glad he refused: though she had not yet got to know the terror of fire, she saw no sense in leaping from one danger to another.

Their sense of time was all disordered. At nightfall the remaining locusts went to roost and it was only when the moon came into view that they realised it was natural night. People started scooping up the insects from the ground to cook and eat. Wairimu was so weary that she drank a little *uji* and fell asleep.

Next morning they saw the full extent of the destruction. The bushes were stripped bare, down to the woody stems, some broken with the beating given them in the dark. Even the grass at the edge of the paths and the flowers in the house garden had been eaten up. They did not know where to start work. The Master looked grey and worn out. He sent the foremen to call them together for a meeting.

'I cannot tell you exactly what will happen,' he said. 'I am grateful that you tried to help, but an enemy of the air is harder to fight than an enemy of flesh and blood. We shall have to see what we can do. First, everybody will stay till the end of the ticket. You will get your money and your posho. I cannot say how any of us will manage to live, because if other places have been devastated as much as this there may not be any vegetables. At the end of the ticket I am afraid some of you will have to go. You will not find it easy to get work, as things are. It may be that I shall have to go myself. Some of you think perhaps that Europeans just get money out of the air, but it is not so. Like you, we get it out of the ground and from the work of our hands and heads. You say, "He has a motor car," but if I took my car to sell in Nairobi tomorrow it would not fetch what would run this place for a month, because more people want to sell cars than are able to buy them. I have to see the Agricultural Officer, and the bank, and those who owe me money on the coffee you have already produced, before I see my way clearly.

'Well, now, the foremen will show you where to start digging in the locust remains when you have used what you can. You will also have to resurface the road inside the estate, because lorries or even trains can slide about on these squashed horrors. Let us all do our best.'

Wairimu saw that it could not last. She asked for her card to be signed off when it was full and left.

She walked to Nyeri to see her people. Plenty were walking now. Everyone was feeling the pinch. She found her brother in the town looking thin and shabby. He had now five children, his wages had been cut and there was no sale for any surplus you could grow. It was good she had come, he said, for their mother was near her end. Father was still upright, but troubled. Kanini had long been married and Njoki was helping the nuns in the hospital. He wondered if they wanted to make a nun out of her – it seemed strange, but perhaps, after all, it was not a bad life, with enough to eat and the other girls for company.

She walked the rest of the way home. The terracing had stopped. Some of the land was bare and the trees fewer. Her mother was lying close to the fireplace. She seemed shrivelled. She had a cloth tied loosely round her body and a blanket drawn round her. Her teeth were nearly all gone and a trickle of saliva ran out of her slack mouth. A tin of *uji* lay untouched beside her.

She is old, thought Wairimu, and then wondered how she could be old. Her brother, the oldest, must be about thirty. At fifty, even allowing for the first few babies to have died, is one already old? The sister-in-law was the only one whose voice seemed to get through to the sick woman, and she herself looked tired, her breasts sagging, her back permanently bent. After several repetitions she managed to convey the message, 'Wairimu has come to see you.' The mother put out a hand towards her daughter, but her eyes hardly focused. In the night, during which none of the grown-ups tried to sleep, the gasping breath at last gave out.

They carried the little body five miles down the mountain and buried it near the church, the priest reading prayers over it. Then they walked back home, and Wairimu's father prepared to sleep in the house as though it had not been desecrated. He had not yet taken a second wife. Where would he now find one? His herds were small and only one of his three daughters had brought him dowry. His son had come home for the funeral, so there was no sleeping-place for Wairimu. She found a corner in a neighbour's house and a day or two afterwards slipped back to her first place of work among the coffee.

Workers had been turned away since the locust invasion two years before had set production back, but she found one of the foremen whom she had known ten years before and who had recommended her. The old Master had gone away and the young Master preferred to work in a bank, so the names were new but the organisation much as before. She got six shillings for a thirty-day ticket (the men got eight), posho and a blanket. The dormitory the girls used to use had been divided up into little rooms for the mature women to share. It was cold and dull compared with Kabete and the attractions of the city nearby, but fair enough as far as work went. Some farms still did not give the blanket in advance of payment, though the law required it, and some had the reputation of forcing girls to work against their will. Strictly females were not to be sent, unless they wished it, too far from home to walk back to sleep there. Of course farmers always denied using force, though many of them could not deny requesting government to use it, but it was sometimes made worth the while of chiefs and headmen to do so, and a man who complained of the treatment of his womenfolk could find himself punished.

This practice had probably come to an end partly through scandals brought to light by some government officers and partly because there was no longer a shortage of labour, but Wanja, Wairimu's room-mate, had been herded into a plantation seven years before, locked in a hut with some other girls and all of them assaulted. She became pregnant, and when her parents complained they were told that their daughter ought to be able to look after herself. She had left the farm as soon as she could, but was ashamed to go home, so had come to this plantation, which had a better reputation. But with a baby it is difficult, of course, to protest your virtue: she had fallen for another child and now felt hemmed in and unmarriageable. They talked about it day in, day out. Wanja seemed hard-working and unassuming. At length a chain of introductions was started which led to her being married, for a token dowry, to Wairimu's father. This was upsetting the order of events with a vengeance, but Wairimu kept in the background and felt satisfaction that two problems should be solved at a go.

She herself did not particularly have problems. The years came and went, came and went. Dull food, dull work, now and again a dull man. But she had no responsibilities, enough to eat, talk round the fire, a place to sit aside and watch the young people dance, occasionally, as times grew better, a chance to switch to piecework and get more money. She knew the uses of extra money.

But then came a new interest, classes. She had learned to read a bit at Kabete but there was not much to read. There was the Harry Thuku pamphlet in Swahili, a booklet of scripture quotations in Kikuyu she had been given at a street corner, and a newspaper she had picked up somewhere with pictures of King George V's Silver Jubilee, but it was in English so she could make out only a few words like *Sunday* and *Queen*. Sometimes she would make a pretext to go to the office and look at the notices on the wall, a calendar, a list of prices, just to make sure her skills were not slipping, though the words did not mean much to her. There were also words written on trucks and machines – people's names, places, *left, danger, no smoking* – and on packets of tea or tins of condensed milk. But when the school came, life became more interesting, and more ambitious people came to ask for work on the plantation. This was about the time they were given a

93

day off to walk into Nyeri and celebrate the coronation of the new king (the one who had been properly advised on his marriage and got children, though unfortunately only girls).

First the Master came with a white missionary and told the workers that, since he had had many requests for a school for the children and a place of worship, he was offering to pay for a schoolmaster and for a tin roof if they were prepared to put up the building. But, since he was going to pay someone who picked no coffee and packed no coffee and carried no coffee, he hoped that all the workers would support him by working harder to cover that man's wages. Everybody cheered, but some asked why 120 should work harder to support an extra one. Wairimu and some of the others knew that the one man would get the pay of four or five labourers and a better house too. But they wanted to learn.

So they joined in building a rectangular mud house for the church, and someone carved a rough cross and put it over the door. The Master brought timber and corrugated iron for the roof, and they asked for a door frame and shutters for the windows, but he said there would be time enough for that when there was anything to put inside.

All the same, he brought more timber, and in their spare time the *fundis* made benches and a blackboard and a table and chair for the teacher. A two-roomed house was built, and the teacher moved in with his own furniture.

The first set of children were all put in one class, whatever their size or sex, as none of them had ever attended formal lessons before, but within a few months they were divided into two groups, according to progress. They wrote on slates and read from the blackboard. Later a few books appeared and were kept under lock and key in the teacher's house.

But the evening school was even better attended than the day school. Ostensibly a baptism class of the Church of Scotland, it attracted many men and boys who wished to learn to read and a few women. Wairimu had to wait for a while until the first women had caught up with her, but she started straight away to attend the Sunday services in Kikuyu. The speakers were always urging people to read the Bible, so she bought little paper editions of the separate gospels, which the elders used to bring round, and was thrilled by the new

94

knowledge she found in them and the absorbing puzzle of working the words out. In 1939 she was baptised Mary.

She had not realised that this too, proper and inevitable as it seemed, would cause distress to her family, for Njoki, at twenty, became a postulant in the Sisters of Mary Immaculate. Her father was proud and even renounced the cow which the fathers of the first novices had claimed ten years earlier. Her married brother and sister also basked in reflected glory. That one member of the family should not simply remain in traditional darkness but court damnation of a Scotchman's devising was hard for them. But Wairimu, bearing no ill-will towards the sisters, nonetheless hugged to herself her new knowledge and her growing horizon.

With the war a lot of the younger men drifted away into the army or to better-paying jobs in transport companies or in the docks at Mombasa. Labour was short and the cost of living going up. To keep them happy, the Master decided to give them meat once a month and vegetables once a week without deducting from their wages. This made him popular, though Wairimu had learned to see that he was still making a good profit from his labour – that *she*, in fact, contributed towards the car, the crude hot water tank over a wood fire, the boarding school fees, the outings to the Club. All the same, he did not, like some, stick to the minimum provision of the law: he took an interest in the school and made advances to one or two families who had sons bright enough to be promoted to intermediate school.

But of course it couldn't last. There was famine and the coffee crop was affected too. Her brother, needing to buy extra food as the harvest dwindled, could not meet the school fees for his two sons, and came to her for help. Fiercely she wanted the girls to read as well, but knew he had reached his limit. The Catholic church would admit illiterates. She tried to teach the girls a little when she went home now and then, but they were not very interested and she did not know how to set about it. The drought did not let up, and many children were getting listless. If it was that bad in Nyeri, then in places that were always on the margin of hunger one knew people were dying. Machakos people had settled in Embu and their relations walked there to save themselves and swarmed over the plantations looking for work, but there was no work. Government had rounded up unemployed men from Nairobi and Mombasa and sent them back to their locations to save the food situation in the towns. But even in the country one had to eat, and no more hands were needed on the farms. The government reduced the maize meal ration for labourers from two pounds to one and a half daily. The Master swore, but said they would have to accept it as there would be inspections. He set some workers to planting vegetable plots to keep the promised issue, as it was not a squatter farm and they had no land of their own. It was better than nothing, but the leaves were limp and tasteless: the meat was from game animals, struggling up towards the mountain in search of better pasture. Wanja came, pregnant again, looking for work, but there was none. Wairimu managed to spare her some flour out of the ration, but it was difficult for the hefty men to leave any for their families. There was no more piecework, since the crop was so poor.

In 1944 the flour ration was to be cut again by some three ounces, and this time the Master refused and said the inspectors could do what they liked if they complained: he could not face his labourers with less than they already had. But everyone was too busy to do much inspecting, and the rain in its time returned.

At last the war was over. Soldiers came back from Somalia, Ethiopia and Burma with heavy pockets and sad faces. Some did not come back. It took time for the ex-servicemen to readjust to ordinary life. They had suffered. But they had also grown used to regular rations and regular pay. Many had shared their sufferings with white servicemen and some few had shared their memories and dreams as well. They were no longer interested in working for a few shillings a month. Some were given technical training. Some used their gratuities to set up shops and transport businesses, but they were inexperienced and did not all succeed. Some sank into apathy with fearful memories behind their eyes. But many of them talked about what they had seen, what they had accomplished and what they had heard about meeting force with force.

Kikuyu newspapers were now available. *Mwenyereri* and *Agikuyu* passed from hand to hand together with some Swahili papers. People who had hardly before looked beyond the ridge were beginning to feel part of a whole. There was no one who did not have a son, a brother or an uncle away at work or in school, no one who had never heard by word of mouth how you loaded a rifle, how you concealed yourself, how you kept a line of communication open. These were the ones who were listened to, not the grandfathers, the few who remembered escaping from Maasai spears or opening up new ground at Kabete.

The ladies were not particularly anxious to hear of these things. Posho and wages they had all come up against one way or another. But they were always interested in presidents and politicians.

'Jomo Kenyatta came back from England in 1946. In February the next year he went to address the people at Ruringa Stadium – Mbiyu Koinange and James Beauttah were there with him. Of course I went. After what I had seen as a girl, I felt I had a right to be present at any political event. And I fell under the spell. From then on I became devoted to Kenyatta. But of course I was only, in their eyes, an ordinary member of the crowd. I did not get invited to the big dinner afterwards and I did not know till much later that the leaders' oath had been given that day. But little by little news of an association and of an oath were being whispered about.

'There was reason enough. The Rift Valley Squatters' Association had been demanding return of their land: they even parked themselves early one morning in the garden of Government House – a sit-in you would call it nowadays. The stand made at Olenguruone was known to us, though the climax of conflict had not yet been reached. There had been a general strike at Mombasa which attracted a lot of attention though it only got limited results. Most people thought Kikuyu skills of organisation had a lot to do with its success. The foreman brought us the partial news which came over the radio. He also told me that there had been a similar strike in the docks before the war and riots a couple of years before that. This was news to me – it shows that our eyes were opening wider as the years passed.

'In fact I narrowly missed seeing the 1947 strike myself. I had often thought of going to Mombasa to have a look round, but for a year or two after the war Africans were not allowed to enter Coast Province from up country without a special permit. I'd been told that a woman can always get by in a port town even if she is past her first youth. After all, I have never looked my age, have I? But I did not know the rules about women having to register for health reasons – and, all said and

97

done, I am not a woman of the streets – so I soon came back again. In any case I found it too hot for comfort.

'The interesting thing is that when I told the police I was a Kikuyu and had come to visit my brother who worked in the docks, but I had lost his address, they straight away directed me to Chege Kibachia, although they were not Kikuyu themselves and I had never then heard of Kibachia. He had resigned from KAU and was then a salesman for the East African Clothing Company, but all the political people still knew him.

'I stayed a day or two to be able to say I'd seen the sea and the palm trees and then got on the train back. You learn something if you travel on our railway. If I had known I would have liked to stay until the strike started. You must have lived through that, Sophia. Some of you people had been organised for a long time. I wish I'd known you then.'

Sophia tossed her head at the thought that she might have known a plantation labourer on the make among men in the docks. But Wairimu's eyes lighted on another picture, of light-skinned girls at the coast working in houses or cafés, gathering outside the Catholic church with hats and handbags, pushing white babies in shaded prams.

It was good to learn new things, and often during those years a story or a song would strike Sophia with its novelty, and the other women, who had heard it long ago and perhaps not yet learned to read, were moved by her enthusiasm. So they would take her about to other churches to give her witness. The story of Ruth was particularly dear to her. In the church she still had the name of a newcomer who had helped many others to believe.

The home was happy, though she had no living child by Henry. His daughter Emma grew to love her and Hawa, though Mariam sulked and grumbled.

They tried sending her to school, but she was humiliated at being with smaller children, though age levels were still fluid, up to the time of Independence, and there were other girls as big as herself in the lower classes. Then Sophia tried her at the machine again and she made some progress, especially when she was allowed to sew a dress for herself, but would always break off when there were other girls to talk to. She sat sullenly in church but refused baptism and took to slipping off to her grandfather's house on Sundays. Then once she was away for two days, and Sophia dared not check with her sisters whether she was telling the truth. Instead she let them arrange for Mariam, then fourteen, to go and stay with the proposed in-laws till she should be ready for marriage. This was just about the time the war ended, so Mariam missed the heady and none too decorous celebrations in the port. They never saw each other again.

The atmosphere lightened without her. Hawa was nearly six and Emma a year older. On Sunday Henry would walk with them to the seaside or bring some of his friends for a meal. They always spoke Swahili and he did not particularly try to impose any pattern from his home place. Sometimes on Saturday afternoons he would stay with the little girls while Sophia went to attend or address a women's meeting somewhere, perhaps bringing back with her orders for dresses or children's clothes.

They still read a Bible passage together and prayed before they went to bed, but Henry was changing. He joked a lot and his language was not always as discreet as a new Christian might think it should be. He became a football enthusiast and kept reminding her that it was about time they started their own team of boys. She had a stillbirth followed by two miscarriages, and though he was gentle with her each time the irritation showed.

He was impatient, too, with the commissions meeting and reports that kept being made about conditions in the town and in the country. The five years they spent together were full of unrest. Everybody knew that the 1939 strike was not the first or most violent upheaval in Mombasa and would not be the last. Had not Ali always said that after the war things would be improved? As more and more workers poured in to assist the war effort, they became more and more conscious that houses were too few, too overcrowded, too small, too expensive. Work grew heavier but the wages remained the same – less than forty shillings a month for labourers – though the war bonuses kept on for a while after the supposed peace had come, and Henry, near the top of the scale of literacy and experience, was getting a hundred and eighty shillings. Sophia was also earning through her sewing machine, so they could count themselves well off, but prices went on rising and shortages created a black market where certain kinds of foods and clothes were completely beyond the reach of the ordinary worker.

Water was a problem, particularly in the hottest weather and the most crowded districts. You had to pay one cent for a tin full at the water-kiosk but the water-carrier charged five cents for delivering it at home. It had never crossed Sophia's mind that she might have to carry water, but the up-country ladies were used to fetching theirs from the river at home and were prepared to go to the kiosks themselves. The water-carriers' strategy, then, was to crowd round the water-point, distracting the operator and jostling other people so as to keep the queues long and impatient until, little by little, the country women would give in and pay the five cents rather than leave their homes unattended while they waited their turn.

Sophia had been sure things would get better after the war ended. Rationing would come to an end, the government would buy what it wanted without having to give it all to the army. New houses would be built and repairs done. Henry was more cautious. Lots of things had been destroyed, he said, in other countries. Many people could not work because they were wounded or undernourished. It would all take time. But surely, thought his wife, wood and cement and *makuti* for the roof are all local materials. We can make electricity here for ourselves. Water can come out of taps in private houses as well as in kiosks. Rice is for eating, not for firing out of guns. Wait, woman, wait, we shall see.

Through 1945 and 1946 they went on seeing. By the middle of January 1947 they had had enough of waiting. A big transport strike was going on in London and making the headlines. (London kept on making the headlines even through the Mombasa strike, because of the big freeze-up that followed, nearly crippling the country that had not moved its fuel stocks in time.) Six soldiers were shot dead at Gilgil and ten wounded when they refused to work, tired of waiting for their demobilisation. (That did not make the headlines.) A congress on prehistory in Nairobi was calling attention to the origin of man in Africa. Rumours of a general strike in Mombasa took second place, with labourers making the absurd claim that they needed two or even three times their present wage to live on. Were they not alive? But

100

even the government admitted that housing conditions were shocking.

Henry nodded his head and approved. Look, the Labour Commissioner was concerned enough to come to the port even before anyone had downed tools. He was known to agree that wages needed to be higher than in Nairobi, because most Mombasa workers could not get food brought from their home areas without paying excessively for transport. (They were, in fact, already getting a few shillings more than in Nairobi, where an employer paying the minimum wage of thirty-eight shillings a month could deduct five shillings if he provided housing and ten more if he gave free rations.)

But although the Commissioner called meetings here and there, to negotiate, although even some African leaders urged workers to hold on and state their complaints before coming out, feelings were running high. The strike was on. To Sophia it made sense: she had more notion of social justice in Medina than of social justice in Jerusalem or Mombasa, but why should it not be the same?

As in 1939, the stoppage was declared illegal, but it was much more widespread, affecting an estimated fifteen thousand workers. There were meetings twice daily of between three and five thousand people, at which strike funds were collected and cooked food sometimes served to the needy. Dock workers and municipal workers held firm – emergency plans for sanitation had to be made, and after a week loudspeakers broadcast an appeal to strikers to allow sweepers to return to work without victimisation because of the health hazard. About two thousand workers on a mainland sugar estate joined in. Extra police and troops were sent to Mombasa, a naval party marched through the streets and a military guard replaced the standing police guard. By the middle of the month two hundred pickets had been arrested for alleged intimidation.

The government was worried, but their attention was distracted by the Rift Valley Province Squatters' petition claiming land in the 'White' Highlands – in February they would stage an early morning sit-in at Government House, and the Olenguruóne crisis was looming. All the same the official side had their resources and claimed sympathy, for employers as well as themselves. Hotels were working on a self-service basis. Italian prisoners of war were made available to man the European bakery. Voluntary labour was unloading the ships and operating the trains. This was made much of in official announcements and pamphlets. As long as the port was in operation, they said, the strike could not be effective: in any case it had not been organised with formal notice and a set of demands specific to each industry. Archdeacon Leonard Beecher, representing African interests alongside Eliud Mathu in Legco, came down from Nairobi and, characteristically, cycled from meeting to meeting, urging workers to return to work so that their demands could be put constitutionally. Mathu himself, it was rumoured, would come.

Henry was tireless in attending meetings. He was talking and joking loudly, intoxicated with the sense of African power, not coming home till he was exhausted with the heat and excitement, calling for bath water and food, hardly bothering to ask where water and food came from in the middle of a strike that left the regular market stinking, the kiosks unmanned, the wayside vendors able to raise their prices at will. And it was all very well, Sophia reminded him, to expect the machine to make up for wages lost – what woman, this month or next, would be able to pay for sewing done or put anything away towards a new dress for Easter? She even suspected that he took a bottle or two of beer while planning campaigns with his friends, just now when he could least afford it and most needed his wits about him.

There is wit and wits. The strikers had been at pains to keep the peace, though a few had been charged with unruly behaviour or threats to non-strikers. So someone had devised a new method. Suppose those blacklegs were detained in a friendly manner, assisted to the barber's chair, shaved in some fancy pattern that would mark them out as special? That would involve no violence, nothing like the tarring and feathering they had read about in more tempestuous countries. A good laugh, and if the fellow was really upset he had only to wear a hat or shave himself completely as though he had come from a funeral. He was not hurt, even if some members of the crowd did shout a warning that next time it would be done with broken beer bottles.

It was no sooner thought of than put into operation, and how could Henry miss a lark like that? Inevitably Henry – senior clerk, Christian gentleman, one who might have been able, thought Sophia, to conduct himself more decently – had to be one of the barbers, one of the arrested, charged, convicted barbers.

Sophia was at home when it happened. She did not feel there was any place for her in these open-air meetings, and though she was in sympathy, of course, it was not bad to keep an eye on your things with all these young idle men roaming around. So neighbours brought the news and took her with them to the court house, police station, remand; she would have been ashamed if she had not been so angry, and did not manage to see her husband but was told the rule was six months for riot, two months for shaving. Two months? And would he get his job back? She went home grieving.

But there was no time to grieve. Of course she must vacate the house. There were only a hundred and forty two-roomed houses on the whole government estate. They would never get another. But equally they could not keep one for a man in prison. She moved back to Damaris's where she had stayed before her marriage and distributed her furniture where there was room for it. Damaris welcomed her and the two children. After all, only two months.

And yet after two months he did not come, and her hopes of his getting reinstated faded. There must have been some mistake. Six months then. She found a room and sewed to all hours. She gave her new address to the people who had moved into her old house, to Damaris, to the church workers, to Henry's office. Ali's old workmates refused to speak to her. The accordion player had been jailed too. Henry seemed to shrink. One tin box held all his spare clothes, the magazines, the church books in Kidabida. The private papers must have been in his pockets. He had sold the accordion long ago. The little girls stopped asking her daily when he would come.

Sophia had hardly noticed when the African schools reopened the Monday after the arrest (Emma had had to remind her) or when Mr Mathu addressed ten thousand people and persuaded them to go back to work if the government would redress their grievances within three months. The strike was over, with an interim award of only a small cash increase on the lowest permanent staff wages. The government, of course, said they could not be bound by a time limit, but the tribunal did start hearing evidence straight away and made their report in June. They gave a few extra benefits and indicated the need for a higher minimum wage, though they did not specify what it should be, as a general salaries' commission had already been appointed to look into that. But Sophia was not paying attention, because the six months was already finished and Henry had not come.

In July Kenyatta turned up in Mombasa, with others, to address a big meeting. Why could not the Kikuyu stick to their own troubles in the Rift Valley, thought Sophia. That Kibachia getting a laugh by saying that next time scabs would get their ears shaved off as well as their hair. (Or so it was reported: he denied it.) Would not that sort of talk make it worse for Henry?

Emma was half-way through standard three. At the end of term Sophia handed her over to a couple going on leave and sent her to her grandmother. They were going on transfer after leave, so she never heard how they travelled or if any news of her husband had reached his home. She never attempted to go there.

She pulled herself together sufficiently to save up news that would interest Henry. For instance, the newspapers kept on saying that the strike leaders stayed in the background, when in fact everybody knew that Chege Kibachia and the KAU were the inspiration behind them. The Mombasa Postmaster said that a wage of forty shillings a month was near starvation point for a single man, let alone a family, and the Port Medical Officer worked out eighty-eight shillings and eighty-three cents as the absolute minimum to feed a couple with two children adequately for a month. (He rather spoiled the effect by saying that if his minimum diet were introduced next day there would not be enough milk on the Island to go round.) One firm was accused of sacking its union members, one supervisor 'had never given a thought' to how his African colleagues managed, one worker claimed that 'the new government' (a catchword of the time) 'belongs to every African'. Henry would be glad that the tribunal took seriously claims that, as well as living at subsistence level, the worker could reasonably wish to go to a cinema occasionally, buy a few magazines, even, in the submission of one witness, give his wife two shillings a month to get her hair done.

But Sophia herself did not particularly want cinemas, magazines or better hair-dos than she could exchange with her Swahili neighbours:

she wanted Henry, and compared to the want of Henry her desire for justice was a small thing, and it did not particularly bother her that the small increases did not procure these amenities for anyone who had not had them before. A cold fury settled upon her. It seemed that it was all for nothing that she had given up the comfortable superiority of that old, Islamic city. She had been promised justice and equality in the new life, and been denied them. She was prepared to wait for Henry, but not for justice. She would protect her feelings more in the future. Hawa was eight, a pretty, happy girl, near the top of her standard two class, though she missed Emma bitterly. Let her read, thought Sophia fiercely, let her get ahead. Let her be rich, and command the power which stops men of their work and wages. We shall not be cowed a third time. But who were 'we' if Henry did not come?

She took the money from the little red book – it had grown over the years, since Henry had provided the house and food money and not required accounting for what she earned so long as she clothed herself and her daughters and bought such things as she fancied for the home. Mombasa still bordered on the countryside and it was possible to get a place to build cheaply. With the money she managed to build a traditional house, big enough for three (she still believed they were three) with a wide working verandah. This saved the rent, and they were able to grow their own bananas and a few vegetables and keep chickens. She was still not satisfied, and scraped and saved until she could get a second sewing machine. She employed a lame man to work this one, making school uniforms from dawn to dusk, and drove him hard. She wanted to be ready when Henry came, but two years passed and he did not come, a third, and there was still no news. She still did not know the way to his home place and a terrible pride possessed her. It was not as though he had nothing to come back to. She was not forty yet and her time for childbearing was not past. Surely he knew, too, that she could earn enough to make up for his loss of seniority? Was there, in fact, nothing to wait for?

Revival had come, and there was a new excitement in the church. But now, between choruses, they would ask for the day and hour of her conversion, and look sad when she could only tell them the year and the slow process of learning. She closed her lips and made

105

splendid dresses for Hawa, and bought a third machine and set the daughter of her uncle, the coffee-seller, to use it, for the girl had disgraced her family and could no longer show shame of having a Christian relation. Sophia remembered that her aunt had taught her needlework long ago, so she allowed the girl to sleep in the back kitchen with her baby, and made no comment when her aunt, heavily veiled, would call in now and then at market time to see her daughter, hoping to escape a beating for it.

The years passed, a dull sequence of shirts and shorts, drill-slips and aprons, until Hawa did well in her KAPE and left standard eight with the glory of a certificate. She could have gone for training as a nurse, but Sophia knew better than her daughter the disgrace of dead bodies and emptying slops and sponging the nakedness of men. The teachers wanted her like them to be a teacher – to go away to a normal school where there were boys as well, and sleep in dormitories with what sort of girls one would prefer not to mention. Hawa rather fancied the idea. But Sophia bade her wait a while and took her to church in the splendid dresses and to the music festival, and to call on her classmates, and pretty soon Wau came up with a good offer. Hawa flushed and looked away and said she wanted to qualify for a job. Wau said that these days girls were not restricted to teaching and nursing: already his company was employing Asian girls as typists instead of men, and the days were coming when African women would go into business too. So when he offered to pay for a course in typing and office practice Hawa smiled and consented. Her mother also made a reasonable bargain in respect of the little red book, and indulged herself in elaborate bridesmaids' dresses and a gown for Hawa which, though dully white, dazzled by its ingenuity. It was the beginning of 1957. People were talking again of freedom and equality. Sophia reserved her judgment. More children were going to school and wanting uniforms. Elaborate decorations had been put up for Princess Margaret's visit, but nothing sparkled in Sophia's eyes like the old *beni* processions and the armistice fireworks. Lighted objects were circling the earth in the upper air. A black man called Kwame had set up a new country called Ghana in West Africa where the cocoa came from. Sophia nursed the little red book and waited to see what would happen.

106

CHAPTER SEVEN

Wairimu resumed her memories.

'There was another strike in Kisumu in 1947. It didn't amount to much, and I wasn't inspired to spend more hard-earned shillings going off to see more water at the other end of Kenya. In any case those days we believed you Luo people ate only fish, and that would not have suited me at all. But it was a sign that things were happening. In July the Colonial Secretary from England – Creech-Jones, that was: they change them faster than *rika* leaders – came to Nyeri and told us he had been sent by the king to listen to our complaints: he did not stay around long enough to do much listening, but we hoped that our leaders had explained all the points.

'I went because I hated to miss anything new, not because I wanted to draw attention to myself. But I was over forty then, though not worn down as my mother had seemed at that age. I could read well and write a little. I knew a lot of Swahili, had been to Nairobi a number of times, had been employed for more than twenty-five years. Very cautiously the foreman approached me, and in 1949 I became a full member of the *chama* – no need to go into that – and a recruiter. I was not, in those sour days, thinking about the rainbow and the golden haze. But, as they say, one thing leads to another.

'I needed a break occasionally between tickets, since there was not much for me to go home for. I'd been to Nairobi once in the late thirties and found it spread out into sets of labour lines: it was hard to keep the excitement of the centre in the landhies and quarters without much money or glamour about them. There were hardly any horse- or bullock-carts left, though someone had an idea to get rickshaws going again in competition with motor traffic. It didn't last long. There seemed fewer Somalis – in fact, of course, there were more inland Africans, about half of them Kikuyu and a quarter Kavirondo. There

107

were nearly ten men to each woman, though some of the workers' wives came for part of each year, after harvest. And though I had once thought myself so sophisticated, I was at a loss now among these women, not knowing where to cross the crowded street or how to arrange my hair in the neat new patterns. I went again on my way back from Mombasa, this time studying carefully the cut of dresses and the suitable occasions for wearing shoes. In 1950, when the city was having its Golden Jubilee, I thought I would go again. Our top leaders were keeping away: ordinary people were afraid that the whole of Kiambu would be swallowed up inside the city boundary, and so they boycotted the celebrations. But I was only an outsider, after all. What harm could there be if I saw the sights and reported back to my local cell?

'Well, I have never seen London, of course, but I am sure Nairobi in those days must have looked like London. There was a big platform outside the Town Hall for the ceremonies and all kinds of police about and soldiers in their smartest uniforms, some of them on horses; there were banners in the streets, and everything remarkably clean. Even in the locations there was some effort to tidy things up, and at Pumwani there was the Royal Guard Simba Scotch led by Edi bin Songoro – that was one *beni* you missed, Sophia.

'The African Advisory Council that was introduced to the Duke of Gloucester included two women – that made me feel good, though I wondered how much advice they had a chance to give. There was a big pageant with people acting out different scenes from Kenya's history as the trailers moved round: most of it was done by Europeans but we had our part in it too. The trade union people had said we ought to stay away, and a lot of people wore their black armbands in protest, but it was difficult for a lot of us to resist a show. Remember that we didn't have any TV in those days and very few people could afford cinemas or outings. Some of our leaders made sure they would not be in Nairobi on Charter Day, but for working men that was not a realistic choice.

'I recognised Harry Thuku again – middle-aged then, a good deal heavier, but as you get older yourself you learn to make allowances for change. He was sitting up on a platform talking to the PCs and the DCs, still a fine figure of a man and, after all, this was one of the things

108

we wanted from him – only one, but still something – to claim familiarity on our behalf. I wondered what had happened to Tairara and the rest – Tairara had got his sentence reduced in 1922, though they never forgave the white lawyer for taking his case on. So I pushed as close as I could in the crowd and began to sing quietly *Kanyegenuri*. But Thuku did not seem to hear me – after all, he was not a young man any more (people were still teasing him about getting married at such an age) and there was a lot of noise going on. I realised then that, although he must have known of Nyanjiru's death, he might not even have known the song, since he had been away in detention all the years it was popular. In any case my loyalty now was to the new *kiama* in which he would have no part.

'I had meant to go home soon after Charter Day, but I was staying with an old friend in Shauri Moyo and she advised me to stay on a bit. We did not talk of the oathing, for she was from Kiambu, and our organisations kept their separate ways, but she wished me to talk to some of the young people about circumcision and our old ways. She also thought I should gather more news to take home to Nyeri with me.

'Perhaps she knew about the big meeting that would be held in Kaloleni Hall in April, where the Africans and Asians got together. They were supposed to be discussing the new policies proposed for Tanganyika, but they dealt with labour problems and freedom as well. Twenty thousand people attended, and the Kenya African Union and the East African Indian National Congress were given a mandate to act together on the resolutions.

'That was great, but it was not, of course, going to be all. Two African councillors had been threatened with arms because they had assented to the Charter celebrations. The United African Traders' Association had also passed resolutions very critical of the City Council. May Day was coming up – you see by then even I was thinking about dates and months rather than seasons and tickets – and the East African Trades Union Congress was not allowed to have a procession. So instead they had a meeting at the Desai Memorial Hall, the one beside the Fire Station. A lot of our freedom was shaped there. You may not even know how strange it seemed then – Asian workmen going on foot to Kaloleni, Africans in suits and ties sitting on a platform in a Hindu hall.

'They made a lot of demands in that meeting, and the discussion was pretty hot. So in the middle of the month Makhan Singh and Fred Kubai were arrested on a technical charge about the registration of the organisation. Almost immediately the general strike started. The organisers called in the name of the TUC for five things which they gave as reasons for the strike. The first demand was for the release of Makhan Singh, Kubai and Kibachia. The second was a minimum monthly wage of one hundred shillings. Then there were some detailed points affecting taxi drivers and a call for the abolition of secret night arrests. But fifth – lastly and largest and hardest to believe – freedom for all workers and for all Africans in East Africa. That was 1950, remember! Since then we have bargained for a lot of things – constitutions, votes, Africanisation, maternity leave, equal pay – but freedom for every worker? Where does that happen? We used to say, *"Gūtirī wīathī, no wathīkanīrī"* – there is no independence, only inter-dependence.

'Strikers were asked to remain in the Shauri Moyo area. That was not so easy, since many lived and worked far from there. It also brought the strongest force of police to Shauri Moyo and Pumwani: some stones were thrown and there were baton charges. Residents were warned that they had better stay indoors during the hours of darkness. Still, up to five thousand men drifted around the area, and many more than that answered the call to strike.

'I don't say – it would be absurd to say – that every one of those thousands knew exactly what was going on. A few were there because they had been threatened by fellow-workers, more than a few returned to work because they had been threatened by employers with dismissal or wage cuts, or enticed by offers of cash which they desperately needed. But every striker knew that he needed and, comparing with rates paid to non-African workers, undoubtedly deserved a hundred shillings a month. Every striker knew that some people who had tried to defend his interests had been put to silence by a government which had quite other interests to defend. Every striker knew that India had got freedom and Gold Coast was demanding

110

freedom and so freedom, whatever it meant, was not an impossible thing to ask for.

'Eight whole days, sisters, the strike went on, even without the trade union leaders to direct it. Convicts were used by the city authorities to empty the dustbins and the lavatory buckets. European ladies served meals in hotels. Essential services were maintained by law. But at Shauri Moyo the ceremonial fire was kept going day and night, and from the house we watched people leaping and dancing round it and piling on branches to keep the flames going. On the night of the ninth day the fire burned itself out. Enough was enough, it seemed to signify. We had not freed those three people – the arguments were still going on, but Singh would start his long detention soon and Kubai escape the net for another two years. We had not got our hundred shillings. We had not got freedom. But we had started a fire.

'The strike spread to Limuru, the Bata factory and other places but the police charges there were very severe and we dreaded hearing about them. Perhaps that was what broke the people's spirit in the end. Then there was the tribal feeling, which the government had always tried to play upon. Some of the pickets were very hard on Luo house servants, threatening to shave people's heads and that kind of thing. Well, I suppose they ought to have refused to work, but of course it was not their land that was endangered by the extension of the city, and everybody ought to know how hard it is for a house servant to strike. He comes face to face with his employer more than a worker in a farm or a factory and he is not part of a big team. If one cook risks losing his job, it doesn't make conditions any better for the cook next door. But because some Luos were intimidated, others enrolled as special constables and the government even thanked the Luo Union for getting these volunteers. To me that was a very sad thing and I expect the enemies of the workers made the most of it. In 1922, when there were so few town workers, they cooperated among themselves. In Mombasa Chege had organised a group in which there were perhaps more Luo than any other inland people. But Chege had been 'deported' as though he were an alien, and now we were looking too much inwards.

'I went back to Nyeri with my eyes and throat still smarting from

111

the tear gas. The first time is the most frightening. Now our sons go to football on a Sunday afternoon without thinking anything of it. I reported what I had seen, but my foreman and the others told me now to stop moving on my own. I was to pass messages and sometimes hide travellers right where I was in the coffee, not to draw attention to myself. My employer already knew me as someone who liked to travel, so now that it seemed clear Kikuyu movements would be more strictly controlled as time went on, I should keep those excuses to use in times of necessity. The words "Mau Mau" were now being frequently seen in the newspapers. At the same time the fear of the "savage African" had just come strongly upon a lot of government people because of the armed clash which had led to several deaths in Baringo over a "breakaway religion". It was a pity, perhaps, that this had to happen while the workers were trying to put their case so reasonably in Nairobi. The same fires were bubbling below ground, but I've no particular fancy for hot steam gushing out myself. I should be all for putting a machine in the middle that you can control by pressing a switch. But they say a child who has never been burned doesn't fear the fire.

'And in spite of being increasingly in the news, we did not seem to be very cautious. Even after a lot of fires had been set in Nyeri town at the beginning of 1952, meetings were being called to oath as many as five hundred people at a time, and there were twenty-five thousand at a mass rally in July. But me, I was very careful. I never missed church – in any case, I enjoyed going to church. I was never late for work, never turned in bad berries: I cut out all the newspaper pictures of the new queen and pasted them on the wall. Because of my age, I was able to instruct the women in the traditional age-group greetings that were being revived and, in spite of never being properly married myself, to help them set up circumcision operations for the girls.

'I was sorry for some of them. They did not know what it was all about and were not going to get the public approval we had had to help us bear the pain. Some also were sewn up too tight – the old skills had grown rusty. Well, some of them have got their two-car households and refrigerators now, and those who need to can deliver in the hospital. That is the way it goes. There is a price for belonging to any age-group.

112

'I lost a lot of good friends in those years – a few in the fighting, others struggling to get their babies born in the camps, some starved out of their homes to trek to distant places. My family survived: it would not do to ask one another how or why. It was Njoki in the convent I was most worried about, since she would find it impossible either to resist or to comprehend attack from either side, but her virgin, after all, is powerful. The sisters were not harmed, and Njoki had her jubilee before she died comfortably in the hospital where she had worked, with all her beads and crucifix about her. One let no tears be seen for those emergency losses. Others I lost respect for, gabbling the solemn oath only to save their skins, or making use of it to aggrandise themselves. But many stood firm, through fire, suspicion, deep double meanings and a web of trust.

'At last we got our wish, freedom, a broadening of the ways much as you all have seen. But the same Master stayed on the coffee. Well, he had also borne much, and Kenyatta had invited them to continue. Until he grew old and wanted to retire, sought a purchaser, a Kikuyu, and we rejoiced. But not for long. We found ourselves turned away, new clansmen brought in: they said we were too political, bargaining, counting hours. Fighting for land and freedom we had not grudged the hours, or money either. But so it was. At seventy one does not expect consideration.

'I came to Nairobi, following my rainbow, swallowing the years of risk and caution, the sweat that trickled when another woman bled from the lashes, the cough that terrified when there was most need of silence, the curfew darkness where each cry for help might be a trap. I came admiring the broad pavements where black girls walked in expensive frocks, the pulsing music in our languages, our parliament, our conference centre, our leaders' statues, our airline and our fleets of buses. Until the sun darkened one day and on the pavements beside the text cards and the cheap mirrors people put forth the pictures of another hero, saved from the hyenas but laid to rest fingerless at Gilgil. I had my little tea kiosk. I watched, for I had practice in watching, but the cough racked me and the kettles grew heavy to lift. Another hero less. I dragged myself up the hill to see, face to face, Jomo Kenyatta lie in state. I saw the fire flaring in the mausoleum for a modern man who had once saved his infant brother, Muigai, from

113

dying alone in the wailing forest. I saw his daughter Wambui in her mayoral robes. And one day I saw my little kiosk kicked to pieces by uniformed men doing their duty to build the nation.

'Rather than weep, I coughed myself into collapse. That was five years ago. They brought me here. Didn't I tell you I was born lucky? My fairy-tale started with a hero on the forest path. It ends where the old queens live happily ever after, and sometimes dance till their slippers are worn out. Priscilla, you never learned this properly. But Bessie, I can teach you the words about the chief of the girls who lived in the coffee:

> *Filipu aromakoguo*
> *Nio matwarithirie munene wa Nyacing'a*
> *Nyacing'a ituire Kahawa-ini.'*

CHAPTER EIGHT

Nekesa dreamed of Kampala. It was all very well for Rahel to say she only dreamed significant messages. Perhaps when she was younger the distinction between dream and reality had been clearer to her – or perhaps she had more command of her thoughts than other people. Those black women who stood up to their menfolk and phrased themselves in terse little syllables – *ok, ol, mit, mak, pok, poth,* sometimes it made her laugh – were possibly better organised than those of the fluent, long-drawn sentences. Nekesa did not count herself one of these. She understood Lubukusu and some of the related dialects that made up Ololuyia, but it had never been a major language of her life and never since early childhood had she visited the home village or shared in the digging of those little overcrowded plots. The language meant to her everlasting rows in the railway quarters where they lived as time and time again her father came home to find no food in the house, her mother either tipsy or still out with one of her fancy men, the children dirty and quarrelling. She was ten and her brother a bit less when they left with their mother for Dundora, beside the quarry. Her father kept the younger children and brought another wife to care for them, but these two, he said, had learned evil ways already and were too much for a decent woman to cope with. That much she had understood in the dialect called of 'home'. But it helped her, later, to get a grasp of Luganda with its long complex greetings and its combination of grunts and hisses.

In her dream she was trudging up one of the long, paved hills of Kampala – she did not know which – with a bunch of bananas balanced on her head, and after a few yards the bananas would fall off and she would be at the bottom again, beginning the long climb. But when she awoke it was to recapture her first excitement at the place and her surprise to find the villages, with their banana groves, tucked between the hills, the separateness of people's lives, as though all the suburbs and labour lines and bazaars and colleges and ministries and parks that made up Nairobi were chopped up into little pieces and scattered up and down the slopes like a nursery school puzzle. She remembered the ladies in their splendid *busuti*s patronising the expensive shops (which African women seldom yet entered in Nairobi, though she did not have much occasion to go to town and see). In contrast she was wearing the very short skirts which were the badge of availability in Kampala, long before miniskirts came in for everybody and swamped the distinction. She thought she knew about men, too, from the earliest years – what else could she learn about out there beside the quarry with no schooling, no land and no peace ever in the house? – but Kampala, that, as the saying goes, was something else again. The young girls who had the energy for it could keep busy throughout the twenty-four hours, and no waste of time on preliminaries either – these men had to get back to the office or drive their buses another stage. She was glad to be saved from it but it was no good wishing one had missed it.

After all, one lived through it and got called to a better way. She would not have had to live on charity now if it had not been for those *askaris* kicking over the brand new stock that she had invested most of her savings in, and hurting her arm so that she had to spend so long in hospital and gradually eat up the rest. But the sisters had helped her to find this place and she had no regrets.

But her brother – it was painful even now to think back to that little boy who, for the sake of school fees, had put up with the rows of home and the weariness of the quarry. As soon as he was eighteen he had joined the army – that was in the early days of the war – gone through the campaigns unhurt, become a drunkard and a boaster. She had met him once or twice during his leaves in Nairobi. Whether he sought her out or came there by accident in his search for pleasure she was not sure, but he got her address and used the name for next of kin. They had lost touch with their real father and the mother was wandering again.

So one day the letter came from Gilgil. Dead. There were no details. She knew something was wrong. She suspected something the clerk was not reading out to her. Where, in any case, could she have buried a body? What, in any case, would she have done with a tin box of men's clothes? What had she to do with newspaper reports and whispers? Something froze in her. Two years after the war ended and a few months before he was due to come back to life, civilian life, she meant. He might have lived through it and got saved. This was when she started thinking of going to Uganda. Of course she knew the Emergency was coming – in the streets and back alleys such knowledge comes to the surface – but there was more to it than that.

She had other brothers, but no idea of what had become of them. She remembered them as small, undifferentiated creatures, and they would hardly remember her at all. And if they could remember, what would she tell them except that a boy could struggle for education, grow up in harsh and self-defeating service, and still be written off by blank words in an envelope. Dead. In too much hurry to start life again. Was it not, after all, better to be a woman, easy come, easy go? When they had no more use for you, at least they left you alone.

Nekesa did not give the nurses any trouble when they examined her. She had dealt with her own life shrewdly enough, attended the special clinic when the illness that made her barren (and, as long as treatment lasted, broke!) recurred several times, early understood that there would be no betrothal offer for her, tailored her desires to possibilities. There had been a fur-fabric coat one time in Kampala, in Nairobi a gilded, full-length mirror that had soon been broken in a brawl. She could not now remember how desperately she had wanted them, or why, but perhaps the longing had been healthy, repressing deeper yearnings that could never be met in the flesh. The ribs had mended where the *askaris* kicked her but the cough still gave her pain. The arm broken twelve years ago had set slightly crooked, but well enough to serve her purposes. She still had a taste for buns and soda when she could afford them, but ate heartily of the daily food and did not complain.

Mama Chunga, though ordinarily placid and helpful, closed up in contrast at the sight of a pencil and paper. Her age? She was not an educated person, expected to think in figures. Over fifty? Well, look at her. Over sixty? Well, yes, probably. Did she remember the Italian war? Was she married then? She had never been married. Working? Yes, she was working as a housemaid. She remembered the troop-

117

ships. So it was Mombasa then? Yes, Mombasa. Was she born there? No, her parents said she was brought there as a small child. From another part of the coast? She did not remember. Did she go to school? She had learned to read and write in a private class. In Swahili? Of course. Her parents? The mother had died when she was a child and the father had gone away to get a job on a ship when she was beginning work. She thought he must have died in the war. Other relations? She did not remember any.

This was a good deal less than the truth. She had always felt a handicap to her father, who for her sake had taken a shore job in a snack bar after her mother died with the next baby. But he was good company, taking her for walks and playing his guitar. He kept up his bit of English and his mess-jacket carefully folded away in the tin trunk against the day he should be free to go to sea as steward again. They boarded in an auntie's house, speaking patois there but Swahili outside: she was darker-skinned than her father and mixed freely with the local children. She was not very quick at lessons.

Papa had told her that it was the extra tips that attracted him back to sea: they would be enough to educate her or, if that did not suit, set her up with a *dot* against her marriage. She used to wonder what was wrong with her, that she should need to take a dowry to her husband when all the neighbouring girls expected to bring wealth to their fathers. But already she sensed that it was more the comradeship of crew quarters he needed than the money, and glamour rubbing off the adventurous passengers, after the disappointment of a sickly wife and a lone surviving daughter. She supposed that he did not want to commit himself to another marriage.

Mimi – that was her name then, and until quite recently she had been addressed by the courtesy title of Mrs Paul, which was close to anonymity enough – began daily work as a nursemaid at fifteen, and when in 1937 she found her first residential job with an elderly European couple, Papa fulfilled his dream at last and set off aboard a coastal cruise ship going up and down to Durban.

The Seychellois community was a warm one, full of aunties: there was some dearth of uncles, as many of them had jobs away, serving on ships or trains, doing maintenance jobs at remote stations which were not very popular with Europeans or camps which had no family quarters. Mimi was considered a pretty girl: she straightened her hair with hot combs and used a lot of oil and light fluttery dresses. The aunties did not always approve, but they did not cut her off. It was only when you married into another group, according to the features you had been born with or your adaptability, that they might stand back a little to help you work out your new identity.

Seychellois house servants used to command a decent wage. Like the Somali, they were considered to need a margin for sophistication. When the elderly couple retired up country, they got Mimi a place with Mr Robert. There was a Swahili cook and a separate house. She would be all right, they said: they would be prepared to leave their wallet with Robert's father, whom they had known for years. Homes were better run when there was a memsahib, but times were hard and many people were reducing their staff. She must make the best of it.

She was making the best of it when Mr Robert started to call her to the house in the evening when he got back from the bar, on the pretext of making him coffee or mending a torn shirt. She was flattered, ambitious, lonely, not ignorant. You had to take your chance. She weighed this one against the sailors in the streets, who made demands on other girls she knew if they did not settle early into their own homes, 'Oh-la-la, parlay-voo?' The alternative lay in the dim, fringed houses of the aunties, full of sewing remnants and sacred pictures. And although Mr Robert had not actually said he would marry her, people lived in hope. He stood apart, for some reason, from his own kind; his shabby house, his clothes were marginal enough. There was no evidence of his having married before, and he was not very young – she realised afterwards that the glazed eyes with deep pouches, the fumbled shaving, the unsteady hand made him look older than he was.

She could not pretend she cared for him deeply: by the time of the first miscarriage she had come to understand how intensely selfish he was. Her father had come to visit her about this time and was more upset than he wanted her to see. He urged her to move elsewhere, but jobs were hard to find and she expected the master's obligation to her to guarantee some protection. There was no other pull on her affections and she thought that a child might touch Mr Robert's heart. But when the next baby died, and the brother- and sister-in-law

119

quarrelled with him – whether because of his liaison with her or his indifference to the child she did not know – she lost hope. Her name was spoiled and she still had nothing to love. Her father's schedule had changed and he now had barely a day or two off between trips. Labour troubles were building up and one was afraid to be caught between a new employer and new pressures outside.

So she dusted the seedy furniture, cooked on the greasy kitchen range (for the cook, with an eye to the future, had got a better job in a forces canteen), grew expert in Alka-seltzer and pick-me-ups. And when Robert made a little more effort to woo her again, expressing sympathy for her loss and contrition that he had not introduced her to his family, she determined to take a chance.

She pulled herself to order: memories must be kept under control. It was necessary to protect oneself against these hopeful girls and their notebooks. Children? Yes, she had had two children. (They would find out from the scar.) For one of them she had had to be cut open. Both had cost her agony. Neither had lived beyond a few months and the doctor had said she could have no more. So of course she could not marry. What had the children died of? (Does this have to go on my clinic card, forty-five years later?) Mombasa is hot and malarial: babies die, that is all. The father? He had taken no interest. (Babies die for lack of an anchor, will, prayer to keep them fast.)

How had she lived? By working, always working, naturally. She was strong until that time she had had pneumonia, from the laundry, and her savings had got finished and so they brought her here. The girls shrugged and did not press her. (Old people may also die for lack of an anchor, will, prayer to keep them fast, except that they have acquired the habit of living, and habit dies hard.) There was not much physically wrong with her now – her wits a bit slow, perhaps. If she had had a house of her own, she could have managed. . . . The report dwelt on temperatures, routines, bowel movements.

Mama Chungu's wits were working all right, working to efface herself. When they picked her up, skin and bone, from the begging place, she had indeed been confused by hunger and despair, had babbled, half-understood, wept and apologised for her isolation, and so had got her new name. But now she had herself well in hand.

Mimi went through her morning sickness during the strike, with

120

the rubbish piled high, stinking and breeding flies, and the strikers wandering about in great gangs, which she felt a menace, Robert getting praised for organising voluntary labour in the docks and all the non-African unemployed eager to join in. By the time the second child was born, Robert was away at the war and the house taken over by naval officers who had their own servants. He had left her a little money for the confinement and she had something saved to keep her going till she recovered enough to look for work: the child had died in the fifth week. Robert never replied to her letter saying it was so. Well, perhaps he never got it. Boats were sinking those days, with people in them and letters, stores and precious unspoken promises and guns and money.

Mimi never saw her father again. The passenger ships, of course, were commandeered and troops were moving all about – Madagascar, Eritrea, India. If a letter or, at worst, a telegram had come it might well have followed the box-holder to some new address. After the war she enquired about the docks without success. She encouraged herself to think of Papa as settled with a young wife and a gratuity, tending a bar in a Seychelles hotel with entertaining stories of his days at sea. But another voice told her that if he had been alive he would have come to look for her. She generally managed to quell the third voice that said he might be lying helpless in a veterans' hospital somewhere or down and out in Beira or Mtwara. The sea is more merciful than the land in keeping its victims to itself. Or, at the very worst, it must be over by now.

Mimi found a lowly job in the naval stores and ignored any man who approached her. She felt tangled with physical pain for a year after the operation, and what was the sense in bearing more pain when no fruit could come of it? There was no child to cherish and to seek money to educate. In any case she felt in her early twenties shrivelled, thin, shrill, dull of hair and skin. People talked around her of politics and strikes and unity coming across the country – Beauttah was already famous, especially in Mombasa, and a great organiser. There was talk of people getting their rights after the war and throwing out the foreigners. Chege had not yet come. Hyder was a name to conjure with. Archbishop Alexander was remembered as a sort of antichrist. She was not interested in talk, but she combed out her woolly hair,

121

spoke only Swahili and resolved to be a Kenyan. But she did not speak of this to those who, twenty years afterwards, made a conscious choice. After all, there had been nowhere else she wanted to go. Sharing a room with a Taita widow, she lived decently enough.

Robert never came to look for her. That could hardly be thought of. But she met him one day at a bus stop in 1946, and he told her he was married and looking for a place to settle when his wife came from England. That she could well understand. British soldiers' wives were competing for places on every ship to come and join their husbands. Even Mr Kenyatta's coming was delayed because he had to wait, like others, for a berth. She answered coldly – Robert did not at first remember to ask what had happened about the baby. But by now her figure was trim again and her hair shining: with the upheaval of the strike next January she lost her job. So finally she agreed to set the new house in order for the memsahib to come, and pretty soon she was being called on to warm the bed as well.

She had no will of her own. She did not even drive a hard bargain. She had never been very good at calculating. He got her foodstuffs reserved for Europeans in the shops and gave her an extra twenty now and then: she lit some candles for her father's safety. When the wife came, he bought her a separate radio, since she no longer had the run of the house.

Robert was attentive to his wife at first and she had no reason to suspect anything. She was a pale woman, often prostrated by the heat and very ignorant of life in Kenya. Mimi exercised her best English to help her understand things in the house, but never outside. When, later on, they moved to Kamiti, she agreed to go too. It would be a change for her and she hoped to live more comfortably under strict observation. She was in her thirties now, and filling out. She thought the memsahib would find her feet in a place where white people were more dominant, and keep her husband up to the mark. But Robert was incorrigible. There was an incident with a female suspect, carefully hushed up. There was coarse talk in front of the nursing sisters, and by now he was loud-mouthed when he strode out to the quarters at night.

It was not only because he took her body and her humiliation for granted that she now resented Robert's intrusion. For the first time since the babies had died she was beginning to feel there was something of her own to protect.

The Taita man used to come with one of the vehicles delivering stores. It was not very clear to her what he was doing. They called him Kinyozi, the barber. He said that he had known her father in the snack bar before the war – that was possible – and had seen her when he used to work in the docks. There was nothing extraordinary about that. He was older than her, with a lined face, a ready smile but eyes that smouldered deep down. He seemed to go out of his way to make conversation, popping up when she was on her way to market or taking a message to one of the memsahib's friends outside the compound. She could not understand it. When he started making advances to her, she froze, and sensed that it was a relief to him that she did so. She felt herself ugly because of the fear and strain under which she lived, and she had never known a man who would turn up for friendly conversation. She had never, after all, claimed to be very bright. What was it, then?

He missed Mombasa, he said. He had had to go away after the strike and felt he had lost the respect of anyone he cared for there. But, even so, one had a commitment to make things better. Did she not think so?

Well, yes, she agreed. One wanted to belong. But she was a simple, uneducated woman, who would find it difficult to get away from her employer. He had spoiled her youth. . . .

Yes, yes, Kinyozi knew that. He seemed to know a lot of things.

So there was nothing she could do, really.

That – he paused – that was not in fact so. If she trusted him – well, he had not had much luck in his dealings with women, he did not want to put pressure on her in any way, they were both mature people, but if – if sometimes he could leave a small packet with her, or occasionally a letter that would be collected by one of the warders, identified by him, just in the spirit of helping. . . .

Of course she did not refuse or even think of refusing. She knew very well what it was about, and suddenly she knew too her need to feed the hatred that was growing in her. But she was very embarrassed the next day when Mr Robert came shouting round her quarters that he heard she was entertaining 'native' men in her room, amounting to an insult to the memsahib as though she were not being paid enough, did not know what was good for her. He started throwing cooking pans about, until the watchman came to investigate and called an officer who edged him away.

The envelope was hidden among her dresses in a wooden box. It was not till the next evening that the sergeant, calling her to the door in noisy protest against women whose bosses disturbed the peace of the whole servants' quarters, while he was only trying to have a peaceful supper with his brother-in-law along the line, was able to collect it with a wink of gratitude.

Two or three more exchanges were made and then one day the driver of the delivery van jeered at her in the road.

'So they got your friend at last.'

'Who got who?' she asked, confused, but confused because of knowing, not of doubt.

'They', he indicated the officers' quarters, 'got your fancy man. Ha, it's not only Kikuyu they've got an eye on, them lot. Watch out for yourself.'

She turned her back and walked away. She did not feel anything towards the man except gratitude that he recognised her commitment, but the sense of failure was strong in her. She would be no more use now.

That was the night the memsahib followed Robert down to the quarters. Next day she wept and screamed and left. Mimi herself could not stand it any longer. She had savings in the Post Office, though she also gave generously towards the support of the Emergency orphans at Dagoretti. She was glad now, fiercely glad, that Robert's children had not lived. She would never have been able to trust them. His wife, too, was better unencumbered. Mimi was glad now that her baptism certificate and her testimonials in a foreign-sounding name left her movements unrestricted. She went to Nairobi where she had the address of one of the aunties. She had drifted away. They thought she had not made much of herself. She never discovered how much they knew about her recent life, but, maintaining a certain reserve, they never held it up against her.

It was not difficult to find work in those days. She had, once more, the advantage of not being a Kenyan. But the laundry work was hard, and, though the money sounded all right, she had for the first time to rent a room by herself, and there were no perks of food or sharing of utensils. She hardly saved anything. The overfurnished houses of the aunties, their elaborate tea-sets and fancy covers, set a standard she was not accustomed to. A sip of sweet sherry now and then, with a biscuit, behind the pantry door, had become a necessity when facing the pasty memsahib in the kitchen. Sixteen years she worked in Ngara as paint crumbled from the shop-fronts and the names over them changed, while Asians joined the queues bound for London and the flats filled up with black families who did their own washing and held their ceremonies in country places far away. The identity card now showed her as a Kenyan born in Mombasa. The rent went up: milk, bread and rice went up too; she needed glasses and false teeth. These came out of the Post Office book. There were bitterly cold winters: she needed thick sweaters, coming out of the steamy heat of the laundry, and a drop of something to keep the spirits up. She bought heavy stockings to cover the swollen veins and they wore out quickly as she stumbled over the roughening pavements amid the ever more intrusive parked vehicles.

When the pneumonia struck, she came back from hospital to lie gasping in her stuffy room, chores done at weekends by schoolgoing children attached to the aunties, always in a hurry. There was no job left for her even if the doctor had passed her as fit enough. The Post Office account dwindled.

She hunted around, not used to insecurity, served in a shop for a few weeks while someone was away having a baby, but was slow and clumsy. Her glasses fell and shattered on the glass counter. In any case they were overdue for renewal and she did not find much difference without them. She minded some children after school until the parents came home from work, but after the first week they never paid her and she had to give it up.

Little by little she secreted her household goods in old bags or, at last, in old newspapers, and sold them, shamefaced, in the street markets, but the rent remained unpaid. Desperate, she cut the flowers from the tiny patch of front garden – half were hers anyway, and the surviving auntie was almost blind – and tried to sell them far away in the town, but they were commonplace and fetched very little. Half-

125

crazed, she stole flowers from distant gardens, a few at a time, hoping to escape attention, but it was noticed and she was taken to the police station and given a warning. Creeping home, she found the house barricaded against her – the auntie had long since surrendered to the mortgage, and her daughters-in-law paid rent for her own apartment in grudging instalments. Mimi's scantily covered bed, a meagre change of clothing, the charcoal burner and a rough box of kitchen utensils were all that remained. She saw the justice of their being locked away.

She still had her ID, proving her to be a Kenyan citizen, some ancient tax receipts and a plastic rainhood tucked into an old-fashioned black silk purse. Believing that you would not be molested if walking purposefully, she set off on a circuit of the town, hardly conscious of hunger but desperate for a cup of tea. After dark an urchin shoved her sprawling, snatching the useless purse, and her dental plate broke as she hit the pavement full face, bruising her nose and chin. She pulled it out and threw away the pieces, checking carefully that she had swallowed none. Where she was going it would be of no advantage to her.

A night watchman found her huddled in a doorway. He let her warm herself at his wood-fire and brought a damp rag to wipe her soiled face. Then he explained to her what to do. It was counsel of despair, but she was grateful for any human counsel. In the morning she dragged herself to the street by the mosque.

The days and nights blurred then into a round of pain and humiliation: she did not know for how long. In fact it was about six weeks before she was picked up in the street in a state of collapse, taken to hospital and from there eventually to the Refuge. She blessed those passers-by who gave her something to eat instead of a coin which she would have first to defend against predators and then make the painful voyage to convert into food and drink at a kiosk. As the big buildings went up and the empty sites were developed, from day to day the eating places of the poor had moved further away from the best begging grounds, across more perilous roads, less warmed by makeshift fires. She hung her head, dreading to meet the eyes of old neighbours, putting off as long as possible the need to pick her way into the public lavatory, treasuring a length of sacking that enabled

126

her to squeeze out in cold water one piece of clothing after another and partly dry it on the vacant lot in the pale morning sun.

But there is mercy, and here she was, retaining part of her mystery, helping Bessie little by little to reach out from her much longer withdrawal, recognisable, wonder of wonders, to Mr Robert's sister-in-law. She must have been badly shaken at the time to retain the picture so clearly in her mind, Mama Chungu thought: she herself could not have described the white lady, probably because there was nothing in her, except her concern for the baby, to cause surprise. (Silly bitch, thought Mama Chungu resentfully, to reveal herself like that. Suppose I had let myself go and asked for a port and lemon or a quilted bed jacket, I might have been out on my ear again.)

She would have preferred to avoid the pain of recognition, and yet it confirmed a continuity in Mimi which Mama Chungu had begun to doubt. Not that these young hussies of nurses needed to know about it, but she had been pretty once and had chosen her side.

Bessie did not return to her line of questioning when Jane came again, but she did manage to speak to her. She felt freer with the young than with these old people who might have knowledge of the struggle and shame which had been locked down below the layer of conscious speech in her – the fire which had engulfed her family when she, in her slow, uncoordinated way, was late in getting them moved from the homestead to the new village; the detention camp where she was herded after wandering out after curfew hopefully in search of them; the hateful guard who had engendered this last, late son upon her; the cousins who had cared for the child, as she could not, in their own, bereaved home, and taught him to be compassionate towards her. They too, she thought belatedly, would miss the boy and might even wonder where she was, if they ever came to Nairobi and saw her house made desolate. She did not know that already an outdoor garage was thriving on the site. A warning instinct had told her not to go back to see if dogs had licked the blood. And she had forgotten, if Leonard had ever told her, that his aunt was blind now and old Ezekiel too weak in the joints to go far from home. They had received Leonard's Post Office book and his civilian clothes. If she had understood this, Bessie would have said that they had the right, for they had sheltered and schooled him, and she had everything she needed. Except the boy.

'I think I may go into a convent,' said Jane, 'when I have finished my training. They always have need of nurses.'

'You are a Catholic, then?' asked Bessie, with a vague memory of incense and crosses and a beautiful lady who had a baby and then was seen to hold him dead and naked in her arms.

'No, not really. But I was at a Catholic school and learned about what they do. After John died, I just wandered about at home, when I had time off, and I always seemed to come on a tall tree, with branches like a cross, calling me. I think that is what it meant.'

'Perhaps,' said Bessie. 'I do not understand much. To be a nun is hard. But this one, Rahel, when she could talk, would always speak of a dead tree. She saw it when she was young and it changed her.'

'So did she take to religion?'

'Oh no. Perhaps they did not even have this religion then, I don't know. She is old. She was married to a soldier and had one son who grew up. I think the others all died. But he ran away, they told me. In a military family it is a great shame to run away. To the rest of us it might seem just like common sense. So he is lost too.'

To succeed in running away might at least soften the memories of those left behind, but they both put the thought away.

'I see,' said Jane, a bit bewildered. 'Perhaps I can ask her when she gets better.'

'Perhaps, but I do not think so. She does not often talk. But then I do not often talk to these old people either. It is because they are jealous of my having a baby.'

'Well, I have two years training still to go.'

'I know you are sad,' said Bessie. Her thoughts had always come slowly, and now she had for many years lost the habit of explaining them to other people. For herself, any hook to hang a picture on was direction enough for thinking – chicken, tea, baby, fire, dress, blood. Baby and blood especially. But this girl had known Leonard. There must be some way, with a great effort, of getting towards her, sucking up the knowledge she had, wrapping it up like a bundle of rags inside the tidy dress they made her wear and wash, wear and wash, wear and wash. She missed her rows of tins filled with secrets – pebbles, bits of charcoal, bright buttons, a photograph. They would never have found which one had the photograph in. But she did not miss them all that badly, because one got used to anything, really. That was what she was trying to say.

'I know you are sad. But you get used to it in time. And there are other – other. . . .' She did not know how to say that from even the ugliest and unkindest guard a child like Leonard could come.

'I know, my mother,' answered Jane, turning away. 'We were not even promised to one another. There are other nice boys. It is not their fault that John was the one to – to – lose his life. But it is not even feeling sad. It is not even wanting. . . . There is a medical student who kept asking me out. I wouldn't have gone anyway because I know he has let down one or two girls before. All the same I know he is good-looking, rich, clever, amusing, by what people say – but it is only knowing, not seeing. It is like at the beginning of your training going to the mortuary frightens you – all those dead bodies, people wailing outside, you feel sick. But after a while you get used to it and all you feel is that it is cold – so cold. You can do anything you have to do there, but always so cold.'

'Cold,' echoed Bessie. 'Cold. You must always keep charcoal. Don't pass a little piece. Keep it by you. It will comfort you. A picture maybe. And keep your clothes on. To keep changing and washing, changing and washing, makes you so cold – cold. And then they take the baby away.'

CHAPTER
NINE

Wairimu slipped outside soon after it was light, unbolting the kitchen
door. She did not expect to sleep much, since she no longer worked
hard or differentiated clearly between dreams and memories, but lay
snugly wrapped in her cot while she heard the heavier women heave
themselves over on creaking springs (had they never lain still on bare
board frames, thinking themselves too good for the easier mat on the
floor?) or spitting into their little tins, and Bessie sobbing night after
night for her lost baby.

She liked to take a quick pee in the garden before anyone could see –
it still felt more natural to her than stooping over the clammy pan
indoors – and had a vague memory that at first light one should be
facing the mountain. Although people told her that it could be seen on
blue January mornings from the ground and easily (easy to whom?)
from the top of those tall buildings, she could not trust her eyes so far.
And it did not matter. Even long ago the blind would be led to the
right position, and nowadays you were taught to look for *Ngai* not
even up in the sky but in your own heart. If it were not so, how would
the Refuge have been built for them by people far away? Even this
young man from Uganda – a green and mushy place, she had heard,
where crocodiles lurked and women grovelled on the ground – came
with a Kikuyu name and an understanding of what old ladies cared
about. The grandson of Waitito? Well, that was all he knew, it was no
good asking for more. Making mistakes began a long time ago, as the
proverb says.

The Somali guard was awake and shifting in his greatcoat. He
would unlock the gate and go off duty when the kitchen helper arrived
with the milk. He never missed the first call to prayer, which perhaps
unconsciously had been Wairimu's signal that day had come. The
chanted syllables rippled through the half-light: though Eastleigh was

never deserted, movement at dawn was subdued, cautious, from figures sleeping in doorways, stirring breakfast porridge in kiosks, trudging from distant suburbs to early duty in town, converging on the bus depot to start up transport for more affluent eight o'clock workers. Later in the day the muezzin would be overpowered by the noise of traffic, trade, education and a thousand radios.

Grudgingly the guard opened the gate.

'Don't you get lost now, granny. My orders are not to let anybody in, but I'm not supposed to let you old girls go out gallivanting either.'

'Go on,' she replied cheerfully. 'You don't know how often I might have tiptoed past you to keep a date on a moonlit night.'

She walked down to the corner kiosk where they sometimes bought bread on allowance days or Vicks or Sloane's liniment ('Whiskers' they called it) but it was not yet open. It was getting light, but a cloudy, grey morning, no blaze of splendour from the east. She turned round the corner where the kids had made a space for playing football, or perhaps kept a space where once the Somali had grazed their herds, moving in to work as butchers, house servants and drivers for the white man's city where a high value was put on the clothed and the literate. She had known a lot of Somali in the old days. . . . She paused to rest as the lights started to go on in the squat houses surrounding courtyards that had begun to colonise the area in the twenties and the tall, balconied flats behind.

As she turned to continue her walk – it was good to be away from the nattering of those old women for a time, and it would be fully light before the porridge was ready and windows thrown open to winkle out the latest of the sleepers – she noticed something lying in the gutter, too big for a dead dog. A drunk? Surely on so cold a night even the farthest gone would have crept to better shelter. She shuffled nearer and bent as far as she dared without risking the sharp pain. It was a young man, brown-skinned, curly-haired but the soft hair messed with blood, well-dressed – not simple robbery, then, to leave the leather jacket, the smart shoes – twisted to an extent that surely indicated death. She did not touch him – she had seen too many deaths: deaths sensed just out of earshot in the forest, deaths outside the police lines in Government Road, deaths in the Emergency, deaths of old people, hungry and forgotten. There was a risk in

131

touching. But she lifted up her voice and the old cry, the cry of mourning, thin and reedy, broke from her, more urgent than the call to prayer.

The curtains in the lighted windows did not move and no doors opened. A dog or two gave a desultory bark and then fell silent. Wairimu felt the impulse to run away and then remembered that her body was no longer capable of doing so. A man in a bus conductor's uniform came hurrying towards her, perhaps late to report on duty. He looked to where she pointed and shrugged.

'Nothing we can do for him, ma. Anyone you know? No? Well, I'll phone police from the depot and you'd better get off home as far as I can see. Where can they find you for a statement? Oh yes, Old Women's Refuge, I know it. But don't you stick your neck out, mother. It won't do him any good.'

She was still gazing at the body as he strode away. There was something familiar about the features though she did not remember seeing the young man before. She bent her knees and picked up something from the gutter just by the dead man's sleeve, took one last look and then trotted back at her best pace to the gate of the Refuge. Suleiman was just leaving but he paused to hear her story and then marched with her into Matron's office to telephone the police. Matron, a scarf over her rollers, was not best pleased, but here was a circumstance she could not say no to.

By the time morning porridge was finished, every person in the house had heard the whole story, and although they did not allow a crowd to form, the police, who were photographing, measuring, sifting round the place of the killing, did so under the baleful stare of a dozen or more old ladies, not one of whom could be hurried in her slow progress towards the purchase of a box of matches, to call on a fever-ridden friend, or to pick up the latest news from the gate of the Maternity Hospital. Even Bessie took her little tin and shuffled after the others, seeming to understand the violent event and the need for stealth. But though she managed to wriggle closer than the others to the body, and to look at it longest, she turned away disappointed, still muttering under her breath, 'My baby, my baby.'

As the passers-by paused, gossiped, moved on, a girl kept walking up and down the road. She was tall and bony. You could almost hear the beads clicking in her long hair against the windcheater. Surely not on the beat – not in the middle of the morning – not on this street – not beside the corpse, for goodness' sake. Nekesa looked at her curiously and a twitch of recognition passed between them, though Nekesa's equivalent younger self would have been wearing a flowered cotton dress and had her hair arranged in skimpy plaits over the line of the skull. Of course the girl was really watching the body, and that flick of the shoulder scarf across her face was to disguise her tears. Nekesa stationed herself on the corner. After all, she knew how.

'Very sad thing,' she remarked as the girl drew level with her. Police were still fussing over the body, trying to keep the crowd back.

'Very sad.'

'You knew him?'

'What are you getting at? Nothing to do with me.'

But she seemed unable to keep her eyes off the place where the body lay.

'You knew him?' asked Nekesa again.

The girl shook her head.

'It might help to find out, you see. If you could give the time or who was with him.'

'I can't. And if I could, why should I bother?'

'Because it's the only thing left to do for him.'

The girl flicked her plaits back and there was a long pause. Then she started to talk.

'He wasn't with me last night or for a long time before. After all, he's a student – he has friends of his own kind: he isn't going to look for a girl like me unless he's pretty low. And unless I were much better off than I am, I wouldn't be able to send the others away and wait to see if his lordship might drop by. Surely you know that?'

'Of course I know it,' said Nekesa. 'You see it in me, I see it in you. I'm old enough to face facts and be no threat to you. Besides, something else happened to me. I'll tell you about it presently. But there is something I want to know from you first.'

'I fancy him, that's all. Did, I should say. Name is Joseph, a university student. You know they don't tell their whole names or where you can find them. But I thought he might be a medical from his hands and – from – from some fancy words he uses. It was the girl in the next room who called me: "Look over the road in a minute and you might see someone you know," she says, only meaning to upset me, because I had no idea. . . . No, she was with her regular boy last night. It was when she was going out to get the milk that she saw him lying there. Why are you so interested, anyway? Do you know him?'

'I'm not sure. I think I know one of his family, but she doesn't call him Joseph and I've not seen him close to. I've no intention of worrying her without being sure. My eyes are not as good as they used to be. And in any case she doesn't always tell the truth. She might be just pretending that he is a connection of hers.'

'Who does tell the truth?'

'I do, for one. Because, you see, the Lord saved me. Me, a cheat, a prostitute, a drinker. True I was getting old, but if I'd had my eyes open it might have happened years earlier. For you too.'

'Oh yeah, oh yeah, I've heard that at street corners before. And then I starve or what? You didn't go on the street because it was fun, I know that. Something pushed you. Me too. You reckon you're going to get me a job as a receptionist/telephonist tomorrow?'

'Well, stranger things have happened – what is your name, now? Judy? I wouldn't rule out the possibility, Judy. I got that way because my mother was sleeping around and my stepfather didn't have much of a job either. There was no school for me and not much training for any girls then, except the few at mission boarding schools. But there are lots of jobs for you girls nowadays. Not enough to go round – I'm not old and silly enough to think that – but enough to give you a hope. I used to fancy myself as the lady in the dry cleaner's; that was the height of my ambition. Good clothes, you know, coming in creased and messy and going out all clean and good to feel. I could have learned enough reading and writing for the tickets and numbers, and I guess that would have suited me fine. That would be child's play to you. You're not twenty yet, surely: time enough to change.'

'I'm eighteen, actually. Mother died. I stayed on in this block with my father and brother. My older sisters work in Nakuru. Father was a drinker – got worse when Mama died and he was sent up for dangerous driving. Of course he won't get a job when he comes out.

134

Brother got killed in 82. Only last year, but I guess we'll always think of it as 82. I'd just finished a typing course – result fair after a third division school certificate: no money to repeat. Where does that get me? The landlord let me keep on one room because he was sorry for me, but I've still got to find the rent, haven't I?'

'Your sisters?'

'One is married to a real holy Joe. Do you think he'd have me soiling his wall-to-wall carpeting? Me – lipstick, ear-rings, a trade word that slips out now and again. The other one has two fatherless kids to support, so they hardly manage to speak to her. Do you think she'd take care of me as well? All right, I won't say it.'

'I'll tell you,' said Nekesa, 'but I can't keep on standing here. Come in the Refuge and sit on my bed. Allowed? What's to stop you? Do you think we're already practising to be a choir of angels or something? Old age isn't infectious unless you let it get you down.'

Judy looked around her, embarrassed. Rahel was apparently asleep in one of the four beds, smelling faintly of urine and breathing noisily through her mouth. Two other beds were neatly made and empty. Nekesa's looked a bit grubby – it was far from inspection day – and there were husks of groundnuts on the cement floor. On top of the locker stood a used enamel mug, a violently coloured picture of the Sacred Heart of Jesus and an ancient Christmas card depicting Santa Claus and a couple of reindeer. Are these the rewards of virtue, the girl thought to herself.

'You see,' said Nekesa comfortably, 'this won't look much to you. For me, it's as good as I've ever had. He gives according to what you ask, you see. For me it was a bit too late to ask for a university student and a couple of kids. A pair of long-lost sisters wouldn't have been too hard for him to rustle up if I'd thought about them in time. You have. But I'd be a bit more ambitious if I were in your place. Don't imagine you're doomed for life at eighteen.'

The girl looked sideways and began chipping at her nail varnish.

'You see, I'd been in Kampala during the Emergency – that's another story. I came back to Nairobi when I was about forty. Things were looking up. *Uhuru* was coming. For one reason and another Kampala was a little bit hot for me at the time. Perhaps somewhere inside me I could see the troubles that were coming to foreigners in Uganda.

'Anyway here I was, all on my own. A lot of my old friends were Kikuyu and had got moved here and there during the bad times. My mother had gone off to Western with one man or another long before, and my brother had died. I hardly knew my dad or the little ones. But I knew what I wanted to do. I had some money saved up and I started a trading pitch at Machakos Bus Stop – that's right, Airport you call it now. I had combs, mirrors, picture frames, handkerchiefs, safety pins, all that kind of thing. Gikomba Market as we know it now had not started then, and though young men had started selling things inside the buses, it had not yet become the racket it is nowadays. Things were very much cheaper then than they are now, but still I had several hundred shillings tied up in stock. I shared a room in a house at Shauri Moyo with a Ugandan friend of mine who had also retired from the game. Pumwani would have been a bit nearer, but we didn't want to be pulled back into the old routine, and there's no upper or lower age limit in Pumwani, as you know.

'I was doing all right and Keziah had a refreshment stall near the stadium. I had my licence to trade and everything – a reformed tart, you might say, but still bitter and rotten-hearted. *Uhuru* came and went, *Jamhuri*, the promise of federation with Tanganyika and Uganda all forgotten, people feeling good, confident, expecting improvement, wanting more and more of the kind of things I had to sell. This went on up to 1971, the time of the great loyalty rally. You won't remember it, of course. Busloads of people coming into Nairobi, excitement, extra refreshment places, police everywhere, suspicion, people afraid for their positions, eager to get a leg up.

'Police came round my stall.

' "Licence? Are you a Kenyan?"

' "Yes, of course."

' "It's been reported that you are from Uganda."

' "I have lived in Uganda, but I have been back in Kenya for eleven years."

' "Husband?"

' "I am not married, sir."

' "Why not?"

136

' "*Why not?* Perhaps I was too fussy."

' "What? Wha-a-a-t?"

'A flying kick. Mirrors broken, combs scattered, kids diving to pick them up.

' "Place of birth?"

' "Nairobi."

' "Where is your father?"

' "Dead for all I know. He turned my mother out when I was a little girl."

' "Oh, like that – I see – like that."

'Arms and batons waving about. I leaned over, trying to protect the glazed portraits of the President, whether out of loyalty or because they were best sellers at the time I did not stop to think. But too late; the whole pile came crashing down, myself on top of it.

' "That's what you call loyalty, is it? Bloody foreign bitch."

'Passengers were crowding round, picking up what they dared. Stallholders hastily packed up and moved away. A bus scraped the fender of a taxi and attention was diverted. People and police moved that way.

'I tried to push myself up but the pain in my right arm made me crumple again. Using my left arm, I managed to get myself sitting straight on the ground. I felt dizzy. Mechanically I began dropping the undamaged items into a carton. Some were kicked away in the dust but people were ashamed to snatch those near at hand when they could see I was hurt. The teenage son of one of my neighbours came to help me. She had picked up her stock in trade and carried it to the far side of the bus park. When the boy saw my condition he ran over to look after her trade while she came to see how I was. She was a *tukutendereza* person and we didn't usually speak more than a word of greeting unless we were begging small change for a note, since I had told her that I was not interested in her appeals to come to Jesus. But right now I was not in a state to reject anything.

'She touched my arm gingerly but let it alone when I winced.

' "You need hospital," she said, "but I don't know how you're going to get there. And you've lost a lot of things. Shall I send Victor to pick up what's left? Is there anywhere you can leave them? I can keep an eye on them while I'm here, but I don't think the two of us will

137

be able to carry them home along with our own stuff. Oh dear, oh dear! And why should they do this to you? You weren't doing any harm."

' "Don't you think your God is punishing me for my sins?" I asked her. At least that's what I meant to say – I hadn't got much control over my voice.

'She looked deeply hurt.

' "Do you think God goes around breaking people's arms and spoiling their pictures?" she asked, really curious. "No wonder you don't think much of me if that's what you think I'm witnessing to. But right now we have to get you treated. Can you afford a taxi if I send Victor with you? He'll walk back, of course."

'My head was still buzzing.

' "If Victor will really help me," I said, "the best thing for him to do would be to go and call Keziah. She will know what to do. Do you know her refreshment stall? It's near the football ground."

' "Yes, I know it. I'll send him straight away. You just sit still but give me a shout if anyone tries to interfere with your things."

'I don't think I ever thanked her. I sat there scraping the broken glass into a heap and putting the pictures and other goods into a carton. I tried to work out the value, but it seemed different each time I counted. It must have been an hour before Keziah got to me but when she did, sensible woman, it was with her own equipment loaded on to a handcart. She quickly added what could be salvaged from my stock and told the young man to take it to our house. We knew that our landlady would take good care of it. Then she bargained with a taxi driver and they took me up to Kenyatta Hospital.

'I had to be admitted with a broken arm and some cracked ribs. Keziah came to see me when she could. She dared not lose trade, especially as she had to pay the whole rent for the next couple of months. But Mama Victor came to see me the very next day. She spoke to some of the saved nurses so that they came to see me too, and every day one or other of the group was around, begging me to praise the Lord. Do you wonder that I did? No one had ever taken that much trouble over me before.

'I went back to work eventually and paid the house rent for the next two months. Keziah had done her share, and she had a child in boarding school to support. I hadn't got much to sell, and for a long time I had to pay a boy to carry my things because of my bad arm. Well, I managed. Then, of course, I had to stop selling on Sundays. People have got slack about this these days but it seemed to me a very clear command. I loved going to the meetings but then there are bus fares, you see, and always clean dresses, everything neat and new. So I wasn't really saving enough to keep my stock up as prices increased. By the time my chest began to trouble me, I could hardly afford to spare the time I needed to rest and go for treatment. Keziah went back to Uganda after the liberation and I never heard what became of her. She hadn't been saved by that time, but the Brethren encouraged me to go on sharing with her and get the message across, and we got along very well. She was afraid I would get upset about her smoking, but it had never been much of a temptation to me and it wasn't the biggest obstacle in her way either. I was so used to it that it didn't bother me, except for being a bit embarrassing if some of the sisters called in and started sniffing. But they were always very polite to her.

'One day in 1980 Mama Victor had to report to the Brethren that I had collapsed in the market and they came to take me home. Of course Victor was grown-up by then and working in the Industrial Area, and all the younger children wanted to read to form four, so with things changing like that their mother did not get much time to help me. As you can imagine, the Brethren discussed me thoroughly, and then they made arrangements for me to come here. So I have been comfortable here for three years.

'You don't think being comfortable is enough? Sure it isn't, in terms of blankets and hot dinners. But being clean and useful before the cross of Jesus, that is another matter. Do you believe me?'

'I believe that you mean every word of it, granny. And I am grateful that you should waste words on a hard nut like me. But whether it could happen again. . . .'

'It keeps on happening, my daughter. Listen – I shall hurt you now: that is the way of grannies with children. Let me for once get out of my skin enough to be a granny. You cared for that boy who is lying dead in the road, didn't you? You thought there was not a chance in a million of your getting on his level, but you still cared. Am I right?'

'Too right.'

'Then that means there is a well of feeling in you not yet dried up and soured as it gets to be – I should know – after all the hot breaths and the pawing. You might never have seen him again, but you still want to cry because his death is a loss to him, not just a loss to you. And if the Lord of Heaven suffers because a loss to you matters more to Him than a loss to Himself, aren't you at least going to listen to His offer? Come now, I will take you to someone who can explain better than I can.'

The girl was thinking, I have not made my bed, and the dirty dishes will be crawling with insects on the table, and before Monday I have to get my pills, and if I went straight back now I might get one more look at him – but all the same she went with Nekesa.

CHAPTER
TEN

Next day, of course, the report came in the newspapers. It was not headline news (this was the prosecution of an assistant minister for debt) and not an eventful day, since neither back street murders nor official bankruptcies were uncommon. But it was of absorbing interest in the home. Wairimu, Suleiman and the bus conductor were all quoted, though not pictured, and Matron had unbent sufficiently to pay for extra copies of the Swahili paper. The dead man had been identified as Joseph Baraka Wau, a third year medical student, aged twenty-three, of Nairobi. His father was being recalled from a business trip to Uganda. The flat in Westlands where he lived during vacations with his younger brother and sister had not been tampered with and his father's car remained in the garage. This was the second time the family had been engulfed in tragedy, as the murdered man's mother and her two older children had perished in a fire eight years before.

Priscilla was the first to read it in full, as she was the fastest reader as well as always the first to be washed and dressed, not like that Wairimu, wandering outside in her night wrapper and headscarf. She sat at the table blinking and twitching her nose, not daring to read aloud as she would soon be asked to do. Evans used to say she looked like a rabbit when she was thinking – how they would laugh then, and he would pretend to lift her by the ears, like a couple of kids playing, until somehow their bodies were engulfed in one another. She slapped herself down for remembering and put away her spectacles. But there was no escape from this knowledge. Suleiman, glorying in his fame, was sticking his head through the window, repeating all the news, and Priscilla found herself already behind Sophia's chair as she let out a piercing scream.

'Baraka, Baraka, son of my daughter, Baraka. Is there no end to the evil that can fall upon this family? Aie-e-e, my grandson Baraka.'

141

The old ladies understood at once, though only Nekesa had had a fearful expectation that it would be so. This was the eldest of the children who had survived the fire which had consumed the big house and killed Sophia's daughter, Hawa, and her children of sixteen and seventeen. The three younger children had been out in the car with their father. Sophia had run out of the kitchen door screaming. She had been cooking on a paraffin stove which overturned and the flames had leaped to an open tin of kerosene in the corner. She had been unhurt but prostrate with grief. Her son-in-law was as one demented, accusing her of arson, witchcraft, insane jealousy. She was examined over and over again by doctors and psychiatrists, questioned by the police, pressed repeatedly to consider whether any deliberate hand, even if not her own, had turned against the family. Why had she not stoppered the kerosene before lighting the stove? She was elderly, easy-going, forgetful, could not recall whether she ordinarily did so or not. Cooked for herself perhaps not more than once a fortnight. Had not mentioned her intention to her daughter. Collapsed again, trembling and sobbing.

Wau would not enter the same room with her, refused any maintenance, urged the children to forget they ever had a granny, only to worship the saintly memory of their mother. It was an evil spirit from the past, he said, that had turned Sophia against her own Christian profession and everything that had followed from it. She had complained the evening before, he said, that the food was too bland and foreign. That was why she had taken it into her head to start cooking as an excuse for setting the fire. She had laughed at the children for wearing European, not Muslim, clothes, and had taunted her son-in-law that she could employ him as a hired driver. Hearing all this at second-hand, she sobbed again, screwing up her wrappers until they tore, withdrawing into a fold of blanket as though it gave her the privacy of a *buibui*.

Truly, she had not much relished the supper, but it was not for her, as a dependant, to grumble. Only because the children had asked, she had told them stories of her early years, what people wore, what they ate, how they celebrated great days. Even nowadays in Eastleigh, she had told them, you could find goats painted pink and blue to be sacrificed instead of Isaac. Isaac was there, right enough, in the Bible.

142

What was the harm in that? And she had promised to show them the goats if their father would drive them over when the time of the feast came, but Wau refused to have anything to do with pagan sacrifices, and she had teased him, saying he could dress up and pretend to be her hired driver if he was ashamed to be seen with his own flesh and blood, but she, though she put faith in the blood of Jesus, could not pretend to be better than the parents who bore her or despise her kinsfolk who still needed to see the light. So they had parted, in a joking mood she felt, and never met again. The court said there was no case for her to answer. She could go. But go where?

Her parental family had cut themselves off from her long ago. Her son Hassan had become a fanatical Muslim, denouncing her conversion, and she did not even know his address. Mariam had gone away to live with her prospective in-laws in 1945. She had sent a message when her first child was born, but it was rumoured that she had been divorced and remarried on one of the islands. Sophia had no idea where she might be. There was nothing to be hoped for in going back to Mombasa.

Sophia declared that she had a bank savings book with over ten thousand shillings in it, but of course that had been destroyed in the fire. The police made enquiries at her Mombasa bank, but no deposit could be traced in any of the names she had ever used. Wau, she maintained, must have got hold of her money and destroyed the evidence. She had no claim on insurance for the house. She was sixty-three at the time of the fire and had no resources for starting another business even if she could have pulled herself together enough to do so. Her personal sewing machine had been burned with the rest. She had never been employed by anyone and even her best friends did not suppose that she could learn to take orders now. The one advantage she had lay in being a convert. She was asked to tell the story many times before boards and committees. As a result she had been admitted to the Refuge and had stayed there eight years, although she was younger and stronger than some of the other residents.

In truth Fatuma had become a Christian, attended baptism classes, been sprinkled with the water and taken her new name because Henry had wished it. She could not honestly say that there had been a hunger for a new faith in her before her appreciation of Henry as a good man and one meant for her. On the other hand she had no doubt that God had sent Henry to be her prophet. Henry was a follower of Issa and she already knew that Issa, whom she would learn to call Jesus, was to be revered. Perhaps it would have been easier to resist the change if she had been a boy and had received all the systematic teaching of Islam. But she was a girl and had picked up her notions of faith along the way, so that the systematic catechism in Bible classes presented a new challenge to her understanding and fell into place bit by bit. More than that, it did not forbid her the pillars, the angels, the foundations of righteousness, the social virtues of charity and compassion to which she had been brought up. It amplified them into a wider charity, a more intimate worship, a framework of forgiveness. As well as celebrating the unloosing of Isaac, it commemorated the unloosing of all through the everlasting son of Abraham. Gradually Sophia came to comprehend these mysteries as well as subscribe to them, and something changed in her and witnessed through her.

But now, as she looked back, the flames flickered in between and the words became a habit in which she still trusted but without delight, and that part of her life no longer seemed real with the urgency of the old town years.

Hawa and her husband prospered. Children were born to them. Wau was transferred to the Nairobi office of his company and Hawa was able to set her feet on the civil service ladder. By 1963 they were living in Ofafa Jerusalem, modelled on an English council estate with fences between the little back gardens. By 1970 they had a house in Woodley, once a sop to the colonial lower middle class. This was where they took Sophia to live with them when the doctor warned her of hypertension. Her business had been running down as factory garments came into competition with local tailors' work. The crippled machinist had died and the man who replaced him demanded higher wages. Her cousin's brood of children spread all over the house, and the eldest came under suspicion when one day the cashbox was found broken and empty. When a new school failed to collect and pay for the uniforms it had ordered she had to break into the bank savings, and medicines and visits to a private doctor bit into the dowry money.

When they persuaded her at last to move to Nairobi, Sophia refused to sell up her home. She feared that the move might not be peaceful.

144

Besides, the company was expanding to uncivilised and inaccessible places. What would become of her health and sensibilities if Wau were transferred to Busia, say, or Kisii? So the niece rented the house, the furniture and the spare machine at a low rate which Wau was to collect for his mother-in-law when he flew down to Mombasa on business every two or three months. But Asha, with every year a new mouth to feed, was often unable to pay in full. After a couple of years Wau found the machine and the furniture gone, the house deserted except for a couple of street boys who had established themselves on the verandah, the structure hardly fit any longer to ask a rent for and rate demands piling up unheeded for who knew how long.

Sophia never believed him. She was always about to make the journey to see for herself, but she had never been on a train and the prospect of an all-day bus journey daunted her more than she would admit. When the Waus had brought her up by car in 1970 she had seen for the first time the scrub country and the inland hills. And when disaster came, she was left penniless and shaken, the curtain of fire coming down, as had previously the curtain of water, to obscure all that went before. Now day after day was the same, except for the quarterly medical check-up and the pills that made her feel more delicate, each time they were changed, than the older women. If she thought back, it was to the sunny scented days, hemmed in by the sea and the fearful angels.

Three days later the newspapers reported that Samuel Kamau was helping the police with their enquiries into the murder, and though the case against him was not complete, it looked strong. He was known to have accosted Joseph Baraka Wau outside the Faculty Library on the day before the murder, seized him roughly by the coat, and threatened to beat him up if he had any more to do with Miss Mary Kamau, a student nurse, Samuel's sister. Miss Kamau admitted that she had been out on several dates with Wau but denied that intimacy had occurred and willingly underwent a clinical test to show that she was not pregnant. She had, however, complained to her brother that Wau had been avoiding her without giving any reason. Kamau admitted to having been in the Sun City Cinema in Eastleigh with some friends on the evening Wau died, although his home was

145

far away on the Kabete Road. Witnesses could attest approximate times for his entering and leaving the cinema.

Kamau said that he had gone to town by no. 9 bus after the show and changed into a *matatu* on Tom Mboya Street to go home. As he lived alone, the time of his arrival could not be checked. Wau's body had been found close to the Old Ladies' Refuge in Eastleigh where his grandmother, Mrs Sophia Mwamba, resided. The father of the deceased, Solomon Wau, however testified that none of his children knew the whereabouts of their grandmother, who had been cleared by the courts of suspicion of arson arising when her daughter and two of her grandchildren had been burned to death in 1975. The surviving grandchildren gave evidence that prior to the enquiry they had no knowledge of where their grandmother lived.

Mrs Mwamba was for the second time judged to have no case to answer. She had her bed in a cubicle shared by three other ladies and had slept normally on the night in question after taking the sedatives prescribed for her. The Refuge was surrounded by high walls and the watchman who locked and guarded the gate had not let anyone in or out. He had not heard any sounds of a struggle from the spot where the body was found, some sixty metres away as the crow flies but farther by road. As loud music was commonly heard in the area as late as 2 a.m. this would probably have masked any such sound. Mrs Mwamba had not accompanied the other ladies who went to the scene of the crime because she 'had had enough of dead bodies', but had broken down in distress as soon as her grandson's name was mentioned. She said that she had not seen the boy since he was fourteen years old. She never talked about her family since the memory of past events was so painful.

No money, identity card, keys or papers had been found on the body, but robbery was not alleged to have been a major motive since an expensive leather jacket and shoes were still intact, and a watch, which appeared to have been broken on striking the ground, remained on the wrist. Enquiries had not suggested any other likely motives. The deceased was generally popular among his acquaintances and fellow students.

Gertrude and Mary, both looking pale and tired, came in their ordinary clothes to call at the Refuge. Gertrude's skin seemed clogged, no light reflected from it any more, her hair bundled up into a plain scarf. Mary glowed more, but defiantly. The old ladies fussed around, some recognising them, others, confused, expecting them to fire questions and conjure insurance payments or new blankets out of thin air.

'You don't look as though you were going to take our temperatures today,' babbled Wairimu for something to say. She knew who they were. 'Are you bringing the babies out of the bushes round the corner then? Enough to put you off men for life, working in the delivery room, some of the girls say.'

'No, Auntie. We haven't finished our training in the wards yet. We just came over for a walk as we are off duty.'

'Well, here we are, as you see. Most of us are not likely to be far away unless they send an ambulance for us, or perhaps a box. Make yourselves at home.'

The girls sought out Priscilla in her corner. She took a tighter hold of herself, knowing why they had come. For what did she know of giving comfort? Trays of tea, polished tables, beautifully ironed collars, those were her trade.

'Mrs Njuguna,' said Mary, after exchange of greetings. 'We have come to you for help. It is her man and my brother. What can we do? As for the one who is gone, we knew him. We are sorry. But not overmastered by sorrow. It was he who provoked Sam to quarrel with him, but it was Sam who would choose to quarrel that way, aloud, before witnesses. It was not in him to hit in the dark and run away.'

'The Bible says that no one knows the heart of a man except the spirit of man that is in him.'

'But this one – this one was different.'

Are we not all different, thought Priscilla, and all sure we know it? Perhaps you too have mistaken your vocation. She thought that he would marry her, but he went away, leaving only the name Waitito for her son. They are scrabbling at the door with knives, those who swore that they would never fear the white man, and a little girl gurgles out her last bloody breath to the accompaniment of police whistles.

'He is your brother, Mary, and your sweetheart, Gertrude. You have to believe that he is different. But there is nothing you can do for him.'

147

'Nothing?'

'Pray if you can. Go on believing when you can no longer pray. Behave as if it were so even when you no longer believe. Only that.'

'Only that?'

'Mary, you have a brother in danger of the law. You have said what was needful to explain his anger, but you cannot follow the course his anger followed. People are trained and paid to do the following. The pulse of shared blood confuses the signals for us. I had a brother. He was imprisoned for the same oath that led people to kill our father – truly or falsely, I do not know. They crushed his balls with pincers and he died of chill and despair in the scrapyard where, out of pity, the boss let him act as watchman. For his confidence was gone and his memory crazed by that dreadful thing to be remembered. Perhaps he did what was once not in him to do. It would not help anyone to find out now. Many years have passed. If it does you good to hear that, then listen. But it would do me no good to be surrounded by people who have heard it and add another shame to their sourness and the burden of their years.'

'But Mrs Njuguna, we did not mean to open up another wound for you. We came because you waited for your husband, you love him. I do not know how to wait, and Mary cannot stop blaming herself.'

'Gertrude, you love Sam: even I can see that, with my eyes dimming and my mind tight shut against emotion. Love can cast out fear but it is not written that love can bring all knowledge. You can wait. It is not so very hard to wait. Thousands do that. The hard thing is to recognise what you are waiting for when it comes and not turn away in revulsion. If Evans were to walk into this room now – old, bald, paunchy, maybe whining his sentences like a priest, or snarling like an animal that has got hold of its prey and finds it no good to eat – what good would it do me? It is my own faithfulness I have cherished, my loss rather than what I have lost. Or instead of waiting you can cut out the painful part of yourself as you medical people snip off a limb, an appendix, a passage to the womb. And then at least you have something left to build with, something a bit less than human but enough for a name, a career, a company. Many do. It is up to you.'

Gertrude was crying openly now. Mary sat as though stunned.

148

'But you never told us. We did not mean to be impertinent. We admired you. We meant no harm.'

'Child, you have not harmed me, nor did I mean to harm you, though I knew I might hurt you: better to do it now when you are so covered with wounds that no new hurt is separate from the others. I hope Sam may be innocent and proved so, but I do not think there is anything you can do about it. The more he sees you grieving, the more conscious he will be of his own grief. But do not ask me how to bear it. I have not been very good at that.'

Gertrude took Priscilla's hand. Bessie hovered, producing a grubby piece of rag from the bosom of her dress, and the girl stood helplessly, holding it in her left hand. Nekesa, more practical, handed Mary a thick wad of tissue.

'I will walk along with you,' said Wairimu. 'I am sure he is going to get off. Nothing bad will happen to him. But Priscilla is upset. She feels things deeply,' she added in a whisper, urging them away. But she was not in time. As they went out of the main door and turned into the drive, Sophia rose from her wicker chair and bore down upon them.

'I see it now,' she screeched at Mary. 'You are the one who threw herself at my grandson's head, are you? Any cheap little nurse thinking she can ensnare a medical student. And then urging on your brother to do this – this.'

She threw her arms aloft, dramatically.

'And you, the apple of his eye. I suppose he wanted to show you how big and tough he was? On a poor, motherless, innocent boy. Not a thought for the grieving family, not a care for anyone outside your own Kikuyu. . . .'

Matron had a firm grip on Sophia's arm and was trying to lead her away with Mama Chungu's help. Both girls were sobbing bitterly. Wairimu led them to the gate.

'Don't blame Priscilla,' she said. 'She is almost a European. She would think it wrong to bend even a little bit of the truth. But me, I'm, I'm sure he's innocent and you won't have to wait long to know it. But remember you have a long path to tread before you come to rest here if God gives you no better. So try to be happy when you come. Some of these my sisters have already taken as much as they can bear.'

149

Matron managed to get Sophia to bed and called a doctor to give her a sedative injection. The Refuge seemed still to vibrate to her screams, and some of the old ladies realised how peaceful it usually was compared with the shouts, insults and alarms that bounced on the outside air of Eastleigh. Why should that be, when nearly all of them had special griefs to bring them here at last and special gifts to have survived so many griefs? Only, perhaps, that each of them had woven through the years a framework of shelter, as the Boran woman keeps the folded structure of her house on camel-back beside her, so that the tent fabric of the Refuge or any other person's home could stretch above it without encroaching on the private place within.

Sophia was breathing heavily. Rahel in the next cubicle creaked and sighed. Supper was served, eaten and cleared away. Bessie was found trying to bundle up a handful of squashy beans in the corner of her wrapper. Mama Chungu was complaining of constipation. Matron, breaking routine, came in for a check on the patients.

'I have left some bread and a thermos of tea in the kitchen,' she told Priscilla, 'in case one of them should wake up and complain of missing supper. But for heaven's sake why did you have to bring those girls here to upset Sophia? Don't we have enough to put up with? I can't understand you.'

'I did not bring them, Matron,' answered Priscilla at her most punctilious, 'but I did not send them away either, if they thought fit to come. We sometimes behave here as if the only problems were old people's pains and memories. Perhaps it does us good to remember that these young ones also have their needs.'

'Indeed, indeed,' cried Matron huffily in Kikuyu, a rare outburst for her and an admission of intimacy. 'Old ladies' problems from morning to night. I live with that. Thirty of you to worry over. It is enough, I tell you, without adding more.'

'But, Matron,' put in Wairimu, 'we appreciate the trouble you take over us. One day you will be old yourself. Then perhaps you will see how grateful we are.'

'One day, one day.' Matron sat down on one of the empty beds and started to massage her ankles. 'Do you think there is an age limit for troubles – do you, now? "Oh, my poor back!" "Oh, my dead children!" "Oh, my sainted husband!" "Oh, my barren womb!" Do

150

you think someone is bound to be happy if she has children, even though they tear her apart and make her almost bleed to death? You are sure of that – those who are so sorry for themselves. And to have a husband, is it all joy, then, those who can remember – a husband like a waxed image, seals on documents, white shiny collars, pomade that rots your pillow-cases, a husband who lives in a brief-case and eats computer rolls for breakfast. And a job – joy of joys, a job where people grumble and snore and scream at you round the clock, and you think you have done well if you have postponed another death for another day, and everyone plays on your sympathy because a well-fed widow with grown-up children must be stuffed to the eyebrows with sympathy – isn't that so? And no one needs sympathy before retiring age, you are all sure of that, it may be written in the constitution for all I know, and in any case grown-up children will be oozing out all the sympathy you might need. Isn't that what you think in this nice emotional corner you have made yourselves? And in a country that's pressed down and running over with kids, why should any old person be short of natural sympathy? Have you asked yourself that?'

'But, Matron,' Priscilla tried to intervene, 'we have not meant to be hard on you. If you do not tell us why you are sad, how are we to know? It is hard for us to be sure even how much you are aware of our separate feelings, for we do not always show. . . .'

'I know, I know, I know. I know as much as I can bear and I don't want to know any more.'

'My younger sister,' said Wairimu cautiously, 'even among ourselves we do not ask everything. It might be too hard for some to tell. We cannot ask you. But we should be honoured by what you may wish to tell us.'

'Oh no, oh no,' repeated Matron, crying quietly. 'There has been enough of telling. If I make myself vulnerable to you two there will be no end to it. Organisation is what you need. Haven't I always said so?'

She stood up and reverted to Swahili, measuring out words like rations.

'Let me know in the morning how those two have slept. Tell those people to keep the volume of the TV down, will you? And tell them I shall lock up the charcoal if they keep burning it at night. It is

151

dangerous. Do I make myself clear? The house burning down and me held responsible, that's all I need. Good night, then.'

And she rustled out, as though it were really a hospital ward and pills and specimens the heaviest of her concerns.

In fact Samuel was released without being brought to court. It happened that he had left a sales folder with some personal letters in it in the Kabete minibus and had run behind, shouting for the driver to stop. He had identified himself by giving the name and address on the letters, so this incident stuck in the conductor's mind. He had scrutinised the passenger carefully before handing over the folder and so was able to identify him and provide an alibi for the approximate time of the murder. Baraka had been seen alive as late as ten o'clock and his broken watch had stopped at half past ten, which fitted in with the police surgeon's estimate of time of death. His drinking companions had not seen him off because they knew that he sometimes called on a girl called Judy somewhere near the place where his body was found.

Samuel found himself trembling as he walked away from remand. He felt soiled to the skin, and was terrified of speaking to anyone before he had been home for a bath and a pot of tea. He held out his fare wordlessly in the *matatu*, afraid he was injuring the market women by being squeezed so closely against them. He still felt physically linked to that man he had once threatened, ignorant as he then was of what a threat implies, a man he had seen only once and come no nearer to touching than the lapel of a tailored jacket which he coveted. A man a little younger than himself, better-looking, he had to admit, cleverer, richer, who had, in that same flesh that now lay gelid in the mortuary, pawed at Mary, demurely greeted Gertrude, withstood with who knew what inner scars the searing knowledge of fire. A man with a father like his own, bowing his head to the jabs of printed words and dusty, dictated statement forms. A boy who had a granny like his own, whose jaw would sag and clatter with incredulity, whose spirit would bend and endure the suffering like any old Kikuyu woman's back heaving under its burdens. Would he ever separate himself from the unfathomed guilt that clung, not to himself but to that boy and the unknown hand that dealt out what he would once have seen as justice?

152

He walked a long way to the telephone box, not daring to enter any neighbour's house and ask to use the phone. He spoke to Gertrude, begging her to see him, and could not take in the fullness of her joy, the completeness of her faith. It was as though – he thought as he flagged down the *matatu* going towards the Nurses' Home – she did not even know that some people let down their loved ones, lost themselves rather than face them again, waited year after year for a certainty that could only fade. And then the conductor, grinning, came by to shake his hand.

It appeared that Sophia *had* seen her grandson. He often visited a friend in Eastleigh and one afternoon she had whispered to Nekesa, as they walked out for a breath of air,

'See, that is Baraka. He does not know me. Probably his father has told him that I am dead or gone to Mombasa. He is a medical student – I am not supposed to know, but I have ways of finding out. He is clever like his mother.'

She knew the soldier too. The old ladies often speculated about him among themselves. One day Sophia whispered in the street as he marched past,

'Do you think your mother may be dying here?' But he did not turn his head. He was still ashamed of running away: that seemed to her obvious. Sophia had not meant to be overheard, but Priscilla was behind with her sharp ears. Another time she had said loudly to Mama Chungu, in the soldier's hearing,

'You see that one getting out of the *matatu*? That is my grandson, a medical student.'

Once she had hissed at the man in front of Nekesa, 'Hey, you, do you not think it was your mother who was sent to the hospital for the students to practise on, and since she came back she has been worse, heh? My son abandoned me because he is a Muslim and sees it as his duty, but you abandoned her because you are a coward, heh?'

Nekesa whispered to her, 'Hush, he may even hit you. There is his stick and even young boys are afraid of him. And when Rahel was well it was up to her to say if she thought it was Vitalis.'

They did not forget, for when so little happens how can you forget any of it? But they did not speak, for when you have been so much hurt you do not open your sore place to any conceivable enemy. You suck up kindness where it comes and let some out when it gives you ease. But you see, as in your young years you never saw, that all your experience presses bitterly upon the present moment and all the things you have shared are separately enfolded in someone else's life. The tug at the cord, the spilt seed and the customary places round the hearth fall away, and sharing becomes a chance neighbourliness or a dangerous revelation.

Bessie remembered a time when the soldier had come at dusk behind her boy, slinking, not with his usual noisy step. She had cried out and the boy had seized the hand raising the iron club and talked soothingly and sent the man away to march out his jealousies. But she did not speak, for grief was dearer to her than speaking.

Nekesa had heard him muttering that death was for the young and cowardice for those who have more sense. But who would want to listen to such words? He passed big people in the street every day, who could take notice if they wished. Let the little people not be answerable for their neighbours.

One day the papers said 'a vagrant' had been found with Baraka's identity card. But he had several other identity cards as well, picked up, he said, outside the day and night clubs, and as he claimed not to be able to read he did not know what to do with them. So they did not charge him, but kept him under psychiatric care.

Mr Wau again began shouting accusations of witchcraft. A celebrated witchfinder was called up from Mombasa and found nothing to the purpose. Matron did not let him in to see Sophia, but he requested a sample of her clothing and for the sake of peace was allowed to examine a wrapper with some of her hairs adhering to it. These he pronounced to be Christian in character and free from malice.

The event was superseded by others. The old ladies kept up their quiet routine. One or two slipped away to die in hospital, one or two more were admitted, examined, clothed, absorbed, a nine-day flurry of gossip and then the broadening of the weight of experience, cessation of questions, harbouring of dreams. They found a separate room for Bessie and tried to see that she took sleeping tablets so that

154

the others were less disturbed. Sophia became a compulsive talker, telling them of the *beni* and the *dansi*, the First World War, the football clubs, the dock strike, the silver jubilee, with tales of djinns and demons and the arts of love. But the curtain of water and the curtain of fire she never touched again.

On the day Rahel was fading from them, Wairimu produced from some hidden place and laid on her pillow a silver paper medal tied with a broken bootlace. The old lady turned her vacant eyes and closed them again.

'Where did you find it?' asked Priscilla.

'Beside the body.'

'She has seen what she can see. Put it away now.'

Solemnly Wairimu picked up the medal and scraped a hole for it next time she went out to test the vegetables growing scrawny under the shadow of the wall.

Rahel's shoulders creaked as she fell back across the pillow, and the pain was too intense to turn. The bawdy wedding-song fell silent behind her slack lips and she was overcome with fear. They had reached the awesome place and the others should have known better than to go on singing. She tried to force her eyes open and seemed to fail, but that could not be, for from where she lay, the petticoat indecently rucked up, the sprawling arm dusty, withered, unoiled, she could see that the fearful tree was now clothed in blossom and birds were singing in the branches.

AFTERWORD

Marjorie Oludhe Macgoye has carved an impressive space for herself in the world of Kenyan literature, a remarkable accomplishment for an Englishwoman who came to her adoptive country when she was twenty-five years old.[1] She chose to make contemporary Kenya, its society and history, the setting and substance of her creative work. Her body of work—particularly her major novels, *Coming to Birth* and *The Present Moment*—constitutes a significant literary achievement in itself, and also in what it contributes to Kenyan literature: the long-muted voices of women, the long-absent sweep and variety of female experience in modern Kenya. The authenticity and sensitivity of her rendering of Kenyan life, more particularly of its working-class and poor women, have earned her the right to style herself as *nyarloka,* or "daughter from across the seas," which is reflected in the title of her first collection of poetry, *Song of Nyarloka and Other Poems.*

While there is a continuity of thematic focus in her fiction before and after *The Present Moment,* this novel represents Macgoye's finest work to date, presenting as it does a rich and complex weave of women's life stories anchored in Kenyan history. The central characters, seven women in a home for the aged homeless, relate or recall their humble lives of privation and constant struggle in the lower reaches of a hierarchical, androcentric, and rapidly changing society. The women's aspirations and circumstances are grounded in and shaped by the history, colonial and postcolonial, of their country. Their valiant attempts to maintain personal identity in the face of these forces mirrors the larger society's efforts to forge a nation out of an arbitrary creation named Kenya Colony.

•

Marjorie Macgoye herself experienced the meshing of identity and place. Born in Southampton, England, in 1928, she came to Kenya in 1954, the year after she obtained her M.A. in English from the University of London. She came initially as an Anglican lay missionary, at the height of the anticolonial Mau Mau insurgency. She lived in African neighborhoods in Nairobi between 1954 and 1960 when she worked for the Church Missionary Society bookstore. In a society where a rigid "color bar" operated, it was "one of the few public places where Africans were welcome and received attention" (*The Weekly Review* 30).

In 1960 Macgoye married a clinical officer, a Luo from Gem location in Nyanza province in western Kenya. This interracial marriage took place when Kenya still remained for the most part a racially segregated colony. It was also a period of heightened tensions between Africans and Europeans as it became apparent that Uhuru, or freedom, was imminent. (Kenya finally achieved independence from the British colonial power in December 1963.)

The Macgoyes moved to Kisumu, where Marjorie cared for their four children and taught high school English part time. Between 1975 and 1980 Macgoye and her family lived in Tanzania where she took up the post of manager of the University of Dar es Salaam bookstore. On returning to Kenya in 1975, she was appointed manager of S.J. Moore, one of Nairobi's major bookstores, and worked there for five years. Later she worked as a publishers' representative in eastern Africa between 1980 and 1982. Since 1983, she has combined her own writing with work as a free-lance editor.

During her early years in Kenya and after her marriage, Macgoye made a special effort to integrate herself into her adopted ethnic and national communities, a process which included learning to speak and write Dholuo and Kiswahili. She internalized the culture of her Kenyan family to a remarkable degree: "her people call her *min* Gem, or wife of Gem" (Ikonya 1994). A Luo critic has remarked with surprise at "the ease with which Marjorie talks about the traditions and customs of her adopted home," which has led people to assume "she must

158

have been born under the African sun" (Obyerodhyambo 6).

Macgoye has differed from most Europeans in pre- and postindependence Kenya, and from their successor African elites, in maintaining throughout her years in Kenya a modestly spare lifestyle, one akin to that of a wide swathe of Kenyan society. She uses public transport and lives in a rented apartment in a lower-middle-class neighborhood on the immediate outskirts of downtown Nairobi. To explain her preoccupations in her fiction with the urban poor, Macgoye harks back to her own English working-class origins: "I come from working people, I write mostly about working people" (letter 5). Typically down-to-earth and attuned to Kenyan realities, she responded sharply to an interviewer's question characterizing her modest lifestyle as one "at variance with that of most people [in Kenya]." Macgoye, realizing that the interviewer was referring to the elite, retorted, "I do not understand what you mean by 'most people' except in the sense that to most Kenyans I look stinking rich" (*Wajibu* 7).

Macgoye's intimacy and empathy with "working people" are evident in her novels, which depict the lives of the poor and outcast in Kenyan society. Evident too is her knowledge of the urban landscape her characters inhabit: the distinctive smells and sights of the streets and marketplaces of Nairobi, the decaying neighborhoods and slums that ring the capital city.

Interestingly, the trajectory of Macgoye's own life resembles that of her heroines in *Coming to Birth* and *The Present Moment.* They leave their homes by choice or, more usually, force of circumstance, and journey to their country's capital; it is a journey that is at once literal, psychological, and symbolic as the characters pursue their quest for a life, a living, and an identity. Macgoye's journey began in a different geographical location; she left her native land in answer to a missionary call to one of her country's African colonies. In Kenya she too "came to birth," as she found her personal and artistic destiny.

The journey to critical recognition was a lengthy one. Macgoye recalls that she experienced "constant rejections up to the mid-60s when my articles and poems started being published in East

African periodicals" (letter 1). Between 1970 and 1977 she published one novel and a collection of her poems. But the first work that brought her wide attention and critical acclaim was *Coming to Birth*, which won the British-based Sinclair Prize in 1986 for a novel of social and political significance, and was published in both East Africa and Britain in 1986. Following almost immediately upon this success, *The Present Moment* was published in 1987. Since then, Macgoye has engaged in a flurry of creative activity, publishing a novella (*Victoria*), two more novels (*Homing In* and *Chira*), and a second collection of poetry. She has also published nonfiction, including *A Story of Kenya* (1986) and *Moral Issues in Kenya* (1996) and children's books.

In the 1960s and 1970s few Kenyan women writers were widely published. The major women writers of the period were fiction writers Rebeka Njau, Grace Ogot, and Miriam Were, and playwright and poet Micere Mugo.[2] From the continent as a whole during that time came women writers Flora Nwapa and Buchi Emecheta (Nigeria), Ama Ata Aidoo (Ghana), Bessie Head (Botswana).[3]

The lack of a major "author-itative" female presence in Kenyan literature, until Macgoye published her major novels in the late 1980s, reflects a larger female social exclusion, the consequence of precolonial, colonial, and postcolonial male assumptions and biases regarding "woman's place" in a male-ordered universe. The dearth of women's writing was itself partly an effect of colonial and postcolonial neglect of women's welfare and development, including scant access to education. Further, women, weighed down with responsibilities of caring for the physical and financial needs of their families, lack the time and supportive networks required for literary production. Even today, male primacy usually reigns in private and public spaces, evidenced by the rarity of a female presence in the country's social, business, and political institutions, and in its policy-making bodies.

In the 1980s there was a flowering of women's fiction around the continent. Women were being educated in larger numbers all over Africa. Consequently, they were more aware of their rights and were articulate in demanding them. They were more determined to survive and better their position in society. These new expectations were reflected in the work of anglophone novelists such as Macgoye, Emecheta, and Lauretta Ngcobo and francophone writers such as Aminata Sow Fall and Mariama Bâ.[4] Crucially, too, there emerged a new generation of critics— African and Western—eager to study and support women's voices out of Africa. They did so at conferences and seminars, in college courses and classrooms, and by devoting critical studies[5] to the work of African women writers.

Despite this progress, the critical-publishing establishment in Africa continued to display an androcentric attitude toward the work of women writers. Revealing of the critical neglect of female writers are three significant studies of "the African Novel" written between the early 1970s and late 1980s. Among them the trio of male critics managed to focus in depth on the work of seventeen African novelists, not one of whom is female.[6]

In *Coming to Birth* and *The Present Moment*, Macgoye sets herself the task of dramatizing how twentieth-century Kenyan history set in motion changes that contributed to the process of women's emancipation in the country. In both novels Macgoye focuses attentively on working-class women struggling to make lives for themselves, to wrest a living and a modicum of autonomy within a rapidly changing society.

The historical scope of *Coming to Birth* is limited to twenty-two years in the life of a single woman, in the years before and after Kenyan independence. *The Present Moment* is more ambitious. In a rich and densely worked text, and for the first time, a Kenyan novelist offers a multifaceted, complex women's perspective on Kenyan history and society over the last century. Macgoye does so by presenting, in their own words or through their memories, the stories of seven women in the Refuge for elderly homeless women. Their lives cover a wide span of Kenyan history: from the early years when British colonial rule was establishing itself, through two world wars, world economic depression, local labor unrest, violent anticolonial resistance, and into the triumphant but profoundly problematic postcolonial period.

In *The Present Moment* history, the engine of societal and polit-

161

ical change, does not function as impersonal force, nor as theater featuring the exploits of "great men." Neither is history in the novel a mere backdrop, the enumeration of significant dates and events signposting a privatized account of the domestic lives of the women protagonists. Rather, Kenyan history—colonial and postcolonial—is the very matrix within which the novel's characters struggle, aspire, suffer, act, and endure. History in *The Present Moment* is that precise location where individual character, choice, contingency, desire, and hope coalesce with the opportunities, tragedies, and possibilities enabled by radical social, cultural, and political change. The personal and public are fused as one plays out within and against the other; women and nation struggle, often against great odds, to "come to birth" by finding an identity.

Moreover, history in *The Present Moment* does not live safely corralled in the past. Priscilla and Rahel uneasily reflect that "one is never quite safe from reminders" (77) as "sounds of the past kept on reverberating" in the present moment (10). In addition to the old women's articulated remembrances, others lie just under the surface, and still others rise unexpectedly and painfully: "But memories . . . need not speak in loud voices. They may gibber at a tantalising distance like a bat in the rafters, or swoop upon you like a moth, soundless but soiling you with a residue of filmy substance" (34–35). Indeed, the weight of their past experiences "presses bitterly upon the present moment" (154).

History has been synonymous with far-reaching social change in African communities such as those of precolonial Kenya. These societies were profoundly shaken, fractured, and irretrievably changed by the intrusion of technologically superior European imperial powers in the late nineteenth and twentieth centuries. While traditional communities were not static, they offered their members a relatively stable and conservative environment. The thematic heart of *The Present Moment* concerns what colonialism and continuing change wrought, for good and ill, in the lives of African women and men.

Change registers in women characters' lives both as loss and as opportunity. With the coming of the new colonial order, as Nduta,

162

owner of the tearoom where Wairimu worked, tells her, "all the old rules [were] set aside" (24). The old village support networks and familial relationships frayed and sometimes snapped under the strain. The chaotic new world of the towns, mushrooming everywhere, provided little safety for women, throwing them back on their own resources. Simultaneously and most crucially, this changing world also presented women with possibilities—an expanding arena for work, mobility, autonomy, choice—that were both a blessing and, especially for earlier generations of women, a curse.

Of the seven protagonists of *The Present Moment,* only Wairimu voluntarily reached out to the new world beyond her village home. The others were forced out by circumstances. Wairimu "goes to the coffee," picking coffee beans on white-owned farms. Her compatriots at the Refuge variously engaged in small business, including prostitution for some, or they went into domestic service for white *bwanas* and *memsahibs.* All led hardscrabble lives, always one misfortune away from disaster and penury.

From one perspective, considering the emotional and material losses they sustained, the women were the victims of change. One could describe the denizens of the Refuge as a sorority of suffering. Their children died or disappeared from their lives. Husbands and lovers died or betrayed and abandoned them. They were forced to eke out a spare living on the bare edges of poverty. They lost their livelihoods through economic depression and the violence visited on them by the minions of the state.

But change can also be understood as an inducement to growth. To survive, individual women relied on their mother wit, skills, and inner resources, and on their network of female friends and relations. However limited the scope allowed them in their precarious lives, these women got to exercise some choice. When Rahel's husband died suddenly, she struck out on her own, rejecting the custom of being "inherited" by one of her late husband's male relatives: "After the town kind of life we lived in quarters, I didn't much like the idea of being inherited by some old man in Uyoma" (38). The widowed Sophia, once named Fatuma, risked her Swahili-Islamic family's disapproval to marry the African Christian man with whom she fell in love. The Seychelloise Mama Chungu's whole life was one open, throbbing wound— dead babies, a callous, abusive white lover, a series of dead-end jobs, hunger, and the humiliation of being driven by desperation to beg in public—yet even she made decisions. Partly prompted by anger at her lover's treatment of her, she undermined his work in the security forces during the Mau Mau insurgency by becoming a message carrier on the African side.

Above all, these seven old women are survivors, individuals who "had special griefs . . . and special gifts to have survived so many griefs" (150). The Vicar notes that "to be eighty years old in Africa is to be tough. Particularly for a woman, because she has learned from childhood to look after others rather than to be looked after" (38).

The Refuge, a Christian-run, charitable old women's home, functions as the site in which the women talk about and reflect on their pasts. It embodies the paradoxes that constitute their lives and experiences. Though spartan, it provides the women with a haven from utter destitution. Here their physical and spiritual needs are ministered to, and within its shelter they create a "lively and comradely" community (55). Despite their bickering, their petty jealousies and resentments, the women offer one another small courtesies and kindnesses which lead Matron to observe that the "community has a strength of its own" (8).

However, the very existence of the Refuge is a testament to social change in Kenyan society. In a period of transition, the women, as Matron notes, were "dwarfed by disasters without any savings or security to relieve them" (36). At the same time, in the absence of children, spouses, siblings, and community, they were bereft of all familial succor and the respect and care accorded the aged in the traditional extended family and community. They have no place to call home. Priscilla reminds Wairimu of this when the latter, in a fit of exasperation at Sophia, demands to know why she is not sent "back to Mombasa." Priscilla tells Wairimu what the latter already knows: "Why didn't they send you and me back to Nyeri? Because there is no one to look after us there" (27). Later in the novel, Rahel alludes to the lost anchorings of home and family ties. "But do you not have any people at all?" Wairimu inquires of Rahel, who responds, "We don't always know. It doesn't seem possible, does it? When we were young, we could not have helped knowing, because everybody was attached to a place" (43–44).

The radical change that the colonial and postcolonial periods wrought in Kenya's indigenous communities in far less than a century—both the mobility and choices it opened up to the novel's characters as well as the sufferings and losses it inflicted on them—is most comprehensively embodied in Wairimu, the oldest and boldest of the novel's protagonists. She stands apart from the others: her restless and questing temperament, and the longings it engendered, meshed well with the historical moment. The new ways were not imposed on her; she grabbed at them hungrily and with both hands. Spunky, adventurous, curious, and mentally agile, she longed for more than the "cloying sameness" (3) afforded by life on the ridge of her rural home in Nyeri.

Wairimu's life story lies at the center of the novel. The opening paragraph simultaneously introduces the reader to the young girl and signals the changes already in process in her rural environment, the icons and heralds of an encroaching alien world of trains and trade and material goods: "On Wairimu's left arm was a metal bangle her brother brought back from Nairobi when he went there to see the train and conduct some mysterious business with rupees and skins" (1).

In old age, Wairimu fondly recalls the young man she met briefly on a village path. Encircled by "a halo of sunlight" (2), Waitito was a "fairy tale" figure to the adolescent girl. His stories of Nairobi and "his shirt and shorts, his wide-brimmed hat and sandals, his knowledge of the world and other ways" (2) marked him as both an emissary from and symbol of that enticing new world. He was the pied piper who fired the young woman's imagination and her desire to explore that beckoning world. But in reality, she appears to have been seduced less by Waitito than by the intoxicating future his stories seemed to promise her. Significantly, this "fairy tale" figure did not carry the girl he seduced away to that new and wondrous world of "dreams" and "marvels"; she had to seek it out and cope with it herself.

Powerfully drawn to that new world, Wairimu set out before a marriage could be arranged for her on her odyssey of exploration, experience, and learning. It took her "to the coffee" near home, then to the big city. In most male-authored African literature, the rural girl who leaves for the city's bright lights can only expect physical and moral ruin. But sexual freedom and experience constitute only part of the young Wairimu's life. The new world she set out to taste and master offered satisfactions for various yearnings: for independence, for participation in the anticolonial struggle, for broadening of the mind, and for freedom to make choices and to learn about and explore her world.

When Wairimu recalls her earlier life in reveries and stories, the narrative assumes the wonderful energy and buoyancy of a young woman "awed," "amazed," "interested" in, and "delighted" by life's possibilities and fully engaged with the world around her. When she arrived in Nairobi, she drank in the sights before her, made plans, set herself goals, and executed decisions. In the process, she blossomed into her own person, forged her own identity.

Initially Wairimu was awed by the big city, but she slowly carved out a niche for herself there. Wairimu's story is a female bildungsroman—the education of a young Kikuyu woman across half a century. Her life was dominated by "learning" of different kinds. We are told that she "reveled in her own ability to learn" (24). She learned from observation of other women's lives. She rejected the traditional hard laboring life of a Kikuyu woman: "the daily tramp for water, digging and shelling, peeling and digging again, bent under firewood." Perceiving that other women live differently, she concludes that "[her] body, too, can be respected":

> Already, at eighteen, I had seen that it is not necessary to being a woman to be bent against the painful forehead-strap, with a little hump down on your spine and danger in bearing children because of it. I have seen hairy white women, big-eyed

166

Indian women, big-nosed Arab women, big-boned, charcoal-black women all standing straight and not lacking for food and fire and water. (55)

In Nairobi Wairimu was as eager to learn "a new concept of elegance" from Somali women as she was to note the independent lives of young white female shop assistants and secretaries who "earned their own money" (25).

She learned Swahili "not in order to be a servant [in European households] . . . but to enter a wider world than the Kikuyu world, to understand Nairobi, . . . to go home with power" (54). She learned from her Sundays spent exploring the big city and from train trips: "You learn something if you travel on our railway," she assures her listeners at the Refuge (98).

In the city, too, Wairimu became politically aware. She plunged into the nascent political life of Nairobi, feeling "an urgent need to participate, to make herself also known. She was about seventeen years old and she too was part of a new world" (23). She was one of the crowd who responded to Harry Thuku's protest meeting against steep colonial taxes and forced female labor. The meeting was dispersed by the police with violence and bloodshed, but Wairimu "learned something about power that day" (49). Some twenty-five years later, she participated in a much larger and bloodier resistance to colonial rule when she joined the Mau Mau movement as member and recruiter. In telling about these experiences, she reveals something of the much-neglected role of Kenyan women in the struggle for justice and freedom. At the Thuku riot in the early twenties, for instance, Wairimu joined "a big group of women." When the men were ready to give up, it was the "women [who] called the men cowards and urged them to fight it out" (47–48). And, long after, Wairimu remembers the heroism of one of the murdered leaders of that doomed meeting:

Not many people were like Mary Nyanjiru, who had a song sung about her even after she died outside the police lines. . . . We used to sing it all the time, and I still sing it now when I need to get my courage up. (54)

167

Wairimu's learning also encompassed the widespread disillusionment of the postcolonial period. The farm where Wairimu picked coffee was bought by a fellow Kikuyu. The workers "rejoiced. But not for long. We found ourselves turned away, new clansmen brought in: they said we were too political, bargaining, counting hours." In telling her story, Wairimu sarcastically notes that "fighting for land and freedom we had not grudged the hours, or money either." She concludes with resignation. "But so it was. At seventy one does not expect consideration" (113). Eventually, Wairimu landed at the Refuge after her "little [tea] kiosk [was] kicked to pieces by uniformed men [municipal police] doing their duty to build the nation" (114).

Central to Wairimu's early life—and what enabled her growing self-confidence and independence—was that she became a wage earner and therefore "a chooser and a doer": "At the end of the month you got some money, and so you were like a man and could do a lot of choosing for yourself" (18). On one of Wairimu's visits home, her mother, commenting on her daughter's single state, suggested that "sometimes it is better to be humiliated than alone." For her part, Wairimu rejoiced that "the dowry of learning" she received from her ex-lover was paid to her rather than to her father. She tried to explain to her father why her ex-lover, James, did not get her "so cheap": "He taught me to read. That is not a little thing. He taught me how to live in a cement house and keep it clean. That is also something people pay money for their daughters to learn" (61). Hugging her "new knowledge and her growing horizon" to herself (95), Wairimu had "learned a lot . . . about how the world works" (57).

Even as a young woman she could appreciate what Waitito gave her in exchange for her virginity:

As I picked [coffee], I thought and thought, and I realised that this was the gift Waitito had given me in return for what he took from me. He had opened a door through which one could see picture after picture, more lively and colourful than the black, dead pictures which get on to each side of a page

168

on a newspaper, and try oneself out on each, accepting or
rejecting. Before there had been pictures—Wairimu, girl—
Wairimu, bride—Wairimu, mother—Wairimu, elder's wife
—Wairimu, grandmother—but nothing to choose between
them, only to be chosen. (54)

The lives of the old women in the Refuge contrast with those
of a new generation of Kenyan women. These young nurses
and community health workers in training already have more choices than Wairimu had. Each nurse cares for an old woman, listens
to her stories, and eventually confides in her. Macgoye has carefully paired younger and older women who share something in
common. Mary reveals to Wairimu her distress over a boyfriend's
betrayal, which summons up for the older woman her own
betrayal by Waitito, the man whom she forgave because he introduced her to a life in which she could make choices. One way in
which Wairimu consoles her younger friend is by making her aware
that she already enjoys more opportunities than Wairimu did in
her youth. Jane bonds with Bessie because both have lost loved
ones in the aftermath of the attempted coup d'état in 1982.
Priscilla, prim and proper because of her own experiences in life—
abandonment by her new husband, Evans, and an incident of bloody
horror during the Emergency—sees in Gertrude her own younger,
robust, and passionate self; this allows her to unbend enough to
reveal her story to the young woman, already engaged to be married to Mary's brother. Nekesa feels an empathy with Judy, the young
prostitute, and encourages her to seek a new life and redemption,
much as Nekesa herself did.

The younger women take for granted opportunities for which
Wairimu's generation had to struggle. When Wairimu had first
come to Nairobi, and after "the golden haze over the city
turn[ed] black and smoky, . . . [and] the dream had turned into
a nightmare" of urban sleaze and danger (49), Nduta coun-
seled: "Go today—go now. The town is not yet ready for you. Unless
you have a man—a husband, best, or a father to speak for you,
but at least a steady man—you get the worst of the bargain here.
. . . One day it may well be different," (50). Six decades later, that

day has come, as Wairimu makes clear to Jane: "I think I would be a nurse if I were young now. But in my day there were only two choices, picking coffee or looking after men" (15). When she relates her own story to Mary, Wairimu explains why she chose to go to the coffee: "It was one way of choosing for yourself. Otherwise for girls there was almost no choice. . . . For girls there were very few school places and as yet little choice. . . . The girl had no alternative to marriage until the coffee came" (17).

Having situated *The Present Moment* within a feminist framework, it becomes necessary to respond to Macgoye's reluctance to identify herself as a feminist writer.[7] In this regard, she is similar to other African women writers who "like to declare that they are not feminists, as if it were a crime to be a feminist" (Ogundipe-Leslie 11). Ogundipe-Leslie remarks on the paradox that "these denials come from unlikely writers such as Bessie Head, Buchi Emecheta, even Mariama Bâ," all of whose repudiations of feminism are belied by the content of their fiction: "Yet, nothing could be more feminist than the writings of these women writers, in their concern for and deep understanding of the experiences and fates of women in society" (11). Ogundipe-Leslie attributes this hesitation of African women writers to accept a feminist label to "the successful intimidation of African women by men over the issues of women's liberation and feminism. Male ridicule, aggression, and backlash have resulted in making women apologetic and have given the term 'feminist' a bad name" (11). Several writers, including Macgoye herself, have articulated their own reasons for rejecting the term—most prominently, its close association with Western feminism, not always at home in an African context.[8]

In such a contradictory situation, perhaps the most productive course a reader of Macgoye's work might follow is that suggested by D. H. Lawrence when he counsels readers to trust the tale, not the teller. Turning to *The Present Moment,* it becomes abundantly evident that Macgoye focuses closely and sympathetically on the difficult lives of her female characters and on their brave efforts to survive in desperate circumstances.

170

Moreover, she has lavished much care, affection, and pride on the most prominent of these characters, Wairimu. Spice is correct when, in his review of *The Present Moment,* he writes:

> Macgoye seems to have most affinity with Wairimu . . . [who] is granted the most developed self-consciousness, so she emerges as the Everywoman figure, the character whose destiny the reader takes to be representative, and around whom the destinies of the other characters group themselves. (4)

Wairimu is a feminist born ahead of her time. She is a strong, quick-witted, resilient woman, and throughout her life she has been curious about the world she lived in and anxious to improve herself. She remains free of self-pity. Boldly, she made her life choices—above all, rejecting the fixed "pictures," or limited roles, set out for women in her community.

The changes which overtook Kenyan society in the twentieth century resulted in the redefinition and extension of the concept of "home," with repercussions, both positive and negative, on the lives of the novel's women characters. Wairimu, a Kikuyu, chose in her youth to leave her rural home to explore the new life on the coffee plantations and in Nairobi. Her younger colleague Nekesa was hardly acquainted with a rural home; Nekesa, a Luhyia "understood Lubukusu and some of the related dialects that made up Ololuyia, but it had never been a major language of her life and never since early childhood had she visited the home village or shared in the digging of those little overcrowded plots" (115).

Most of the protagonists' experiences away from their rural homes were unremittingly harsh. Nekesa was a prostitute in Kampala, Uganda, for much of her life. Wairimu's "golden haze" became besmirched. Bessie eked out a precarious existence in the slums of Eastleigh after her rural home was destroyed during the anticolonial insurgency. Mama Chungu was reduced to increasingly menial and exhausting jobs, and finally to begging in the streets. Lacking are the safety nets of home on the ridges and in the villages. Children die or disappear, as do siblings, spouses, and lovers. The women have to summon up their own meager resources just to survive, and they are especially vulnerable in old age. Just ending up at the Refuge is a concession of defeat.

Yet the new opportunities and possibilities for women which also developed in this era altered women's sense of "home." Mobility, owing to coercion or choice, widened the horizons, consciousness, and skills of the women in their youth. As an army wife, Rahel followed her husband to the barracks far from their rural home and "learned to read there and to look after a military house" (13). Wairimu had more choice and independence and learned more than she would have had she stayed at home: "She could not settle back to life within the ridge. That would neither expel her fear nor satisfy even the narrowest part of her dream" (50).

In *The Present Moment,* mobility is only one agent of change in an already complex definition of "home." In common with most other African countries, Kenya, paradoxically, is an artificial creation. The nation's geographic outlines were determined by European great powers' colonial rivalries in the late nineteenth century. In the "scramble for Africa," many indigenous communities were divided by imperially imposed borders. The new borders often brought together a multitude of ethnicities: native, colonial, and immigrant. In any given African colony, the colonized ethnic groups had to build alliances among themselves, often despite old antipathies, in order to eject the colonizers. In the novel, we see the development of this more inclusive consciousness and coalition building begin quite early on, after the Thuku rally ends in failure:

> In fact, what was happening was Nairobi drawing together, becoming, on the African side, a community. . . . Most of us were Kikuyu, it is true, in that meeting, but everybody knew what was going on, even the Somali and the Luo kept their children home from school and their wives from mar-

ket that day. . . . The ground was ready and the community began to grow. (46)

The Refuge itself epitomizes the changing nature of "home." As an institution for elderly homeless women, it is a product of the new society where charity must sometimes provide what the family and community once did. The very need for an institution of this kind tells us something about the social changes that have overtaken traditional African communities. Natural communities of "filiation"—in which the group into which one is born assures one's ties, status, and welfare for life—have gradually been replaced by a society increasingly marked by "affiliation"—in which individuals choose to ally themselves with a group of relative or total strangers, for example with one or another Christian religious denomination, or a trade union.

Simultaneously, the Refuge functions as a microcosm of the nation's ethnic heterogeneity. Of the seven protagonists, three are Kikuyu, and one each Luo, Luhyia, Swahili, and Seychelloise. At the Refuge, they live out a larger, more commodious and inclusive conception of "home," one which encompasses a Kenyan nation of various ethnicities. The nation's heterogeneity is most evident in Sophia's life story. She is a Swahili who comes from Mombasa's Old Town, mostly inhabited by Arab Muslims who "considered themselves a cut above the inland people, Christians or pagans, kaffirs all, except for a few who had seen the light and were beginning to follow civilised ways" (31). In order to counter Arab Kenyan legislative power and to win better wages and labor conditions, the Muslim Swahilis (a coastal people, the product of African-Arab intermarriage over the centuries), including Sophia's husband, Ali, a docker, throw their political lot in with upcountry Africans, many of whom are Christian: "So Swahilis had begun to talk about unity with inland Africans, and once one started to think about them as brothers it was impossible not to see that they were suffering" (31). Later, after her husband's death and after she has traveled a bit, Sophia can begin to move beyond her provincial insularity:

She smiled and tried to think about Kenya. She had been
a short way up and down the coast but never a dozen miles
inland. But some of the women she talked with in the market had come from as far as Kisumu, two nights' journey
on the train, to visit their husbands working in the docks.
All this was Kenya and all those people were Kenya too. (66)

The women at the Refuge do indulge in petty bickering and
stereotype one another. Rahel, a Luo, harbors unflattering views
of Kikuyus, thinking of "the terrible bent backs of their burdened
women" in contrast to the Luo women with their "graceful carriage and a steadily balanced water-pot" (14). Wairimu complains
about Sophia: "fat and flabby and flaunting herself like a young
girl. Look at her hands—never did a hard day's work in her life.
And all those bangles—*jingili, jingili, jingili!*" (27). Sophia
despises all her mates as "faded old ladies," lacking in sophistication and whose Swahili is "dull and devoid of ornament" (32–33).

But alongside the squabbling, a sisterhood develops among
these old women. A fine example of this solidarity and care for
one another occurs at the beginning of the novel:

"[Rahel] is very weak," frowned one of the nurses. . . .
"Don't you think she would be better in hospital?"
"No," said Wairimu firmly. "She likes the company of people she knows. She is better here with us. . . ."
"But isn't it depressing for the rest of you?"
"She got worse last time they took her to hospital," put
in Sophia. "And it's not depressing to have her here. What
would be depressing is to think that we would be kicked out
if we got like her." (7)

The author underlines the redefining and widening of "home"
and "community" by enmeshing the characters in a network of
links, most of which they themselves—and the reader—become
aware of only as the mysteries in the novel are gradually revealed.
Reverend Andrew, who visits the Refuge, might be the son of Evans,
the husband who deserted Priscilla. The half-crazy Vitalis who

parades outside the Refuge might be Rahel's missing son. Sophia might have unwittingly precipitated the murder of her own grandson, a medical student, when she maliciously hinted, within Vitalis's hearing, that Rahel's condition has worsened after she was "experimented" on by medical students at the nearby hospital; the author suggests that Vitalis was the murderer. It is likely that Henry/Kinyozi, Sophia's second husband and the one who left her, is the freedom fighter whose cause Mama Chungu aided, but neither woman speaks about him. The sheer number and weight of coincidences linking the characters seems implausible from a realistic point of view. But Macgoye seems to be suggesting a deeper truth concerning how Kenyans are all linked in one way or another, echoing Priscilla's employer's view that "in one place or another we were all strangers and pilgrims" (65).

Like the sisal rope that Rahel dreams her long-dead uncle is braiding (4), the novel's narrative is structured around the life stories of its seven main characters; their stories constitute the skeins and strands of a shared history, but one approached from different locations, cultures, experiences and animated by differing temperaments and aspirations.

In a culture and literature where women's voices have long been muffled and marginalized, the seven central characters directly address their life stories to one another, to various individuals who visit the Refuge, and to themselves, retrospectively. Their stories are not filtered through the single, authoritative voice of an omniscient narrator. Macgoye captures with remarkable fidelity the very cadences of Kenyan speech in all its variety. The author's voice and sophistication do not distort or overwhelm the voices of her humble characters.

Further, there is an immediacy to the characters' stories. As the narrative shifts from the storytelling site of the Refuge, in the novel's "present," to the places and scenes of the women's event-filled past lives, the young women within the old women come alive in all their complexity, and mesh with the present of the Refuge. Time becomes multilayered in *The Present Moment,* without sacrificing realism, authenticity, and vitality.

175

An important aspect of the author's art in shaping the novel, and of its richness, is the multilayered quality of mundane objects. The Refuge, for example, is the very real home of the novel's protagonists and the "venue" of their storytelling. Viewed from another angle, the Refuge might be seen as a microcosm of contemporary Kenyan society. The tree is another image with multiple meanings, which sometimes shift and collide with one another. The "image of the dead tree" (3) that Rahel recalls in old age might stand for the neglected and abandoned traditional culture. Later, when the sorrowing young woman Jane, whose boyfriend has been killed, thinks a vision of the cross beckons her to give her life in service as a nun, the tree segues into the Christian symbol: "After John died, I just wandered about at home, when I had time off, and I always seemed to come on a tall tree, with branches like a cross, calling me. I think that is what it meant" (128). The novel closes with the dying Rahel again seeing "the fearful tree," but shorn of its menace; now, "clothed in blossom" and with "birds . . . singing in the branches," it becomes a symbol of hope, even triumph (155).

The novel's structure creates space for social "voices from below" of the marginalized in more than one way: these are not only women's voices but also the voices of the poor. Most often, these voices are drowned out, and these people are spoken for by the privileged—the educated, moneyed, politically powerful—who dominate the means of communication in any society. This has been especially true in authoritarian Kenya both under colonial and postcolonial rulers. Spice notes of the novel's protagonists that the text "bears witness to the predicament of a true underclass" (4).

Macgoye is quite aware of what she is doing in providing a "forum" in her novel for those voices of the "underclass"—old, poor, homeless women, the least powerful or noticed in society—as they tell the stories of their lives. Through her central character, Wairimu, the author characterizes these stories:

> The stories we learned when we were children were all
> about big people—braver, stronger, fiercer, cleverer, even wicked-

176

er, than anyone we knew. The ordinary people got passed off as hares or hyenas or birds. But if we knew the secrets of those little people, or the littleness of the big people—what they were afraid of, what they were mean over, what they wasted— then there would be the true story of our people. (88)

Important, too, is that in recalling their past lives, the old women re-create themselves, give a shape and significance to what most would regard as lives of meager import or interest. With their stories and memories, the old women build a figurative structure around themselves—a structure which confers dignity on them even as it creates an inviolate interior space for meaning, privacy, and peace. This "structure" is at the same time the novel and Macgoye's own art—the weave of memory, experience, history—at work:

> Each of [the old women] had woven through the years a framework of shelter, as the Boran woman keeps the folded structure of her house on camel-back beside her, so that the tent fabric of the Refuge . . . could stretch above it without encroaching on the private place within. (150)

The novel's form assumes importance in another way. Through her characters' stories, Macgoye dramatizes how "the present moment" has been shaped by historical constraint and opportunity, by individual circumstance and choice. Part of the challenge "the present moment" poses to readers—particularly to Kenyan readers—is the challenge of nationhood, of living in a pluralistic society. They are confronted with issues such as the need to balance competing loyalties to clan, class, and community with the vision of an inclusive and just society; to create a Kenyan mosaic from numerous ethnicities, cultures, and histories. Macgoye's heterogeneous weaving of the historical and personal, in addition to demonstrating the interconnectedness of Kenyan lives, creates just such a mosaic.[8]

Mikhail Bakhtin's notion of the polyphonic and the dialogical inheres in the very structure of *The Present Moment*.[9] The women's stories, individually and collectively, refract each other and provide a different angle from which they and the reader can view a single historical event. Each story modulates and extends, adds to, even at times undermines all the rest. History is not monolithic, but variously experienced and endured. In coming to understand this, the characters are better able to accommodate their individual selves to a relatively harmonious existence within the heterogeneous community of the Refuge. For example, Rahel, a Luo, concedes that the brunt of colonial dispossession and oppression fell on the Kikuyu. Referring to the harsh time of the Emergency and the Kikuyu insurgency against the colonizers, Rahel remarks to Priscilla: "But I admit it was a tough time for you in the fifties. . . . We were taught to feel superior to [the Kikuyu freedom fighters] and with their jobs and houses falling our way it wasn't too hard" (35).

Similarly, all the main characters are centrally or tangentially involved in or affected by the Mau Mau movement. But their responses to memories of the movement differ radically. Priscilla and Wairimu are both Kikuyu from Nyeri. The former anxiously represses memories of the Emergency because during that period she suffered a searing and traumatizing experience: the white family she and her father worked for was attacked by Mau Mau fighters; Priscilla's father and the young white child she looked after were brutally murdered; the child's screams and the blood from her slit throat continue to haunt Priscilla. Wairimu was a member of and recruiter for the Mau Mau movement. She too has memories of some of the darkness of that time, of "the silent garrote and the evening roadblock" (45), and of the loss of good friends. But for Wairimu the insurgency represented a necessary fight for freedom:

> One let no tears be seen for those emergency losses. Others I lost respect for, gabbling the solemn oath only to save their skins, or making use of it to aggrandise themselves. But many stood firm, through fire, suspicion, deep double meanings and a web of trust. (113)

The novel's main characters are all nominally Christians, but the promptings and circumstances that led to their adoption of this alien faith were rather different. Sophia, a Muslim, converted for love of her second husband. Nekesa, once a prostitute, was moved to embrace her faith owing to the kindness and care shown to her by a Christian group when she was injured and helpless: "Every day one or other of the group was around, begging me to praise the Lord. Do you wonder that I did? No one had ever taken that much trouble over me before" (138). Nekesa's religious earnestness ("The New Testament was all she wanted to hear. She had come to it late and couldn't have enough of it," [89]) is in sharp contrast to Wairimu's pragmatism. The latter was seemingly motivated to accept Christianity as much by the opportunity it gave her to learn to read and gain knowledge as by personal conviction: "Ostensibly a baptism class of the Church of Scotland, [the evening school on the coffee farm where she worked] attracted many men and boys who wished to learn to read and a few women. . . . [Wairimu] was thrilled by the new knowledge she found in [the gospels] and the absorbing puzzle of working the words out. In 1939 she was baptised Mary" (94–95). Wairimu was able to hold in easy balance her Christian faith on the one hand, and on the other, her nationalist fervor and her role within the anti-Christian Mau Mau movement: "[In 1952] meetings were being called to oath as many as five hundred people at a time. . . . But me, I was very careful. I never missed church— in any case, I enjoyed going to church" (112).

The style of *The Present Moment* is characterized by simplicity of language, a seeming artlessness that belies the patterning involved in a work of art. The intricate plot ties the characters' present to their past, links their lives, and anchors them in the turbulent history of their country in the twentieth century.

Finally, the gentle underlying force of *The Present Moment,* as of all Macgoye's fiction, is the author's compassionate tone and inclusive vision, which is possibly influenced by her strong Christian faith. For understandable reasons, much African fiction has displayed a bitterness toward the colonial past and bleak disillusionment with and antagonism toward the postcolonial

179

present. Macgoye is concerned with important social, political, and gender issues in *The Present Moment,* but her authorial persona is not programmatic, shrill, or hectoring. This is not to say that Macgoye's critical judgment is blunted by "niceness." Her insights are sharp and she can be tart, even when the subject is close to her own heart. But nothing human is alien to her, and no voice is ignored or excluded, not the weakest or most abrasive of characters. Macgoye's is a quiet voice. She shows, not tells. She dramatizes how issues play out in the lives of these individual women, and the identity and the vision of each woman is accepted and gathered into the whole in Macgoye's generous telling.

Valerie Kibera
Ontario, Canada
June 2000

Notes

1. Just how remarkable Macgoye's position is becomes evident when one compares her work with that of two other European writers—Isak Dinesen (Karen Blixen) and Elspeth Huxley—who lived in Kenya for long periods of time and whose Kenya-based works (*Out of Africa* and *Shadows on the Grass* by Dinesen, *The Flame Trees of Thika* by Huxley) are much admired in the West. Both authors write lovingly about their years in Kenya. Neither was totally unsympathetic to her African "characters." But, given their own situation as part of the white ruling class in a British colony, they could present only the colonial, European perspective of their times. Neither Dinesen's or Huxley's work is without interest or artistic merit. But it is irrelevant today in a way that Macgoye's is not.

2. See Njau's *Ripples in the Pool*, Ogot's *The Promised Land, Land Without Thunder*, and *The Other Woman*, Were's *The Eighth Wife* and *Your Heart Is My Altar*, and Mugo, *Daughter of My People, Sing!* and *The Long Illness of Ex-Chief Kiti*.

3. See, for example, Nwapa's *Efuru* and *Idu*; Head's *When Rain Clouds Gather, Maru, A Question of Power*, and *The Collector of Treasures*; Aidoo's *Our Sister Killjoy: or, Reflections from a Black-Eyed Squint*; Emecheta's *Second-Class Citizen, In the Ditch, The Slave Girl, The Joys of Motherhood* and *Double Yoke*.

4. See Ngcobo's *Cross of Gold* and *And They Didn't Die*; Fall's *The Beggars' Strike*; Bâ's *So Long a Letter* and *Scarlet Song*.

5. Prominent among these critical studies are a study by Oladele Taiwo and two collections, one edited by Peterson, the other by Jones.

6. Critical works that entirely neglect women writers include Palmer, Gakwandi, and Gikandi. Brown's *Women Writers in Black Africa* was a welcome exception.

7. Macgoye comments on feminism in her interview with Telleh-Lartey, in Ikonya's profile, and in her letter to the author.

8. Perhaps because of her insider outsider status in her adoptive country, Macgoye is especially attuned to the ethnic heterogeneity and cultural hybridity of Kenyan society. She reared her own children on the assumption that they should be able to steer their way with grace and flexibility "in a polyglot country where they are going to meet people with wide disparities of lifestyle and belief" (*Wajibu* 7).

9. Mikhail Bakhtin's dialogism, with its notion of the heteroglossic nature of human life and art, enables especially rewarding readings of literary texts such as Macgoye's, which reflect our present world of overlapping, hybrid, and interdependent cultures. See particularly *The Dialogic Imagination* and *Problems of Dostoevsky's Poetics*.

Works Cited

Aidoo, Ama Ata. *Changes*. 1991. New York: Feminist Press at CUNY, 1993.

———. *Our Sister Killjoy: or, Reflections from a Black-Eyed Squint*. London: Longman, 1977.

Bâ, Mariama. *Scarlet Song*. Trans. Dorothy S. Blair. Harlow, Eng.: Longman, 1986.

———. *So Long a Letter*. Trans. Modupé Bodé-Thomas. London: Heinemann, 1981.

Bakhtin, Mikhail. *The Dialogic Imagination: Four Essays*. Trans. Caryl Emerson and Michael Holquist. Austin: University of Texas P, 1981.

———. *Problems of Dostoevsky's Poetics*. Trans. Caryl Emerson. Minneapolis: University of Minnesota P, 1984.

Brown, Lloyd W. *Women Writers in Black Africa*. Westport, CT: Greenwood, 1981.

Dinesen, Isak. *Out of Africa*. New York: Modern Library; London: Putnam, 1937.

———. *Shadows on the Grass*. London: Joseph, 1960.

Emecheta, Buchi. *Double Yoke*. New York: Braziller; London: Ogwugwu Afor, 1982.

———. *In the Ditch*. London: Barrie, 1972.

———. *The Joys of Motherhood*. New York: Braziller; London: Heinemann, 1979.

———. *Second-Class Citizen*. London: Allison, 1974.

———. *The Slave Girl*. New York: Braziller, 1977.

Fall, Aminata Sow. *The Beggars' Strike, or, The Dregs of Society.* Trans. Dorothy S. Blair. Harlow, Eng.: Longman, 1981.

Gakwandi, Shatto Arthur. *The Novel and Contemporary Experience in Africa.* London: Heinemann, 1977.

Gikandi, Simon. *Reading the African Novel.* London: Currey; Portsmouth, N.H.: Heinemann, 1987.

Head, Bessie. *The Collector of Treasures.* London: Heinemann, 1977.

———. *Maru.* New York: McCall; London: Gollancz, 1971.

———. *A Question of Power.* London: Davis-Poynter, 1973.

———. *When Rain Clouds Gather.* London: Gollancz, 1969.

Huxley, Elspeth. *The Flame Trees of Thika: Memories of an African Childhood.* New York: Morrow; London: Chatto, 1959.

Ikonya, Philo. "Marjorie Macgoye, the Evergreen Author." *The Sunday Nation* (Nairobi) 1 May 1994.

"An Individual Response to the Challenges of Modern Life." *Wajibu: A Journal of Social and Religious Concern*, vol. 4, no. 4 (November–December 1989): 6–8.

Jones, Eldred Durosimi, Eustance Palmer, and Marjorie Jones eds. *Women in African Literature Today.* London: Currey, 1987.

Macgoye, Marjorie, O. *Chira.* Nairobi: East African Educational Publishers, 1997.

———. *Coming to Birth.* Nairobi: Heinemann, 1986.

———. *Homing In.* Naitrobi: East African Educational Publishers, 1994.

———. Letter to the author. 1 January 2000.

———. *Moral Issues in Kenya: A Personal View.* Nairobi: Uzima, 1996.

———. *Song of Nyarloka and Other Poems.* Nairobi: Oxford University Press, 1977.

———. *The Story of Kenya: A Nation in the Making.* Nairobi: Oxford University Press, 1986.

————. *Victoria and Murder in Majent go.* London: Macmillan, 1993.

Ngcobo, Lauretta. *And They Didn't Die.* 1991. New York: Feminist Press at CUNY, 1999.

————. *Cross of Gold.* London: Longman, 1981.

Njau, Rebeka. *Ripples in the Pool.* Nairobi: Transafrica, 1975.

Nwapa, Flora. *Efuru.* London: Heinemann, 1966.

————. *Idu.* London: Heinemann, 1970.

Obyerodhyambo, Oby. "Marjorie Oludhe Macgoye: Child of Two Worlds Approaches Seventy." *Sunaa* (1998): 6–7.

Ogot, Grace. *Land Without Thunder.* Nairobi: East African Publishing House, 1968.

————. *The Promised Land.* Nairobi: East African Publishing House, 1966.

Ogundipe-Leslie, Molara. "The Female Writer and Her Commitment." *African Literature Today,* 15. (1987): 5–13.

Oladele, Taiwo. *Female Novelists of Modern Africa.* New York: St. Martin's, 1985.

Palmer, Eustace. *An Introduction to the African Novel.* New York: Africana; London: Heinemann, 1972.

Petersen, Kristen H., and Anna Rutherford, eds. *A Double Colonialisation: Colonial and Postcolonial Women's Writing.* Sydney, N.S.W.: Dangaroo Press, 1986.

"Profile of Marjorie Oludhe Macgoye." *The Weekly Review* (Nairobi) 12 September 1986: 29–30.

Spice, Nicholas. "Looking After Men." *London Review of Books* 9 July 1987: 4–5.

HISTORICAL
CONTEXT

Precolonial African Societies

The forty ethnic groups recognized in Kenya today represent a wide range of linguistic and cultural backgrounds. The Kikuyu, Luyia, Luo, and Kalenjin peoples are the largest in numbers; others include the Gusii, Kamba, Maasai, Mijikenda, Samburu, Somali, and Turkana. Some peoples, especially the Kikuyu in the more fertile southern half of the country, combined subsistence agriculture with raising cattle and other livestock in scattered settlements of families related by patrilineal ties and ruled by councils of elders. They formed broadly patriarchal societies, where the senior man in a family was recognized as having the right to control land and other resources and to reallocate them when necessary. Wives gained rights to land or cattle only through a viable marriage to a man of the lineage.

These were by no means isolated societies, but continuously proliferating communities with localized leadership. Regular patterns of trade and intermarriage forged links between neighboring peoples; ceremonies of blood brotherhood created fictional kinship ties across ethnic lines to stimulate trade. Ethnic identities thus tended to be rather fluid, as changing patterns of trade, rainfall, disease, or enemy raiding parties might prompt families to move away and join a different group. Colonial political and economic structures later tended to freeze these rather loose associations into more permanent ethnic identities and to pit them against one another.

A rather different situation prevailed along the Indian Ocean coast. Swahili society, like the Swahili language, is the product of a profound interaction of Arab/Persian and African elements that took place over centuries. Founded more than a thousand years ago, Mombasa was the largest Swahili settlement along the Kenya coast and had absorbed immigrant traders and sailors for centuries. More recent Omani Arab immigrants (whose numbers increased measurably in the middle and later 1800s) considered themselves superior to their darker Swahili cousins, an attitude that led to occasional conflict under colonial rule.

The Swahili generally saw themselves as urban dwellers, followed the ways of Islam, and marked themselves off by language, dress, and behavior from their up-country neighbors. By the early twentieth century, Mombasa was a cosmopolitan city with a mixture of Swahili, other African, Arab, and Asian inhabitants, and a small number of Europeans. The Swahili language became a lingua franca among Africans of different backgrounds throughout the hinterland as well.

The Imposition of British Colonial Rule

The British ruled Kenya from 1895 to 1963, a period covering only two or three generations, yet the long-term impact on African societies was substantial. For the agricultural peoples of western and central Kenya, two aspects of colonial rule had the greatest effect on their lives: the constant demand for land and for cheap labor and the active presence of Christian missionaries.

British interests in East Africa were originally commercial and strategic. Thus one of the first colonial projects in Kenya was the construction of a railway from Mombasa to the shores of Lake Victoria to provide regular access to Uganda. Begun in 1896, the Uganda Railway ultimately shaped both the economic geography and the political history of the Kenya colony. Alarmed by the vast expenses of railroad construction, colonial officials hoped to generate revenue by using the railroad to carry agricultural products for export. They assumed that only white farmers could adequately develop the territory and moved quickly to attract white immigrants, primarily from Britain and from South Africa.

More than five thousand Europeans had come by 1914. Settlers were rewarded with large tracts of the most fertile agricultural land, the so-called White Highlands, at low cost. The White Highlands covered roughly 7.5 million acres of land in central

Kenya, including many areas claimed by the Kikuyu and their neighbors. At its height in 1950, the white population in Kenya consisted of some twenty-nine thousand people.

British colonial officials helped provide the cheap labor that settlers demanded through restricting land available for African use, imposing "hut taxes" on the African population, and instructing to local officials to "encourage" men in their area to meet the labor needs of local white settlers—encouragement that sometimes involved the use of force. A formal labor registration system was developed in 1921 whereby all Africans over sixteen were required to carry a *kipande,* or labor pass, which listed the dates and terms of their current wage employment. At first the law was applied only to men and to women who worked or traveled outside their home area. Men who were found without their pass or whose card showed they were not currently employed could be forced to work on white-owned plantations. Young women sometimes worked for white settlers as well; it was widely believed that their manual dexterity made them ideal for picking delicate coffee berries and tea leaves.

Settlers often avoided labor shortages by allowing African "squatters" to live on their farms—to build temporary huts, plant small gardens to feed their families, and keep a number of livestock—in exchange for working a specified number of days during the year. By 1945, nearly one-fourth of the Kikuyu population was living as squatters on white-owned land.

Africans living near Mombasa were able to work for white employers as daily "casual labor" at the port of Kilindini and elsewhere on terms that allowed them to choose when they would work. Especially during the early decades of colonial rule, coastal men often refused long-term contracts, working on their own farms during key parts of the agricultural season and only presenting themselves for daily labor during the off seasons. They were also free to participate in the lively *beni* dance processions and competitions that were a highlight of coastal society. But men from central and western Kenya were forced to travel long distances and to work on contracts lasting from three to six months. Their wives were generally left behind in the rural areas, expected to fend for themselves and to continue the same levels of agricultural production despite the withdrawal of male labor.

Christian missionaries, representing many different denominations, poured into Kenya from Europe and North America. In the early years they were often members of the Church Missionary Society (Anglican), the White Fathers (Roman Catholic), or the Church of Scotland Missionary Society (Presbyterian). Despite the importance of African lay teachers in the spread of Christianity, mission churches kept key positions within their hierarchy firmly in in the hands of white missionaries; this tendency later sparked the growth of a number of separatist African churches.

Besides propagating the faith, missions were critical suppliers of education, health care, and social services in rural areas. While government efforts in both education and health care were oriented toward the needs of the white population, mission stations operated schools, rural clinics, and orphanages for Africans. Those who persevered in mission educational systems had access to better-paying white-collar jobs, but African families knew the mission schools would turn their children away from traditional beliefs. Some missionaries encouraged early Christian converts to move away from their extended families and form separate Christian villages, sometimes around a mission station. Conversion thus tore apart the social fabric of a number of rural communities in the early days of colonial rule. In Mombasa and other Swahili towns, families sent their children to Islamic *madrasas* (koranic schools) instead. Despite African demands, a network of government-supported secular schools did not become a reality until the 1950s.

World War I and the Interwar Period

The demand for African labor escalated dramatically in 1914 when World War I came to East Africa. Despite a few German raids across the border, most of the actual fighting took place in neighboring Tanzania—then called Tanganyika and a German territory —and in Mozambique. Some 250,000 Kenyan men were conscripted into military service for the war. While a few served with the prestigious Kenya African Rifles (KAR, or "Keya"), the great majority served as porters in the Carrier Corps. Neighborhoods in East Africa still named "Kariakor" reflect the location of these wartime barracks. About one-fifth of the Kenyan men conscripted for war-time service never returned home, dying more often from malnutrition and disease than from battle wounds. Those who survived came back to Kenya with a new willingness to demand political and economic change. Colonial officials feared these new attitudes and determined to attract more white settlers to maintain the status quo. An official "soldier-settler" scheme offered qualified British veterans a chance to take up substantial farms at nominal cost, and more than twelve hundred additional farms were allocated under the scheme.

Despite the increased settler presence and demands for labor, many African farmers prospered during the 1920s as they grew cash crops for local markets and for export. The Great Depression greatly reduced those chances for prosperity, however, as worldwide demand for agricultural exports declined, jobs for Africans dried up, and white employers unilaterally slashed wages. Meanwhile a series of measures gave European settlers increased control over African squatters. A 1937 ordinance, for example, allowed settlers to limit the number of acres that squatters could cultivate on their own, eliminate squatter livestock, and increase the number of working days per year from 180 to 270. The interruption of the Second World War gave the squatters a certain grace period, but settler pressure for control resumed with a vengeance after 1945, forcing many squatters back to the reserves and provoking their participation in the resistance movement. In 1946–47 a group of Kikuyu ex-squatters at Olenguruone actively challenged government restrictions on their farming and took oaths of unity to protect their rights. Ultimately evicted by colonial officials in 1950, the Olenguruone settlers had close ties with the Kikuyu Central Association (KCA); through these experiences the squatter movement became politicized and the squatters helped to radicalize the KCA.

World War II and the Rise of African Nationalism

The difficult years of the Depression were soon followed by the crisis of World War II. Kenyans were required to fight with British forces against the Italians in Ethiopia and Somalia and against the Japanese in Burma. This time most of them were trained in the use of weapons in combat. Kenya's primary contribution to the war effort, however, was to provide extensive food supplies for the troops. African homesteads were ordered to sacrifice livestock and crops as "voluntary" contributions to a war effort they understood little about. The war years also witnessed government attempts to silence potential opposition by banning African newspapers and political movements.

The years following World War II saw a great increase in racial tensions and political conflict. Kenyan soldiers who returned home had a new sense of European vulnerabilities and expected to be treated with greater respect for their war service; they also returned with substantial pay packets and great expectations. At the same time, white settlers who had enlisted, or who had stepped in to replace colonial officials called up for the war effort, fully expected to be rewarded for their sacrifices and to have a greater say in the colony's affairs. These conflicting expectations would collide violently in the late 1940s and throughout the 1950s as white settlers confronted greater African militancy in both labor organizations and political movements.

While Nairobi was a British colonial city, with clusters of African neighborhoods scattered around a white official and residential core, Mombasa remained very much the African town it had been for centuries. That is perhaps why the organized Kenyan labor movement centered around the workers of Mombasa, under the able leadership of men like the Luo Tom Mboya and the Indian Makhan Singh. Labor protests at the port of Mombasa beginning in the 1930s culminated in widespread general strikes in 1939, 1947, and 1957, each of which effectively shut down the port and other public operations within Mombasa, and often spread to Nairobi as well. Each strike gained workers some concessions and higher wages, though never as much as they had demanded.

192

The roots of Kenyan political nationalism lay in the 1920s, when a range of locally based organizations were formed to protest such issues as land alienation, the *kipande* system, hut taxes, forced labor, and the appointment of African chiefs who lacked local legitimacy. One of the best known of these protest organizations was the Young Kikuyu Association, led by Harry Thuku. When Thuku was arrested for sedition in 1922, hundreds of his supporters surrounded the Nairobi police station and demanded his release; when they refused to disperse, twenty-five people were killed in Kenya's first large-scale political riot. Thuku was then exiled to British Somalia and his organization banned. A newly named Kikuyu Central Association with similar concerns was formed in 1925. When some Christian missions tried to undermine the Kikuyu tradition of female circumcision by prohibiting initiated girls from attending school, the KCA helped establish an informal network of "independent" schools. By 1939 the KCA had become the colony's main protest organization and was able to continue underground operations despite its formal banning during World War II.

Nationalist pressures gained momentum with Jomo Kenyatta's return to Kenya in 1946 after years of study abroad. Widely recognized as the leader of Kikuyu nationalism, Kenyatta was president of the new Kenya African Union (KAU). While other ethnic groups shared many of the same colonial grievances, Kikuyu dominance within KAU and the shaping of the culture of resistance to reflect Kikuyu traditions—including the widespread use of oaths to recruit new members and bind them to secrecy— meant that the nationalist revolt was primarily, though not entirely, a Kikuyu affair.

The Mau Mau Revolt and Kenyan Independence

The Kenyan government declared a State of Emergency in 1952, following sporadic outbreaks of violence targeted at Europeans and African loyalists. The brutal crackdown on African dissent sparked a widespread anticolonial revolt that is known as Mau Mau. Putting martial law in place—including imposing curfews and detaining suspects without trial—colonial police arrested several hundred Kikuyu political activists in the Nairobi area, including Kenyatta himself. Thousands of Kikuyu in Nairobi were forcibly repatriated to the rural areas. Losing their key leaders at one blow, the movement went underground and developed a more decentralized leadership in rural areas. Hundreds of Kikuyu men and some women fled to the forests of Mt. Kenya and the Aberdares, where they formed the military arm of the Mau Mau movement, the Land and Freedom Army, and staged guerrilla raids on British command centers and loyalist farms.

While several white settler families were attacked and the greater white community lived in fear, those who suffered most during the 1950s were clearly the Kikuyu themselves. Perhaps 100,000 Kikuyu men and women were arrested and held in detention camps where they were beaten and required to perform hard labor. Great hardships also faced those who remained on the land. Perhaps a million Kikuyu were forced to abandon their existing homes and build new houses in concentrated settlements in an attempt to cut off peasant support for the guerrilla fighters. Made up primarily of old men, women, and children, these stockaded villages were usually surrounded by barbed-wire fencing and a deep trench, and were guarded by armed loyalists.

Kikuyu women were active in support of the Mau Mau struggle, one important example being the women's organization Maendeleo ya Wanawake (Progress for Women). Originally founded by European women in the 1950s, Maendeleo helped improve the lives of African women through training in domestic arts and science. After independence Maendeleo helped women learn crafts which could generate income for their families, and gave them a collective voice in society and politics. In 1989, perhaps because of the success of that independent voice, the Kenyan government absorbed Maendeleo into the dominant party, making it essentially the women's branch of the Kenyan African National Union (KANU), despite the independent Kenyan governement having been largely a men's affair.

The State of Emergency was finally lifted in 1960. After nearly a decade of struggle, some fifteen thousand Africans had died, while at most a hundred Europeans had been killed. Mau

Mau suspects kept in detention often returned home to find their farms and cattle reallocated to loyalists. The disruption of African life in central Kenya had been severe. But while the Land and Freedom Army might have lost the battle, in the sense that effective military challenge was largely put down within a few years, they had essentially won the war. The costs of continued colonial control were simply too high for British officials, and negotiations began to settle the terms and process of the transition to Kenyan political independence; African representatives were first elected to the Legislative Council (LegCo) in 1957.

Most white settlers gave in bitterly and withdrew in the early 1960s, selling their farms and leaving Kenya. A few stayed on, and the first minister of agriculture in the new government was a European. The independent Kenyan government purchased many abandoned white farms to make them available for landless peasants; in practice most farms were purchased by members of the new African elite, who relied on tenant farmers to provide labor.

In December 1963, Kenya became an independent nation under the political leadership of Jomo Kenyatta, with a democratically elected Legislative Council. In December 1964 a republican constitution was adopted and Kenyatta became president. Despite the rhetoric of the radical nationalists, the new Kenyan government declared its commitment to capitalism and to private property. Kenyatta assured world leaders that his would not be a "gangster government," and urged Kenyans to forget the past. The powerful Kenyan labor organizations were ultimately folded into the Kenyan African National Union, the dominant political party, as KANU leaders felt a new and fragile nation could not afford confrontation with workers.

Only a month after formal independence, a short-lived mutiny occurred at the Nairobi headquarters of the Kenya African Rifles in January 1964, and British troops quickly restored order. Kenyatta moved swiftly to improve wages and barracks conditions for the rank and file and to promote Africans within the KAR to positions previously held by whites.

President Kenyatta ruled the country until his death in 1978.

A smaller ethnic group, the Kalenjin, came to enjoy the fruits of power under his successor, Daniel arap Moi. Kenya's population has increased rapidly in recent years, while the changing terms of trade for agricultural products since the early 1980s have led to a generally stagnant rural economy. A coup attempt in 1982—the most serious threat faced by the new nation—was sparked by air force officers who attacked Moi's government for corruption and economic mismanagement. Forces loyal to the government restored order after a few days. Since the end of the Cold War, the United States and other Western nations have pushed the Moi regime to reduce corruption, impose economic reforms, and permit a more open political system. Moi capitulated to international pressure in late 1991 and announced that opposition political parties could form and compete in national elections. In the face of the relative weakness of the ethnically fragmented and under-funded opposition, the regime has continued its repression of dissent, including the use of government-funded ethnic violence to convince ordinary Kenyans that they are safer clinging to the status quo.

Jean Hay
Boston, June 2000

CONTEMPORARY WOMEN'S FICTION
FROM AROUND THE WORLD
from The Feminist Press at The City University of New York

Allegra Maud Goldman, a novel by Edith Konecky. $9.95 paper.

Almost Touching the Skies: Women's Coming of Age Stories. $15.95 paper. $35.00 cloth.

Apples from the Desert: Selected Stories, by Savyon Liebrecht. $13.95 paper. $19.95 cloth.

Bamboo Shoots After the Rain: Contemporary Stories by Women Writers of Taiwan. $14.95 paper. $35.00 cloth.

Bearing Life: Women's Writings on Childlessness. $23.95 cloth.

Changes: A Love Story, a novel by Ama Ata Aidoo. $12.95 paper.

Coming to Birth, a novel by Marjorie Oludhe Macgoye. $11.95 paper. $30.00 cloth.

Confessions of Madame Psyche, a novel by Dorothy Bryant. $18.95 paper. $30.00 cloth.

David's Story, a novel by Zoë Wicomb. $19.95 cloth.

An Estate of Memory, a novel by Ilona Karmel. $11.95 paper.

A Matter of Time, a novel by Shashi Deshpande. $21.95 cloth.

Mulberry and Peach: Two Women of China, a novel by Hualing Nieh. $12.95 paper.

No Sweetness Here and Other Stories, by Ama Ata Aidoo. $10.95 paper. $29.00 cloth.

Paper Fish, a novel by Tina De Rosa. $9.95 paper. $20.00 cloth.

The Present Moment, a novel by Marjorie Oludhe Macgoye. $11.95 paper. $30.00 cloth.

Reena and Other Stories, by Paule Marshall. $11.95 paper.

The Silent Duchess, a novel by Dacia Maraini. $14.95 paper. $19.95 cloth.

The Tree and the Vine, a novel by Dola de Jong. $9.95 paper, $27.95 cloth.

Truth Tales: Contemporary Stories by Women Writers of India. $12.95 paper. $35.00 cloth.

Two Dreams: New and Selected Stories, by Shirley Geok-lin Lim. $10.95 paper.

What Did Miss Darrington See? An Anthology of Feminist Supernatural Fiction. $14.95 paper.

Winter's Edge, a novel by Valerie Miner. $10.95 paper.

With Wings: An Anthology of Literature by and About Women with Disabilities. $14.95 paper.

Women Working: An Anthology of Stories and Poems. $13.95 paper.

Women Writing in India: 600 B.C. to the Present. Volume I: 600 B.C. to the Early Twentieth Century. $29.95 paper. *Volume II: The Twentieth Century.* $29.95 paper.

You Can't Get Lost in Cape Town, a novel by Zoë Wicomb. $13.95 paper. $42.00 cloth.

To receive a free catalog of The Feminist Press's 200 titles, call or write The Feminist Press at The City University of New York, The Graduate Center, 365 Fifth Avenue, New York, NY 10016; phone: (212) 817-7920; fax: (212) 987-4008. Feminist Press books are available at bookstores or can be ordered directly. Send check or money order (in U.S. dollars drawn on a U.S. bank) payable to The Feminist Press. Please add $4.00 shipping and handling for the first book and $1.00 for each additional book. VISA, Mastercard, and American Express are accepted for telephone orders. Prices subject to change.